PRAISE FOR THE COMMANDER

The Commander: Last Enemy Series Prequel by Dan E. Hendrickson is the story of a tenacious man whose only thought is to win. Commander Jacob Edwards is a man of many different talents, which is the reason why he is called upon to handle the most difficult tasks. As the captain of the Coast Guard, he had his work cut out for him when he and his team came face to face with terrorists who just wouldn't quit and murderers looking for the next kill. Jacob and his team have to put their heads together to stop this chaos from increasing and spreading out. But it is not easy and even a man as daring as Jacob Edwards needs allies. He does not know who he can trust and who he can rely on. He has secrets to protect, orders to complete, and lives to save. Can he do it all?

This high-octane action novel is pretty amazing. From the moment The Commander begins and Jacob enters the scene, you will know that it is about to get heavy. Jacob Edwards is the kind of character who will command your attention from the very beginning. Dan E. Hendrickson did an amazing job at building the tension and making sure the reader was there in the moment with Jacob as he chased down the perpetrators. He was observant and really not subtle with his words (I loved that about him). He had his own personality and his seniority at his job was not going to change that for him. I enjoyed how immersed I was in the story. I was transported right beside Jacob and living the situations with him. The descriptions were vivid and the imagery was phenomenal. I loved this book and I'm pretty sure it gave me an adrenaline rush for hours after I finished it! This is a must-read for anyone who enjoys high-pressure, action novels that keep you up at night and hoping that the story never ends.

—Reviewed By Rabia Tanveer for Readers' Favorite

For three years, Lt. Commander Jacob Edwards of the United States Coast Guard has been part of a naval pirate task force in the Caribbean. He is fit and strong, a man who does a five-mile run every morning. He is the best that Captain Tommy Williams has, so when Tommy calls on Jacob to take care of a crisis in the Gulf of Mexico, the last thing Jacob can think about is getting embroiled in a mess far greater than anything he could have imagined—mass murder, sabotage, and terrorism. Plus, he has to be very discreet about his job when he receives the command directly from the President of the United States. Can Jacob be at the center stage of the president's war on drugs, human trafficking, and reported "upticks in pirate activity in that sector," without drawing attention to himself? The Commander: Last Enemy Series Prequel by Dan E. Hendrickson is a compelling military thriller with very high stakes for the protagonist.

The author shows a lot of understanding of the operations of the Coast Guard and writes a story that features very compelling characters, plucked from government agencies like Homeland Security. The themes of drugs, human trafficking, and terrorism are ingeniously developed. The prose, in itself, is delightful. Dan E. Hendrickson has a gift for crafting characters that are human and believable. The protagonist is a family man and readers will enjoy the relationship he has with Danielle, his nine-year-old daughter. Characters have solid backgrounds, are likable, and it is interesting to watch them evolve through the narrative. The Commander: Last Enemy Series Prequel is a beautifully written and engaging tale that grabs the attention of the reader from the first page and never lets it go.

—Reviewed By Christian Sia for Readers' Favorite

The Commander is a work of fiction in the action and adventure sub-genres which is aimed at adult readers, penned by author Dan E. Hendrickson. A prequel in the Last Enemy

Series, the book follows the adventures of Commander Jacob Edwards, a highly skilled agent of a classified military task force. Given the captain's chair of the freshly refurbished ship First Responder, Commander Edwards is deployed to the Gulf of Mexico after a crisis sends the region into chaos. As he and his crew contend with saboteurs and terrorists, Commander Edwards must complete a separate mission issued with the utmost secrecy by the President himself.

Author Dan E. Hendrickson has crafted a superb work of adventure fiction which perfectly introduces readers to commander Jacob Edwards and sets up his prime role in future books in the Last Enemy series extremely well. One of the things that most impressed me about this book was the close attention to character development from Hendrickson, whose sharp dialogue and attentive narration ensures that we have insight into Jacob's brilliant mind and his capabilities as a hero. The pace of the novel moves from exposition scenes to action scenes with plenty of twists and turns, and the use of atmospheric language and detailed descriptive techniques during the action ensures a cinematic feel to the adventure as a whole. Overall, I would certainly recommend The Commander to fans of the Last Enemy series and newcomers eager to be introduced to a hero they can really root for.

—**Reviewed By K.C. Finn for Readers' Favorite**

Dan Hendrickson's The Commander is a story of a valiant man named Jacob Edwards. Lt. Commander Jacob Edwards could be described as the younger version of "The Living Legend" Captain Tommy Williams. Captain Tommy Williams has earned the title of a legend because he was the most successful SEAL team leader to date. Similarly, Commander Jacob Edwards was the best operative on the field which prompted the comparison between the two. Few people have witnessed Commander

Jacob's astounding leadership skills, so only a few understood why he was suddenly promoted as the commander of a Hamilton-class cutter, the First Responder. He was, after all, the first person who was still at a low rank to be suddenly promoted to commander. The shakedown cruise of First Responder was the beginning of a secret mission filled with murder and terrorism. Will Commander Edwards be able to handle all the challenges thrown at him without being discovered?

The Commander by Dan Hendrickson is an engaging story that reels you in with every page turned. It's a well-written piece full of valuable, unforgettable lessons. The main character, Commander Edwards, was an exceptional protagonist - no matter what trouble he faced, he kept proving to everyone that he wasn't someone they should mess with or underestimate. Despite his strong character, he was also a leader full of compassion, truly a commendable man. He cared for his crew like they were his family and made sure that all his decisions would be for everyone's safety. He's a great example of what a leader should be. The antagonists in the novel were also memorable because of their heartless ways. If I were given a chance, I would like to punch them at least once! I was hoping they'd be caught by Commander Edwards and be in prison for the rest of their lives, but they were always so well prepared. Still, I understand that an exceptional protagonist needs an equally exceptional antagonist to make a story great. I also have faith that Commander Edwards will one day catch them and teach them a lesson they will never forget! I can't wait for the next book because this was definitely worth the read. Great work!

—Reviewed By Trisha Dawn for Readers' Favorite

In The Commander by Dan E. Hendrickson, Lieutenant Commander Jacob Edwards has just taken command of the Hamilton Class Cutter, First Responder as the captain of the US

Coast Guard when news of a possible terrorist attack in the Gulf of Mexico reaches the White House. Captain Tommy Williams sends Jacob to investigate and deal with the situation. As the true extent and severity of the situation unfold, Jacob realizes there is a link to the possibility of a terrorist attack on a US oil rig, and a missing ship carrying children. Behind the sabotage are the Saudi Royal Family, the Russian underworld, and a notorious pirate assassin. As the First Responder races to the oil rig, time is quickly running out. Jacob must use every skill he has learned to resolve the impending catastrophe while obeying an order from the President to keep his movements confidential.

Since reading other books in The Last Enemy series, I was looking forward to more exciting exploits from Jacob Edwards and The Commander by Dan E. Hendrickson definitely lived up to all my expectations. There are new and intriguing characters, as well as many old favorites. Natasha is a real psychopath. I never thought there could be a character more despicable than Dominik, but she was evil to the core. Jacob's relationship with his daughter was endearing as they shared so many tender moments together; this was contrasted perfectly with his relationship with his enemies. I love Jacob as a protagonist. Although his character is flawed, it makes him even more relatable and his morals and character are impeccable. The action begins immediately and takes you on a roller coaster of excitement with so many interesting and strong sub-plots. I thought I could second guess how the plot would unfold by now, but the author always takes me down a path I was not expecting. His brilliance at creating tension and conflicts in the story are enviable and so satisfying as a reader. I read the final third of this novel with my heart pounding, as all the loose ends were tied up with immaculate literary genius. I cannot rate this author highly enough and would recommend his novels to everyone.

—Reviewed By Lesley Jones for Readers' Favorite

Jacob Edwards has seized his new role in command of the First Responder for the United States Coast Guard as part of his new and well-earned promotion. Shortly after the newly refurbished vessel takes to sea, Edwards is put to the test in a barrage of troublesome events that may prove too much for even Commander Edwards to overcome. Heated acts of international terrorism, blackmail, and drug-fueled aggression not only put Edwards in danger of losing his life but also bring trust and loyalty into question. It's a dangerous game, and the outcome may be death, but certainly not glory.

Dan E. Hendrickson has done it again; The Commander is a well-crafted piece full of action, suspense, and undertones of family, friendship, loyalty, and doing what is right when that's not always so clear. I was impressed with the clear amount of knowledge and research that Hendrickson has clearly put into The Commander. I compare Hendrickson's writing with that of Tom Clancy; a descriptive and engaging military master-piece. Immediately from the first chapter, Hendrickson pulled me in with tense action, then I built relationships with the characters as I got to know them, then I pored through the book to discover how everything plays out. Suspenseful action is complemented by well-structured characters and a fine-tuned plot. A quality read for any action-thriller lover.

—Reviewed By Joshua Soule for Readers' Favorite

THE
COMMANDER

by
DAN E. HENDRICKSON

ISBN: 9781734518740

DEDICATION

This one goes to my son Lieutenant Carl Hendrickson of the United States Coast Guard. Buddy you are part of a fantastic organization that protects and serves it country in dynamically huge and diverse ways. I am so proud of you and all that you do. My character Jacob Edwards is just how I see you.

THANK YOU

First and foremost, I thank God almighty for inspiration and support in all of my life endeavors. Then I want to thank my wife Cheryl and my daughter Rebeccah for their efforts in helping me put this manuscript together. Tom Hyman for his fantastic insight and tutelage in editing and helping me finely tune this story. Teresa Jackson for her help in editing. And Danny Salter for putting in the final touches and copy editing.

CONTENTS

CHAPTER ONE

MARCH 1, 2003
DADDY, DAUGHTER TIME FIRST, THEN WORK

"Daddy, I think I can beat you this time."

"Prove it," answers the father of the wiry, blonde-haired girl nipping at his heels.

Lt. Commander Jacob Edwards of the United States Coast Guard loves his morning run along the coastline of Falcon Lake. At 6' 2" and weighing in at 210 pounds of muscle and bone, with dark brown hair and deep green eyes, he is the spitting image of his father, Jim Edwards, who—along with Jacob's mother, Linda—owns and operates one of the biggest automobile wholesale businesses on the East Coast.

Since being assigned here three years ago as part of the newly formed Coast Guard/Naval pirate task force in the Caribbean, Jacob has taken these five-mile runs every morning before going to work on the lake. He loves the quiet solitude, but sometimes his nine-year-old daughter, Danielle, will join him for about the first mile. She's a real spunky monkey and always tries to outrun him if she can, before she has to stop and catch her breath. It's on those mornings that he usually lets her opt out of their morning routine of practicing hand-to-hand self-defense techniques for half an hour before she goes to school. This morning, she makes it for a whole mile. His wife, Mary, is following the pair in her car, and she sees that Danielle has had enough, so she pulls up to a stop and waves her over. Danielle gives her dad a fist bump and gets in the car.

Jacob waves at them and continues his run. Graduating at the top of his group in the Naval Special Ops training program earned him his first command and a promotion. He now commands a patrol cutter and the pirate/smuggler task force on Falcon Lake. He had originally hoped to get assigned to South Africa to help with the pirate problem down there, but Captain Tommy Williams convinced Jacob's superiors he would be more useful in this region because most of his previous assignments had been in the Caribbean, and he knew the culture down here pretty well. Mary was ecstatic about the idea because it meant that she and Danielle could be close to her parents in South Padre Island, where her father serves as the commander of Station Brazos for the Coast Guard.

One mile before his run is over, Jacob is rounding the corner of the boardwalk when he sees the dark silhouette of a familiar yacht, one that he and his crew chased into Mexican waters the day before. He quickly spots the entrance to the pier that the yacht is about to depart from, and sprints to the end to catch it before it launches. While running, he gets out his cell phone and calls his cutter pilot to tell him to launch ASAP. There's no answer, so he texts the information and hopes the pilot sees it while he is checking in for work. When he gets to the end of the pier, the yacht has already pulled away.

Jacob is sure they have dropped off a shipment of drugs and probably picked up cash and firearms to take back to their Mexican cartel bosses. He looks around the end of the dock and sees a jet ski rental stand with the proprietor out front setting up for the day's business. He walks over to the man and pulls out his Coast Guard ID that he keeps with his cell phone in a zippered pocket on his running shirt. "Excuse me, señor, my name is Lt. Commander Jacob Edwards of the United States Coast Guard." He points to the yacht that has just left. "That's a criminal smuggler we've been chasing for some time. I need one of your jet skis to catch them."

The man just stares for a few seconds and then looks over at the yacht leaving the port. He turns back to Jacob, reaches down to grab a set of keys and hands them to him. "It's the last one at the end. That is the fastest one I have. I have never seen anyone try to chase a boat with one of these things. It sounds dangerous, Captain."

"It's lieutenant commander, and thanks," he says as he grabs the keys and sprints to the jet ski. He does not have his .45 1911 duty pistol with him, so he scans the area for anything that would substitute as a weapon and grabs a long-handled hammer with a large, forked claw on one end used for pulling large nails. He quickly puts it in the storage compartment, jumps on, hits the ignition, and maneuvers the jet ski out of the dock. When he turns around to wave and thank the owner, he sees the man pointing a video camera at him. "I'll put this whole thing on YouTube!" he yells at Jacob. "It'll be great for business."

Jacob rolls his eyes and waves back, thinking to himself, *not when Captain Williams sees it. He'll have it taken down in a heartbeat.*

Jacob never really thought a jet ski was something he would operate in the middle of Falcon Lake while on duty, but it was the only thing available. He and his crew have been trying to catch these guys for months, and if he lets them get away this time, chances are he'll never get another shot. His patrol cutter and crew are still docked five miles east, at the Coast Guard station. He looks down and sees a text from Chief Petty Officer John Maxim: "On our way. Where are you now?"

Jacob is not as proficient as his nine-year-old daughter at texting with one hand, so he hits the redial button. When the chief answers, he yells, "I borrowed a jet ski at the dock, and I'm in pursuit! They'll be in Mexican waters in ten minutes. Hurry!" He disconnects before Maxim can respond. It's still barely dawn, and the lake is dark. He can see that the yacht is moving at a leisurely pace, trying not to attract any attention. But still, he knows that his patrol cutter is at least fifteen minutes away, going at top speed. He has to figure out some way to slow the pirates down, or they'll get away again. He's close enough now that he can make out two people on the lower deck and one on the upper deck, piloting the craft. He can also tell that they have not heard him yet because of the noise from their own turbo diesel engine.

Jacob turns his throttle to maximum, watches the roll of the water behind the yacht, and at just the right time hits the *off* switch and glides into the yacht's aft end. He grabs the ladder leading to the lower deck with both hands while bracing his knees against the handlebars of the jet ski. He knows that he can't keep hold of both for long, but he has a plan. Next to the ladder is a rescue tube connected to a long nylon rope. He grabs the tube with one hand and drops it over the handlebars. He wraps the rope around the bars twice and then releases his knees from the jet ski. He secures the rope so that the jet ski does not drift out of reach and then grabs the hammer from the compartment and bangs a hole in the front of the jet ski near the bottom. When he lets go of the jet ski, it drifts away from the yacht as he slowly lets more slack out of the nylon rope, but it is held tight with the rope when it becomes taut. He looks back and can see that it is already sinking because of the hole he put in it. The drag caused by the jet ski being towed by the yacht only quickens the sinking process.

That should buy me a little time, Jacob thinks to himself. He is a little dumbfounded that no one has noticed him yet, but when his head creeps over the edge of the deck and he sees two of the passengers, the reason is apparent. Directly under the pilot house, two Mexican men are drinking shots of tequila and laughing. Jacob's Spanish has gotten a lot better over the last ten years since being married to Mary and being around her parents so much, so he understands what they are saying. The men are complimenting themselves for having outsmarted the stupid *cabrones* on the Coast Guard patrol boat once again. Jacob does not see any weapons near either of the two men, so he hoists himself over the side of the railing onto the deck and says in a loud, jovial voice, "I wouldn't get too self-complimentary just yet. Maybe we should just turn this tug around, dock, and wait for those idiot Coast Guard guys to come and arrest you."

Both men get wide-eyed, then cautiously move toward Jacob. Jacob knows that if they get into Mexican waters, it's over. He will have to escape and probably lose these guys forever. But when the pilot suddenly turns the throttle up to maximum, something wonderful happens. The back of the yacht dips deep in the water, and they slow down instead of speeding up. Jacob figures that since they are still in a shallow part of the lake, the jet ski he tied to the yacht must have sunk low enough below the surface to get tangled on something.

Before Jacob can revel in his victory, he looks up and sees the pilot of the yacht on the upper deck pointing a shotgun at him.

"I know you," the man sneers. "You're the commander of the United States Coast Guard patrol boat. None of those *cabrones* will touch us as long as we have you." He looks down at one of his men and yells, "Cut that rope and let's get out of here!" Before the man can move, something rocks the yacht and Jacob sees an opportunity. He takes the hammer he is still holding and throws it at the pilot. It strikes his midsection, causing the shotgun to go off, and the man falls over.

Jacob dives for the closest man and tackles him. He sends two piston-like jabs into the man's jaw, knocking him out cold. He rolls to the side as the other man tries to bash his head in with an oar he has picked up, but Jacob has been in the Coast Guard for about sixteen years now, and most of that time he has been at sea, so he quickly gains his feet, grabs the oar from his assailant and uses the shaft end to jab him in the stomach and head. The would-be attacker falls over screaming, holding his broken nose.

Jacob knows he has to get to the upper deck and shut down the engines before the yacht sinks. He runs toward the stairs. Two steps from the upper deck he finds himself staring down the barrel of the same shotgun that confronted him earlier. Jacob has stared down the barrel of oblivion a few times in his military career, and he has learned that the smallest of things can work to one's advantage, if you seize the opportunity. This time, the man on the lower deck provides the opportunity with a loud groan as he rolls to one side. For a millisecond, the man with the shotgun looks down at his friend.

Jacob reaches up and pushes the shotgun barrel out of his face and jumps up onto the upper deck. The shotgun goes off while Jacob is still holding the metal barrel. The heat is intense, and he feels his palm burning. He growls and smashes the man on the upper deck square in the jaw with a devastating right cross. Jacob drops the shotgun from his left hand and picks it up with his right, points the weapon at his would-be attacker, and tells him to power down the yacht before it sinks. As the yacht powers down, he hears the sirens from his Coast Guard patrol cutter to his left. When he looks over, he sees Chief Maxim and Lt. Commander Chuck Yeager, his second-in-command for the Falcon Lake task force, standing on the deck, waving at him. Chuck shows his big, pearly whites as he hollers across the water. "Maxim said you might be in trouble! He asked me to come along. Looks like those other guys need more help than you do, buddy." He laughs and looks over at the nylon rope coming out of the water. "I am afraid to ask what's on the other end of that, but knowing you, it will cost someone in Uncle Sam's accounting office some big bucks, right?"

Three Hours Later, Falcon Lake Coast Guard Station

Jacob and Chuck are finishing up the paperwork on the arrests they made this morning. The pilot of the smuggler's boat turned out to be the head of the whole ring on Falcon Lake for the Mexican cartels operating in the area. Mainly because of Chuck's brilliant detective work, they could backtrack the boat's shipment of drugs into the United States before it left the dock. They have been working for three years to take this guy down and both are relieved it's over. Chuck leans back in his chair and puts his hands behind his head and smiles at his best friend. "Sixteen years we've been together, huh, buddy?"

Jacob looks up from his desk and chuckles. "Don't forget about our last year at Kings Point, where I had to put up with that awful snoring of yours when we were roommates."

Chuck feigns hurt feelings. "Buddy, Nancy says it doesn't bother her, and she'll have to put up with it for life."

Jacob drops his pen and stands straight up from his desk with an ear-to-ear grin on his face. "You finally popped the question, and she actually said yes?" As Jacob makes his way over to give his best friend a congratulatory bear hug, Chuck's eyes get as big as saucers as he braces himself for one of those trash-compactor experiences with Jacob that no one ever gets used to.

As soon as Jacob lets him go, he catches his breath, smiles, and points at his face. "Geez. How could she say no to this?"

Jacob punches his buddy in the shoulder. "So, it appears that we have done everything the commandant and Captain Williams wanted us here for. Are you going to request a transfer, Chuck?"

Chuck furtively eyes his buddy, trying to gauge how Jacob will react to what he is preparing to tell him. "Jacob, I've been sitting on this for about a week now. Captain Williams called me and offered me something that I don't want to turn down. Since we're both at our sixteen-year mark in the Guard, he wants me to consider not reenlisting and joining the FBI. He says he can have me in the next class at Quantico this fall."

A little stunned, Jacob sits there processing what he has just heard. He and Chuck have been inseparable since they graduated from The United States Merchant Marine Academy at Kings Point. Chuck was his best friend, Danielle's godfather, and the best man at his wedding. Chuck was also there with him on that yacht down in Honduras twelve years ago, and he knows he would never have made it through the aftershock of holding that little thirteen-year-old girl in his arms until she died without Chuck's support.

He laces his fingers together behind his head and blows out a puff of air. "You know, Chuck, investigating is your long suit. The FBI would be a perfect fit. I just thought you and I would be together for our whole twenty."

Chuck lets out a long, heavy sigh. He knows what's on Jacob's mind. They both had to deal with what they saw down off the Honduras coast when they boarded the Mexican finance minister's yacht. When they were just two junior lieutenants on their first assignment aboard a Hamilton-class cutter, neither of them was prepared for what they saw when they boarded. But when Jacob held that little girl as she died, something broke deep within him. He almost lost his mind over the incident.

The next year was rough on both of them. Jacob got into a lot of fights, both on and off duty. He never really ever picked any fights, but he could not walk by and let someone get bullied, especially children.

Chuck knows there were three big reasons Jacob could get control of his temper with bullies. First is the birth of his daughter, Danielle, and the speedy recovery of his wife, Mary, after a very rough pregnancy. Next is when they were invited to be a part of Navy SEAL Captain Tommy Williams's special six-month SEAL tactical training program. Captain Williams took a special liking to Jacob because he applied himself to the training like no one the SEAL team commander had ever seen before. He really helped Jacob channel his aggression in ways that molded him into a superb soldier and officer. Finally, there is Chuck and Jacob's friendship.

Before he can respond, Jacob surprises him by saying, "You do what you got to do, Chuck. Whatever you decide, I'll support it."

Chuck knows this will be hard for Jacob, but he also knows that Jacob is ready for bigger things, and so is he. Chuck and Captain Williams talked about this very thing just the other day. He does not want Jacob to know this, but Captain Williams has been talking to the Coast Guard commandant, Admiral Rogers, about Jacob commanding a Hamilton-class cutter here soon. That will mean another promotion for his buddy that might ruffle a lot of brass feathers, but the commandant really likes Jacob, and after what Jacob and Chuck just pulled off on Falcon Lake, he can probably get away with the maneuver and put Jacob in the captain's seat.

Chuck has to chortle a little when he thinks about Captain Tommy Williams. In the navy, they called him "The Living Legend," or "The Legend" for short. Although you never want to use that term around him personally, it was given to him because Tommy was the most successful SEAL team leader to date. Funny thing is, that's all you ever heard. They considered anything that the man did top secret, so nobody really knew what he had done to earn such a reputation—that is until they served with him or were trained by him. Those who did, knew it was a well-earned reputation.

Tommy has developed quite a network comprised of his trainees over the last ten years in the intelligence, military, and law enforcement communities. His school was originally designed to give said agencies some skill sets he had developed while serving as a SEAL over the years. The brass saw it as an opportunity to get those three different entities working together in joint cooperation from time to time. Thus, Tommy had access to people like the commandant of the Coast Guard, the director of the FBI, and others, to make suggestions and help with their operations. When Chuck showed Captain Williams that he understood this, that is when he suggested that Chuck consider being an FBI agent; and the more Chuck thought about it, the more he liked the idea.

Jacob, on the other hand, is a born leader. It always blows Chuck's mind how the man could keep several functions of an operation working simultaneously with brilliant coordination. He also genuinely loves the people he serves with, and that made him someone everybody wanted to follow. He knows that Jacob will be just fine without him watching his back. He has not seen the man lose his temper in years, and he keeps getting better at his job.

Chuck winks at Jacob. "I got to go, buddy. The future Mrs. Yeager wants to go pick out wedding rings this afternoon." They shake hands, and Chuck turns to leave. He stops at the door and looks back at Jacob. "I'm taking applications for best man. Know of any good candidates around?" He ducks and barely avoids getting hit in the side of the head with a half-full water bottle. "OK, buddy, if you insist. But I'll be three times more demanding than you were, and there better be lots of beer and a girl jumping out of a cake at some point."

He quickly opens the door and darts out as another water bottle hits the door as it closes.

Jacob gets up to collect the two bottles he flung at his best friend. As he is emptying the contents into the sink, his desk phone rings. "Falcon Lake Coast Guard Patrol, Lt. Commander Edwards. May I help you?"

"Nice work, kid. Looks like you and Chuck did everything Commandant Rogers and I wanted you to do."

Jacob knows that Captain Williams is not officially his commanding officer, but since the commandant gives his intelligence operations full cooperation, he treats him as such. "Thanks, Captain. We lucked out this morning. I wasn't even on patrol, yet when I saw those guys leaving the dock while I was running...uh, about the jet ski, I can talk to my dad. He would probably replace it if I begged him enough. Then you wouldn't have to go through all that red tape with those black ops accountants you're always complaining about."

Captain Tommy Williams—of the United States Navy and a former SEAL team commander—bursts out laughing, because he's already been on the phone with the owner and has promised him two brand-new jet skis like the one Jacob ruined, if he would turn over the footage he took of Jacob boarding and capturing the smugglers' boat on the lake.

"Don't sweat it, kid. It's handled. Lucky for you, only the owner of the jet ski and that slime-ball cartel man and his compadres will ever know how you took them down. Quick thinking out there. Damn risky, too. If it was anyone else, I'd be chewing their ass out for a month for that stunt. But with you, what's the point? You'd just do the same thing again if you thought it would work."

Jacob blows out a puff of air in relief as he considers how this enigmatic officer that he has worked with for so many years always seems one step ahead of any situation. He leans back in his chair, puts his left hand behind his head, and says, "So what's the plan now, Captain? Are we staying here, or moving on?"

"Commandant Rogers wants Chief Maxim to take over patrolling Falcon Lake. To be honest, kid, unless Mexico does something on the other side of the lake, we are basically at a stalemate with what we can accomplish there. What we really need is someone like you and Yeager to clean up over there. Until that happens, we'll just play guard dog on our side and wait. As for you, Commandant

Rogers and I want you back in the Caribbean with more resources to work with."

Jacob knows he needs to dig a little to get answers, because Captain Williams is not a part of the Coast Guard command structure and can't officially tell him his next assignment, but he might give him a heads-up. "So, what do they have in mind, Captain?"

"Kid, I'll leave that little surprise to the commandant, but I suggest you wrap your head around people calling you *commander*."

Jacob tries to press for more info, but in his usual elusive way, Tommy brushes him off and ends the conversation.

CHAPTER TWO
POLITICS, MEDALS, PROMOTIONS

That Evening, United States Coast Guard Command, Washington DC, Office of the Commandant

Harry Rogers is probably the most well-rounded and experienced officer in the Coast Guard. After graduating from the United States Coast Guard Academy in 1970, he spent most of his first ten years on assignments at sea. Then he took on senior officer positions, eventually commanding two Hamilton-class cutters and three sectors before he came back to Washington DC to be promoted to admiral and appointed as Vice Commandant of the

United States Coast Guard. Now he sits in the hot seat. Just six months ago, his predecessor retired and insisted that Harry take his spot. The president and the secretary of Homeland Security agreed, so here he sits. What he does not understand is how a pencil-pushing desk jockey like Rear Admiral James Harrington could ever get his old job. Nobody bothered to ask Harry what he thought; they just saddled him with the blowhard. So, here he sits with the man, arguing over Harry's latest promotion and command decision.

"Commandant, I think this is preposterous. The man has only been a lieutenant commander for less than three years, and now you want to promote him to commander and give him a Hamilton to boot? We hardly ever give that ship to that rank unless he is just about to make captain. What will the rest of the Guard think, sir? My son is already four years into his commander's rank and is third in line to make captain in the whole service. He's been the XO on *First Responder* for over a year and a half. If anyone should get that ship, he should."

Harry rolls his eyes and inwardly sighs. He thinks to himself, *now I know what's really blowing up James's skirt.* "Look, James, Will is a capable officer and a superb administrator, but his CO doesn't have your enthusiasm for him taking on *First Responder*. It's not that he thinks he can't handle command in normal times, but we're talking about South Texas, Mexico, and Central America here. With the president's war on drugs, human trafficking, and reported upticks in pirate activity in that sector, we need a commander who has combat and law enforcement experience."

James stands up and points an accusing finger at his superior. "Will has been to the War College in central Pennsylvania. His marks were some of the best in his class. He earned his master's degree before he made lieutenant commander. This other guy—what's his name—Edwards? He hasn't even gone back to school yet. We rarely pull out the captain's chair unless a candidate has at least a master's degree, Commandant. Besides, hasn't he been a little busy playing sea cop for three years, chasing two-bit smugglers on that little lake and stuff?"

Harry has gotten used to Harrington's temper and does his best to diffuse it to avoid having to blow the man's hair back by pulling rank. He reaches under a pile of papers and pulls out a document. "James, Lt. Commander Edwards earned his master's degree in Maritime Law Enforcement two months ago from a Coast Guard-approved online university." He hands him the document over his desk. As Harrington grabs it, Harry smiles and says, "Pay special attention to the GPA that Edwards kept throughout his entire curriculum."

Harrington sits back down in his chair and pulls out his reading glasses. As he scans through the document, he notes several compliments given to Edwards on his insightful and imaginative essays that he turned in over the last two years. Then he comes to the GPA. He does a double-take at the score—4.0. A perfect straight-A grade point average. He lowers his glasses and looks at his superior. "Will never did better than a 3.5, but he went to the War College. This is just an online university."

Harry is ready for that and tells James to look at the list of professors that teach the courses Jacob took online. Seven out of ten of them are associate professors with tenure at the same college Will went to.

James is stone-faced as he looks the commandant straight in the eyes. "I will not see my son passed over like this. I have friends in the Senate who owe me and my family favors. If you continue down this path, I'll reach out to them."

Harry knows full well of James's government connections. He is the son of the late New Jersey senator, Bill Harrington, and his family has lots of ties in different government circles. So now he has to pull out his best pitch to get what he wants and keep the peace. "James, we both know that *First Responder* is due for a complete shakedown next month. I am having Lt. Commander Edwards transferred to Sector New Orleans, where that process will take place. We have already approved Commander Will Harrington's promotion and he will receive notice of that in two days. He is to report to Sector New Orleans, where Admiral Bishop will indoctrinate your son into the duties and responsibilities of sector command in his territory. When that is complete, Captain William Harrington will assume command of Sector Corpus Christi, Texas, and will be the commanding officer that Commander Jacob Edwards will answer to as the captain of *First Responder*."

James doesn't like everything he's hearing, but he's got his daddy's political bone and knows a good compromise when he hears it. It dawns on him that with this new assignment, his son will be the youngest officer to assume a sector command. That is a feather in the Harrington family's cap. "Commandant, considering this new development with my son, I see no more reason to oppose Lt. Commander Edwards's promotion and his being given command of *First Responder*. Although someone should inform that cowboy that he better be careful to dot all his I's and cross all his T's, because under Captain William Harrington's command, we will tolerate no shenanigans."

James stands, smugly salutes his superior, and walks out of his office.

As Harry watches his second-in-command close the door, he lets out a huge sigh of relief. He really does not mind giving Corpus Christi to Will Harrington. The man has shown himself to be an excellent administrator. He has also blossomed into a very intelligent and confident Coast Guard officer; and if they can just keep him from being too influenced by his self-important blowhard father, he'll turn out just fine. As he ponders these things, the buzz of his private cell phone from the corner of his desk catches his attention. The indicator display says unknown, but he knows exactly who is calling him. He picks it up and answers the call.

"Captain Williams, your timing is impeccable. Harrington just left my office moments ago."

"Did everything go the way you wanted it to, sir?"

Harry leans back in his chair and looks up with a sly grin on his face. "The day I can't handle that self-seeking aristocrat is the day I call it quits. Yes, he's pacified, and Jacob will be in command of *First Responder* within the month."

"Sir, it was only a suggestion. It's your command, and we would support any decision you made about Edwards. But thanks, and I don't think you will regret it, either. Jacob can handle anything you throw at him."

"He's one of my favorites, too, Tommy. Did you tell him about *First Responder?*"

"No sir, I did not. That's your place, not mine. But I need to remind you that if he is to remain one of our operatives, I will at times have to work around Will Harrington. We will always brief you in advance, and it will always be your call whether or not we can use Jacob, but Will Harrington must remain out of that loop."

"Don't worry, Tommy. The secretary of Homeland Security and I signed on to this deal fully aware of the intricacies. As long as The Living Legend is in command of this secret, intraoperative military/law enforcement thing you have going, we're willing to work with you. Thank you, Captain." Harry swiftly hangs up the phone before Captain Tommy Williams can rebuff his use of the label that he hates so much. He smiles and picks up some documents from his desk labeled "Commander Jacob Edwards, Commanding Officer of *First Responder.*" He inwardly chuckles. *OK, Jacob, let's see about sitting you down in the captain's chair.*

Two days later, Starr County, Texas, Home of Jacob, Mary, and Danielle Edwards

Jacob sits with his nine-year-old daughter, Danielle, on his lap as his wife, Mary, leans on his shoulder. The three are on the back porch of their little two-bedroom, ranch-style house watching the beautiful Texas sunset. He has just told them about Chuck and Nancy's engagement, and about Chuck's decision to leave the Guard and become an FBI agent

"Daddy, are we still going to see Uncle Chuck?"

Jacob pats Danielle's head affectionately. "Of course, honey. We're just not going to be living close to one another anymore. But Nancy wants you and your mother to be in the wedding. Mommy's going to be the Matron of Honor and you'll be a flower girl."

"What are you going to do, Daddy?"

"I have the same job at Uncle Chuck's wedding that he had at mine. Best Man."

Mary sits up and looks seriously at Jacob's face. "Have you heard yet what we'll do?" Before Jacob can respond, the phone in the house rings. Mary gets up and answers it. One minute later she hurries back out. "Jacob, it's Commandant Rogers!"

Danielle hops off her dad's lap and Jacob gets up to answer the phone.

"Commandant Rogers, Lt. Commander Jacob Edwards. What can I do for you, sir?"

"Nice work you and Yeager pulled off down there in Falcon Lake, son. We've done all we can there. Now it's up to the Mexicans."

"Captain Williams said the same thing, sir. Lt. Commander Yeager already told me what he's doing next. I'm hoping you called to let me know what is next for me, so I can tell my girls."

"Jacob, you've really turned heads lately. Even the Joint Chiefs of Staff know who you are and what you guys just pulled off. Now, son, you better sit down, because this one will shock you."

Jacob takes a big gulp and pulls out the kitchen chair and sits. "Go ahead, sir."

"Well, for one, as of today you are now Commander Jacob Edwards. And two, you will assume command of the Hamilton-class cutter, *First Responder,* after she gets out of refit in New Orleans."

There is a ten-second pause as now-Commander Edwards processes what he was just told by the commandant of the Coast Guard. He looks up and sees Mary and Danielle standing in the kitchen doorway with anxious looks on their faces. Jacob catches his breath, holds up a hand to stave off questions from the girls, and says, "Sir, you know I just reached my sixteen-year mark. I have never even heard of someone commanding a Hamilton without at least twenty years under their belt and four stripes on their shoulders. How is this going to look to the rest of the Guard, sir?"

Harry laughs heartily. "Don't worry, Jacob. Every admiral in the Guard gave me their personal approval on this. Hell, the president himself contacted the secretary of Homeland Security today to make sure I gave you the news. We all want this to happen, and I think you know why."

Jacob gets a sly grin on his face and remembers his conversation with Captain Williams the other day. "So, The Legend wants to have access to a Hamilton in the Caribbean, huh? That makes sense when I think about it.

Few people understand what's going on in those waters better than Chuck and me. Now that Chuck's going to the FBI, I'm what's left."

"You were always my first choice, Jacob. Chuck's a superior officer and one of the finest investigators we've ever had, but you know how to command, and that's what a Hamilton needs at the helm. There is more to this. You're right that your sudden advancement in rank and position could ruffle a lot of feathers, but Captain Williams and I came up with a solution that will even smooth that one out. You and Chuck are to be decorated. We will award you both with the Coast Guard Cross, which as you know is the highest honor we can give out."

Jacob stands straight up out of his chair. "But sir, that medal has never been awarded to anyone yet!"

"Calm down, Jacob. I know what you're thinking. No one is supposed to know what you and Chuck were really doing down there. But now that it's over and we've done all we can in that region, Captain Williams and I both agree that it's OK to let the rest of the world in on some of the stuff you boys had to go through to clean up all the cartel activity there. Besides, God knows that after all the shit Tommy's had you guys in over the last nine years, you both deserve ten more of those damn things, and you know it, too. I need this to make my decision to put you in the captain's chair go unchallenged. There's just not a hell of a lot of good men with your particular talents and knowledge that can do this for us. Besides, the president himself wants this, and you don't have a choice. Am I understood, Commander?"

Jacob takes a big gulp, a little taken aback at being reprimanded and being called by his new rank all at the same time. "Yes sir, Commandant. Not a problem. As soon as I get my orders I'll report as directed, sir."

One Month Later, Coast Guard Sector, New Orleans

Jacob and Chuck are standing on a platform next to Commandant Admiral Harry Rogers and Vice Commandant Admiral James Harrington, as the secretary of Homeland Security is addressing the crowd of over 250 people seated and standing around the stage. News crews from half a dozen agencies are filming the event, and in the crowd are Mary and Danielle, along with Jacob's mother and father, Jim and Linda Edwards. The fact that Captain Tommy Williams is in the back of the crowd wearing sunglasses and in his civilian clothes does not escape Jacob's or Chuck's attention. Jacob sees that the secretary is about to finish his speech and prepares for what comes next.

"Now, for performances above and beyond the call of duty; unprecedented law enforcement and military achievement; and undying perseverance and adherence to the highest standards of service to one's country and its people, I hereby award the distinguished Coast Guard Cross to Commander Jacob Edwards and Lt. Commander Chuck Yeager."

The secretary steps away from the podium and joins the two admirals. The commandant hands the medals to him. He pins the first one on Chuck and the second one on Jacob. He turns around and claps. The whole crowd stands up, clapping and cheering too.

An hour later, Jacob is sitting at a table outside the New Orleans Coast Guard HQ, enjoying refreshments with Mary and Danielle; his parents, Jim and Linda; Mary's parents, Chief Roberto Garcia and his wife, Isabella; and Chuck and his fiancée, Nancy. The mood is light and mirthful as the group is talking about how Jacob and Chuck will now be doing different things.

Chuck leans back in his chair and puts an affectionate arm around Nancy. "Well, now that she is out of medical school, I figure it's time to step back and take it easy for a while. After her first internship, she'll be making double what I will at the FBI. I might just settle for some soft desk assignment somewhere and coast on into retirement." Everyone laughs except for Nancy, who playfully punches him in the ribs.

Jacob leans forward. "Yeah, and the first time some mysterious unsolvable crime happens, Inspector Clouseau here won't be able to contain himself and will fumble his way into catching whatever idiot bad guy was unfortunate enough to get on his misguided radar."

Chuck winks, and with his best Peter Sellers imitation says, "And then once again the case will be sol-ved!!"

As everyone is laughing, a loud, commanding voice interrupts from behind them. "Commander Edwards, a moment of your time, please."

Jacob turns around in his chair to see the Vice Commandant, Admiral James Harrington, standing with a younger-looking captain whom Jacob recognizes from photographs as Captain William Harrington, the admiral's son, and his new commanding officer. Jacob, Chuck, and Chief Garcia all stand and salute as the admiral waves Jacob over.

Jacob stands at attention in front of the vice commandant a little longer than is necessary. Finally, Captain Harrington tells Jacob to stand at ease, but before he can reach out to shake Jacob's hand, the Vice Commandant gruffly interrupts. "Commander, I think it is appropriate that you meet your new commanding officer." He points his right index finger to his son and says, "This is *Captain* William Harrington, the next commander of Sector Corpus Christi. Now, both of you have been rather abruptly promoted and given responsibilities traditionally beyond your seniority. However, Commander, unlike you, the captain here is third-generation Coast Guard and comes from an affluent and well-connected family in Washington political circles."

He moves up a little closer to Jacob so no one but him and his son can hear. "What I am saying, Commander, is that if you want to survive this little exhibition of politics and flamboyancy, you will submit to Captain Harrington's tutelage and management of your career. I have taught him how to navigate these slippery roads of the military-political games around here, and you would do well to heed my admonition in this." Without even acknowledging Jacob, he turns to his son and shakes his hand as he grasps his shoulder. "I leave the rest to you, Captain Harrington." With that, the admiral gives his back to Jacob and strolls off.

The commander and the captain stare at one another for a few seconds, and then Will busts out laughing as he reaches out and grasps Jacob's hand. "I'm sorry, Commander. Sometimes my dad can be a little over the top. Congratulations on the Coast Guard Star and the promotion. I guess we're both in a little over our heads. Tell you what—you cover my ass and I'll do the same for you. Maybe after a while we can look like we deserve what fate just threw our way. What do you say?"

Jacob visibly relaxes and returns the handshake. They both walk back over to where the Edwards and Yeager parties are eating, and Jacob introduces them all to his new commanding officer.

Roberto and Chuck stand up and salute first and then shake his hand. Chuck then looks at the captain and says, as he begins to put two and two together, "Wait a minute. A friend of mine, LTJG. Alex Maelstrom, got transferred to *First Responder* three months ago. You were the XO on that ship, right?"

Will smiles. "Yes, and it's Lieutenant Maelstrom as of today, and he is one of the few who will continue on with Commander Edwards here on *First Responder*. Captain Billings has just received his promotion to admiral and his appointment as the new commanding officer of the Coast Guard Academy. One might say the Guard is getting the same shakedown that *First Responder* is. Hopefully, all these changes will just make for a better Guard and a safer country."

Roberto picks up his drink and raises it in the air. "I will drink to that, Captain. Here's to bigger and better things for the Guard."

Everyone raises their drinks, including Captain Harrington who says, "For the Guard."

Captain Harrington finishes the toast and excuses himself from the group. Jacob settles back down, and as he is about to take a bite of his sandwich, Chuck raises an eyebrow and motions for Jacob to turn around. Jacob turns his head and sees a lieutenant commander and a very attractive, dark-haired woman standing behind him. He recognizes both of them from the personal dossier he was given of *First Responder's* crew and their families. He stands, turns around, and gives the man and his wife a smile. The lieutenant commander stiffens, throws a smart salute and says, "Commander Edwards, I'm Lt. Commander..."

"Larry Phillips, and this is your wife, Rhonda. You're now my XO on *First Responder*. It's a pleasure to meet you both," Jacob says, finishing the officer's sentence. He returns the salute and reaches out to shake the man's hand. Jacob then looks back at his wife and daughter and says, "Lt. Commander, Mrs. Phillips, this is my wife, Mary, and my daughter, Danielle."

Jacob puts his hand on Phillips's shoulder and says, "It is a pleasure to finally meet you and your beautiful wife, Larry. I have read your file and I'm looking forward to serving with you on *First Responder*."

Phillips thanks Jacob profusely then smiles at his wife. "OK, Rhonda, let's leave the commander to enjoy his family and guests."

Jacob reaches over and grabs Mary's hand, kisses it, then looks back at Chuck and Nancy. "Every CO that guy has ever had has made notations on his record that he is one of the most dedicated and brightest officers they had ever worked with. That's the premise from which I plan to start our working relationship."

CHAPTER THREE

DEALS STRUCK, PLANS MADE

Office of Prince Abuella Hasheen;
Member of the Saudi Royal Family and
Largest Oil Mogul in the Middle East

Peter Rasmov sits next to his uncle Boris, who is talking to one of the richest men in the world. Peter has been on extended assignment for his uncle down in the Caribbean for almost a decade now. Being the lieutenant of the infamous pirate assassin and madman, Dominik Thrace, has been the biggest roller coaster ride of his young life. He has lived from one marauding adventure to another with the undefeated underworld cage fighter. Killing, raping, and pillaging, along with some drug and gun smuggling and assassination work thrown in, was just business as usual in Thrace's crew. Though Dominik is intimidating and even frightening, to Peter there will be no one who evokes more fear and blind loyalty in him than his uncle Boris.

"Peter, how well connected is our network from Padre Island to New Orleans?"

Peter quickly shakes the reverie from his mind and stands to look at the map that Uncle Boris and Prince Abuella Hasheen are poring over. He takes a pointer stick from the bottom of the board and points at different locations. "It's mostly fishing companies and oil rig employee transport companies up and down the Texas coast. We have the same in Louisiana, plus two tourist cruise ships that go between that port, Houston, Corpus Christi, and Mexico. The latter, as you know, have been effective in moving product and personnel from one location to another undetected. As you have arranged, these networks can be tied only to local assets and have nothing that could connect them to any of your other interests, Uncle."

Boris steps up and asks for the pointer, then motions for Peter to sit down again. He draws an imaginary arc around the perimeter of the Gulf. "So, you see, Prince, we have a network in place that could access many of the larger platforms easily and without suspicion. As for the cruise ship line, human sacrifices can be an effective measure if needed to dramatize and publicize an operation." He puts the pointer down, and in a very rare gesture for Boris Rasmov, he smiles. "I believe we can accomplish this for you with no danger of exposing you or your organizations."

The prince ponders the map for a few seconds and then mimics Boris's smile. "Your reputation for attention to detail and objective analyses is not without merit. Pedro Guerra's recommendation of your services is fortunate." He holds both hands out in an agreeing gesture. "I believe we have a deal. Let's proceed as planned." Boris smiles again and gives a slight nod of his head as he gestures to Peter to follow him out. As he is leaving, the prince says, "One more request, if you do not mind, Boris."

"Anything, Prince Hasheen. Only say the word."

The prince walks over to Peter and puts his hand on the young man's shoulder. "I understand that your nephew here has been Dominik Thrace's lieutenant for the last few years, and that he has been trained by him. Is that so?"

Boris looks quizzically at the prince. "That is true. Peter here is only the second person we have forced Dominik to have the patience to train without killing. The first was the son of a rather enigmatic client of mine in Central America. Unlike Peter here, the man's son was only fourteen when he was trained. Although I am told he has grown into a very competent fighter, he has not grown to be the accomplished killer my nephew has. Why do you ask?"

Prince Hasheen raises his right hand and waves it in the air in a nonchalant gesture. "I lost some of my best fighters and millions of dollars in betting against Santiago's devil, Dominik Thrace, during his reign of terror in Maximillian's famous cage fights. I have a very promising young contender whom I very much want to see do well in there. Since they retired your Dominik from the circuit and he is not available, I would consider it a deep personal favor if you would allow your nephew to contend with him for, say, ten minutes? Whoever puts the other down or gains a yield in that time wins. What do you say, Boris?"

Without even looking at Peter, Boris agrees to the proposal. He then focuses on his nephew. "Prepare yourself, and do not disappoint me."

The prince motions them to an adjoining chamber that has a complete MMA-style pentagon ring and elevated spectator seats outside the cage. He has Boris take a seat while he motions Peter to go to a side room where he can change and prepare.

Twenty minutes later, Peter and another man enter the ring, along with an older military officer whom Boris surmises will act as referee. Both fighters are similar in height and stature. They are both very muscular in a wiry way that reveals they did not earn their bulging, muscular frames from bodybuilding all day, but in preparing for and performing hand-to-hand combat. When Peter comes around the ring and presents his back to Boris and Hasheen, several long, dark red furrows of scars stand out on it. Hasheen pulls his vodka martini glass away from his lips and asks Boris, "Did Dominik give those to your nephew while training him?"

Boris shows the slightest crease of a smile. "Peter was my pupil long before he ever met Dominik Thrace. He proved to be a very stubborn child. I often found it necessary to discipline him in an attention-getting manner. I eventually got through to him and he became quite competent in the skill sets I imparted. Thrace has had him for over nine years now. I am told Peter is the only man that has ever lasted over ten minutes with him without being killed."

The military officer has Peter and the other combatant face each other. "When one of you doesn't get up or yields, the other wins. That is the only rule." He yells "Begin!" and steps back. Prince Hasheen's man is fast, and he steps in tight with a left/right strike to Peter's face, both vertical punches. When Peter tries to counterstrike with a right cross of his own, the man ties up his arm with a curved palm block and then uses the momentum of the block to thrust another vertical fist into Peter's sternum, followed by a palm strike to his face, which knocks him down. Peter immediately rolls backward and gains his feet. He looks at his opponent, who is now advancing toward him in a traditional Wing Chun stance.

It is hard to gain a strike on a Wing Chun fighter by coming at them straight on with punches or kicks, but if one can figure out the timing of the other, there are openings that can present themselves if one is quick and observant. Peter mimics his opponent's stance and moves in for a traditional exchange of tan sau and bong sau Wing Chun blocks and strikes with Hasheen's man. Peter is just as quick as his opponent, and both men begin to display a beautiful demonstration of traditional, high-speed Wing Chun sparring, with each man occasionally landing a vertical punch or palm strike. Peter bides his time as he brings his opponent to an almost textbook-perfect sparring routine where each move is a calculated and predictable response to the other's.

When the traditional flow of punches and blocks are at their peak, and it almost seems like both opponents are fighting at lightning speed, Peter breaks with the routine, presses his whole body into the man's perimeter, moves both of his arms in a vertical arc and then lifts them straight up and outward, bringing his opponent's arms and hands with them. He then smashes his forehead into his opponent's face, shattering his nose. The man screams and reaches up to cup his face with both hands. But before he can, Peter puts his right hand up by his left ear, palm facing out, arching his whole body as he twists his open hand to face the knuckles outward. He then catapults a backhanded strike into the man's left jaw right below the ear, knocking him out cold.

Without waiting for the referee to say who won, Peter turns and walks over to his uncle Boris and Prince Hasheen. On the way, he grabs a cup of water and a towel to wipe his face. He steps up to the men, takes a long drink, and wipes blood from his mouth. "Your man shows ability and skill, but you need to expand his fighting horizons. He is a true master of Wing Chun Kung Fu, but he needs to learn how to adapt and change. Dominik Thrace would have killed him in sixty seconds."

Boris's expression is unreadable as he turns to the prince for a response. Hasheen sits there fighting with his disappointment over the match, but gains his composure and responds. "Your nephew is remarkable, Boris. I congratulate both you and Thrace on what you have accomplished with him. I believe that we have concluded our business for the day. Both of you have my full confidence that our next business endeavor will be enormously successful and profitable. Boris, whatever you need in capital or resources, you need only ask. My people will be at your disposal."

Prince Hasheen says his goodbyes and excuses himself. The same military officer who acted as referee then escorts Boris and Peter to the door, where their car and driver are waiting. Boris looks over at his nephew sternly. "We need to be very careful how we proceed with this contract. Prince Hasheen is one of the richest and most powerful men in the world, but I fear this endeavor may be too big for him to pull off, even with our help. We need only make sure we are covered for any eventuality. I need his money to complete setting up my services to the crime families on the east coast of the United States. The Mexican and South American cartels are all on board, and we are on the verge of having the most aggressive money-laundering service in the Americas. Hasheen wants to own the world oil markets. If we can make that so, then all is well. But if this fails, which it could, I still need his money. Do you understand, Peter?"

"Yes, Uncle, but aren't there strict rules inside the council that no one can break, and especially one who is still a pledge like yourself?"

Boris is both pleased and amused with his nephew's insight. "Peter, Prince Hasheen is not a member of the council I am now pledged to join. His group is a different entity with which we, more times than not, have been at war over the centuries. Even now, factions within both our camps sponsor different sides in the conflict going on in the Gulf. No repercussions will come from the council I am associated with, should circumstances force us to aggressively deal with the good prince."

As they drive away, Boris tells his nephew to catch the first flight he can back to Moscow and report to his father about getting the proper personnel for the upcoming mission.

Chapter Four

Tying up Loose Ends and Getting Ready to Launch

July 3, 2004, United States Coast Guard Shipyard, New Orleans, Louisiana

Commander Edwards walks up the dock, inspecting his new command. *First Responder* is sporting a brand-new paint job. They finished installing its new engines and the OTO Melara gun system. Jacob served on this Hamilton before. His first assignment out of the academy was on *First Responder*. He and Chuck came on together as ensigns, and they both stayed long enough to make lieutenant junior grade, or LTJG. This was the ship he served on when they came across the Mexican finance minister's yacht off Honduras back in '96. He still remembers Captain Billings ordering him and Chuck to take a skiff over and investigate. What they found still haunts him to this day—an entire family slaughtered.

"She's looking damn good. Should get another ten years out of her."

Jacob turns to see his old commanding officer and the former captain of *First Responder* standing behind him. Jacob first smiles then immediately comes to attention and salutes Admiral Billings. He returns the salute and tells Jacob, "At ease. I wanted to see her one more time before I passed her off to you, son. She's a good ship and will get the job done. Don't be afraid to push her, Jacob." He laughs and winks. "She doesn't like it when you go easy on her."

"I'll give her my best, sir."

Admiral Billings puts his hand on Jacob's shoulder. "You give your crew your best, son. We call these contraptions 'her,' but we all know they are just a tool. Your command is your people. Never forget that, and you'll be the skipper that the commandant and I know you can be."

"Thank you, sir. I'll do my best to be like the captain *First Responder* has always had."

Billings winks. "You be a *better* captain, like I know you can be. That's what will make me happy. Take care, Jacob. Come by and see me sometime." They shake hands again and Jacob promises to visit the new Coast Guard Academy superintendent soon.

Jacob turns and makes his way to the gangplank of his new ship. As he approaches the deck, he sees his next

XO, Lt. Commander Larry Phillips, talking to one of the ship's gunnery chiefs and a seaman. Phillips turns and sees Jacob approaching, and calls everyone to attention. They salute their new commander and he returns the gesture. Phillips says, "Commander, this is our Gunnery Chief Petty Officer Arin Thompson, and this is his new assistant apprentice, Seaman Marvin Schuette. We've just installed the new OTO Melara gun, and Chief Petty Officer Thompson here was just drilling the seaman on its maintenance."

Jacob is about ready to tell the men to carry on so he can talk privately with his new XO when he notices Schuette is sporting quite a shiner on his left eye. "You run into a door or something, seaman?"

The man nervously reaches up and touches his eye then shyly looks at Chief Thompson. The chief just nods and tells him to tell the commander what happened. Schuette looks at Jacob. "Commander, the chief and a few other guys on the crew heard about one of the gunnies over at the Marine Corps base offering to have Coast Guard enlisted men come over and join his hand-to-hand combat training. This happened when he was showing a disarm-and-take-down move on me to the group."

Jacob steps close to Schuette and looks directly into the injured eye. He's had a lot of experience triaging injuries when he and Chuck were out on special assignment with Captain Williams and wants to make sure there is no retina damage to that eye. He steps back and looks directly at Lt. Commander Phillips. "Have this man report to a doctor for an eye exam before we leave

41

on our shakedown cruise next week. I don't see any real damage, but I'm not a doctor."

Phillips looks over at Chief Thompson, who tells both officers it will be handled right away. Jacob smiles and pats Schuette on the back.

"Thank you, men, carry on. Lt. Commander, let's take a tour."

For the next four hours, Jacob has Phillips show him every square inch of *First Responder*, introducing him to all the department heads and most of the enlisted men. He is very thorough in his inspection of all the upgraded systems the ship received in its recent overhaul.

That Evening, Edwards's Apartment Complex

Jacob and Danielle are in the pool area of their apartment complex, off to the side on the grass. He has her on a fifteen-foot plank that is six inches wide and raised two feet off the ground on cinder blocks. Jacob is standing in front of his daughter, straddling the plank and holding up two martial arts striking-focus pads, one in each hand. They are working on balance and striking with both the hands and the feet. She steps forward on the plank, does a tight cartwheel, lands, and then either performs a spinning back fist to the pad or a turning hook kick, all while maintaining her balance and issuing the proper power in the technique. Every once in a while, Jacob tries to touch Danielle on the head or stomach with a pad, and she blocks whatever he's throwing at her. So far, she has fallen off the plank only once and her father has not connected with any of his strikes.

They have been going at it for about an hour now, and the duo has attracted quite an audience comprised of children from around the complex, with a few adults to boot. From the back of the spectators, they hear a familiar voice excusing herself through the crowd. Mary walks up to her family and watches her daughter perform a flawless cartwheel followed by a spinning hook kick that lands squarely into Jacob's focus pad. "I think that is enough father-daughter ninja training for today. You two clean up this stuff here and let's go enjoy this nice free pool while we can."

Jacob and Danielle know better than to keep Mary from enjoying her pool time with her family, so they both immediately do what she says. As they are putting the planks back in the shed next to the pool, Danielle giggles and says, "Daddy, does Mommy outrank Commandant Rogers?"

Jacob laughs. "You know, spunky monkey, that's a good question. Let me think on that one awhile. Come on, let's go get our swimsuits on." Since Jacob's assignment in New Orleans is only temporary until *First Responder* gets out of refit, they are only spending the summer there. Mary could have opted to move down by Corpus Christi and find a house, but she and Jacob decided instead that it would be better to keep the family together while Jacob prepares for his next command.

One hour later, Jacob and Mary are lounging by the poolside, enjoying iced tea while they watch Danielle practice her diving. Mary rubs Jacob's forearm. "You two have more energy than any ten people I know. Look at her—one hour doing all that ninja stuff with you and now she'll work that diving board until we drag her off to bed. The only reason you're not out there with her is that I made you sit here to keep me company."

Jacob rolls his eyes and leans over to kiss his wife. "Baby, you'll always be my number one." As he leans back in his chair, he sees Danielle giving the old "please get a room" stare from the diving board. Just as Jacob puts both hands up in a comedic, "you caught us" gesture, his cell phone rings. He looks down to see that the call is from his XO, Phillips.

"Larry, what's up?"

"Commander, it's Chief Thompson. He's at the base infirmary with a broken arm. Apparently, he went back to talk to the sergeant at the hand-to-hand combat training, and things got heated while they were sparring, and the guy broke the chief's arm. Doc says it's a compound fracture and the chief will be out for six weeks."

Jacob rolls his eyes and then grinds his teeth. "Dammit, Larry, it's less than a week before our shakedown cruise. I'll be there in thirty minutes."

Mary stands and puts both hands on his cheeks. "You keep your temper in check, Commander. My daddy always says, keep your head cool so you're sailing on calm seas."

He thanks her for the advice, waves goodbye to Danielle and heads to the apartment to change.

Danielle dives off the board and swims over to the side of the pool where her mother is standing. She shyly looks up at her mother. "We almost had him for the whole day. That's pretty good, huh?"

Mary smiles and wraps an affectionate arm around her daughter as they head back to the apartment.

About half an hour after he hung up with Larry Phillips, Jacob makes it to the infirmary and finds Chief Thompson sitting up on an examination table with his arm in a cast. He checks with the attending doctor first, a Coast Guard Lt. Commander MD, who shows Jacob where the fracture is on a computer screen. As he points to the section of the arm that is broken, he explains, "If this were any more severe, I would recommend surgery and pins. But I think it will mend nicely if the chief takes it easy for six weeks and then does physical therapy when we take the cast off." Jacob thanks the doctor and then walks over to Chief Thompson.

"OK, chief, tell me everything and don't leave out any details."

"Well, Commander, I went to have a talk with Gunny Jones over at the Marine Corps base earlier today. He's the hand-to-hand trainer over there, and I caught him right during one of his sessions. As I came in the gym, he spots me right away and asks me what I wanted. So I tell him I want to talk about how he knocked around Seaman Schuette the other day, and that I also found out Schuette was not the first Coast Guard enlisted guy he's beat up during training. He gets all cocky with me and says someone's got to teach us puddle pirates how to toughen up, and to quit crying about it. I don't like it when they call us that, so I asked him if he wanted to give me a tough-guy lesson. We get out on the mat and for about the first ninety seconds I was doing good, even threw him to the mat twice. But then he jumps up and round-kicks me in the side of the head, lands and back-fists me on the other side, sidekicks me in the stomach, and grabs my arm and throws me down with a shoulder throw. Then he goes down hard with me, pulls my arm up his inner thigh like he's going for a submission but yanks it down across his leg, and that's when it breaks. The pain was so bad I passed out and later woke up here."

Lt. Commander Larry Phillips is standing behind them and Jacob turns to him. "What's been done about the gunny?"

Larry shrugs. "Nothing yet, Commander. The chief wanted to wait for you to get here before he decides whether to press charges or not. I know that guy can't be allowed to go around beating up people under the pretense of combat training, but he's a gunny and has probably done some good things for his country. What do you recommend, Commander?"

Jacob is glad that Chief Thompson said what he did and now knows what he's got to do. Jacob excuses himself from the others and asks the doctor if there is a private office available for him to make a phone call. The doctor directs him to one on the side of the infirmary, and Jacob closes and locks the door. He gets out his cell phone and dials an unpublished phone number he committed to memory a long time ago. "Captain Williams, you told me to call you the next time I wanted to rip someone's head off in a non government-sanctioned way. Well, I am calling, and I do."

Tommy takes a deep breath. "It's been a long time since I've heard you this mad, kid. What's going on?"

Jacob tells him the whole story about Gunny Jones and his bullying of the Coast Guard personnel and breaking Chief Thompson's arm. There is a long pause on the other end as Jacob waits for a response. "Jacob, you're talking about Gunnery Sergeant Rick Jones, stationed at the Marine Corps base near the Coast Guard base, right?"

"Yes Captain, that's the guy." Tommy burst out laughing, and Jacob pulls the phone away from his ear. "What the hell is so funny, Captain? That asshole just laid up *First Responder's* gunnery officer for her shakedown cruise next week."

Tommy gets control of himself and responds. "I'm sorry, kid, it's just that when it comes to you, I am forced to believe in serendipity. Rick Jones is one of my assets in that area, and when it comes to any special ops we do down there, you're his commanding officer."

Jacob sits down in the chair behind the doctor's desk, leans back, and blows out a puff of hot air. "I think you better tell me everything I need to know about this guy. And start with why someone with his kind of training is going around beating up my men, sir."

Tommy tells Jacob that Rick Jones entered the training just prior to 9/11 in 2000. After graduating, he was deployed to the Middle East. Toward the end of that tour, he and his platoon were ambushed and forced to retreat to the sea and their transport. But when they got there, the enemy had destroyed their vessel. They called for emergency evac and the only one available was a Coast Guard PSU security patrol boat a few miles away. They responded as soon as they could, but Jones lost half his platoon while waiting. Jones has held a grudge ever since then. He never found out what took the PSU unit so long.

"Tommy looked into it, and that same boat was evacuating a family from a war zone to safety when they got the call. They got them to safety, and when they took off to get Jones and his crew, they ended up being fired on and losing two seamen in the fight, but they got what was left of the platoon out of there. Later, Jones wanted to go back and retrieve his fallen comrades, but the Coast Guard skipper refused, telling him it was too dangerous. Jones almost caused a mutiny on the boat before some of his own men restrained him. He was a master sergeant then and got busted back to staff sergeant over the incident. He recently got promoted to gunnery sergeant and was given that post in New Orleans. Tommy has had him on stand-down for special ops since the Gulf. "The reason I say you make me believe in serendipity, kid, is you would be Jones's last chance to prove he can be a team player and be of any value to us. I was going to wait until your shakedown cruise was over before I introduced you two to each other. He just needs someone to knock sense into that thick jarhead of his. To be honest with you, kid, you're about the only one I have that could do it. That one is as tough as they come and meaner than a rattlesnake to boot."

With a mischievous grin, Jacob asks, "Does he know I work for you, or would he recognize me if he saw me?"

"No, kid, he does not know you're one of my operatives. But whether he would recognize you or not, I can't say. You were just in the news two weeks ago, but he may not pay too much attention to Coast Guard stuff. Why do you ask?"

"Well, he opened it up for us 'puddle pirates' to participate in some of his hand-to-hand combat training. So maybe I'll pay his class a visit and see if I can't instruct the instructor."

"Kid, that's all enlisted personnel in Jones's class. If you go in there pretending to be an enlisted man, he could bring you up on charges."

"Don't worry, Captain. I'm just going over there to instruct the instructor, and then he and I will have a private talk about how we both have a mutual, favorite navy captain friend in common."

"OK, Commander, but you keep that hothead of yours in check. He's a good man, and one hell of a soldier. I want him salvaged, not put out of commission. Understood?"

Jacob gives a "yes, sir" to Captain Williams and hangs up the phone. He then goes back out and asks Chief Thompson for Seaman Schuette's cell phone number. The last thing Jacob does that night before going home is to go back to his office in the Coast Guard complex across from the infirmary and use his desktop computer to look up the whole incident Tommy had told him about earlier with Gunny Jones and the Coast Guard rescue boat in the Gulf two years ago. He finds pictures and files pertaining to the incident, downloads and prints them, then sticks them in his briefcase and heads home.

The Next Evening, Marine Corps Base New Orleans

Jacob and Schuette get out of Jacob's 2001 Ford Taurus, grab their workout gear and then head over to the gym where Gunny Jones is conducting his personal combat class. As they are walking into the gym, Jacob asks, "So where you from, Schuette?"

Schuette gets a huge grin on his face as he answers the question. "Well, Commander, I'm glad you asked me. I'm from Sheridan, Wyoming."

Jacob stops, turns toward Schuette, puts both of his hands on the seaman's shoulders and lightly shakes him. "No kidding! I was born in Sheridan and lived in Story, Wyoming, until I was four years old. My dad was born and raised in Sheridan."

Schuette laughs. "I know! My grandpa on my mom's side is Lt. Al Freeburger of the sheriff's department there. He trained your dad when he was a deputy back in the early seventies. Mom said he loves your dad like a son, but he never talks to anyone about those days. Do you know why?"

Jacob chuckles. "Beats the hell out of me, Schuette. Mom and Dad refused to tell me anything about those days. After a while, I stopped asking. Look, seaman, we need to walk in separately. I don't want to announce who I am, and I don't want you to lie to anyone about me or my rank."

Schuette gives Jacob a quick "yes, sir," salutes, and runs ahead to get into the gym. Jacob comes in a few minutes later and locates the locker room. As he is changing, he notices two men from his ship. He puts a finger to his lips and quietly says "shhh," and they nod their heads and hurry into the gym. Once Jacob gets his practice gear on, he grabs his MMA grappling gloves and heads in. As he approaches the group, there are about thirty men seated around a large wrestling mat with one man in the center of the mat, waiting for everyone to quiet down and get settled.

The man is Gunny Rick Jones. He is a wiry and muscular African American, about 6'3" and two hundred pounds. He definitely has the hardened look of a seasoned combat veteran. As Jacob steps on the mat, he immediately notices that it is a thick, foam rubber wrestling mat, and makes a mental note about how that will affect the sparring. Wrestling mats are good for doing a lot of throwing and grappling, but they don't lend well to quick footwork, and he remembers how Chief Thompson said Gunny Jones used quite a few kicks in his fight against him.

Gunny Jones tells everyone to be quiet and take a seat. "My name is Gunnery Sergeant Rick Jones. You can call me Gunny Jones in this gym. Colonel Hardcastle, commanding officer of this base, wanted me to invite the puddle pirates next door to take part in some of these sessions. I didn't like the idea, but rank has its privileges, and the colonel got his way. I see that we have more gluttons for punishment returning from over there, even after I taught one of their loud-mouthed chiefs a lesson the other day. Turns out the poor guy broke his arm." Gunny Jones scans the room as some of the other Marines laugh. He then focuses on Jacob and says, "You, the big Coastie in the back. I don't recognize you. Why don't you stand up and introduce yourself?"

As soon as Gunny Jones addresses him, Jacob puts his grappling gloves on and stands up. "Name's Jacob. Chief Thompson sends his regards. He thought you and I could be pals."

A wicked grin goes across the gunny's face and he walks over to get a closer look at the new Coast Guard guy. He stands there for a few seconds, examining him. "So, what are you, some kind of Coast Guard intramural base boxing champion sent over to teach poor little Gunny Jones a lesson he won't forget?"

Jacob pushes down the old rage that wants to erupt and replaces it with an ice-cold determination in the pit of his stomach, which is what Captain Williams taught him to do. The effect always heightened his senses and steadied his mind before a fight, so there is no chance in hell he's letting the rage get to him. He nods. "Something like that. Let's dispense with all the bullshit and get right to it. What do you say, Gunny?"

Gunny Jones steps back and with a half-smile looks around. "If any of you puddle pirates in the room recognize this man from the base next door, raise your hand." Six very nervous hands go up. Jones looks over at Schuette and says, "You know this guy, Schuette? Do you think he can kick my ass?"

Schuette shrugs his shoulders. "I know him, and he's stationed here in New Orleans with the Coast Guard. Whether he can kick your ass or not, I have no clue."

Gunny Jones looks around the room again, smiles, then directs his attention back to Jacob. "OK, champ, it's your funeral. Care to join me in the middle?"

"Sure."

"The only rule here, Jacob, is that you either go down or you yield. We train for real combat here, got it?"

Jacob winks and says, "Got it, Gunny. Now please stop flapping your gums like a little schoolgirl and fight."

Gunny Jones glares at Jacob. "You son of a bitch, I'll tear you in half."

He steps in tight to Jacob with a lead-hand back fist that is easily blocked, but then Gunny jumps straight up in the air and twists his body, shoulders first, then hips, and finally his right foot impacts Jacob's face with a perfect crescent kick. He lands right foot forward, and before Jacob can recover, Jones does another jump-spin and catapults a left sidekick into Jacob's midsection. When he lands, he grabs Jacob's arm and sets him up for a hip throw, which he almost accomplishes. But with lightning-fast speed, Jacob moves in close while Jones is turned sideways, rakes him across the face with his left hand and then karate-chops him on the neck with his right. Jones goes down to one knee to compensate for the blow.

Jacob quickly replays the last few seconds in his mind and realizes he is dealing with a proficient Taekwondo kicker here, who is also good at judo. Being trained in Taekwondo explains the man's ability to kick well from off these mats, because most of his maneuvers are airborne, which that form of martial art is famous for. Instead of attacking, Jacob goes back two steps. It's a very smart move because Jones is only half-feigning the disorientation. From a kneeling position, Jones jumps straight up in the air and arches his right foot in a crescent kick sweep that barely misses Jacob's nose. When Jones lands from the maneuver, Jacob pops him in the ribs with a quick kung fu-style sidekick that does not require the twisting of the supporting leg's back heel for power.

Jacob knows that speed and flexibility are his main allies now. Because the mat hinders his feet from twisting efficiently, he has to stay on the balls of his feet and step quickly and strike from a stagnant stance. His Wing Chun is a little rusty, but he uses its stance to maneuver, and in fist fighting he has never met his equal. He then steps in and unleashes a series of six fast, hard, and straight kung fu vertical punches to Jones's face and body. The power and speed of the punches completely overwhelm Gunny and as he is falling, Jacob grabs his right arm with his left hand and steps in, arching his right arm under Jones's. He crouches down low, puts his right foot on the inside of Jones, and uses his hips to lift the man straight up off the ground. Jacob then twists his hips and shoulders, catapulting Jones to the mat. He uses his right arm to twist Jones's hand into a devastatingly painful wrist lock and turns him over on his stomach. While maintaining the wrist lock, he kneels on Jones's arm right at the elbow and pulls it up. Jones lets out a scream, and Jacob puts his face right down by his ear and says, "Gunny, do you know what you're supposed to do with a man when you have him in a lock like this in a training exercise?" He then releases the tension on the wrist and stands up. "You're supposed to let him go, you arrogant bastard. Now get on your feet."

As the humiliated Gunny gets up, everyone hears an authoritative "Atten-hut!" They all turn to the entrance of the gym, and standing in the doorway is Colonel Ralph Hardcastle, the Marine Corps base's CO. Next to him is Captain Tommy Williams of the United States Navy.

Everyone, including Jacob, stands up and salutes the two officers. Jacob gets a slight smirk on his face as he recognizes Captain Williams, and the gesture is returned in kind by the captain. The colonel walks straight up to Gunny Jones and gets one inch from his nose as he says, "Gunny, get all of these men out of here, *now!*"

Jones salutes. "Yes sir, Colonel. You heard him, everyone out!"

The whole group vacates, but Captain Williams looks over at Jacob. "Not you, Commander Edwards. We want to talk to you, too."

Gunny Jones's face goes ashen when he hears that the man he just sparred with and who just kicked his ass in front of all his men is a commander. As the men are leaving, two Marines go over to Seaman Schuette and ask him who Jacob is. Schuette tells them he's the captain of the Coast Guard cutter, *First Responder,* and his commanding officer. One of the Marines breaks out laughing. "You mean to tell me your CO came over here to teach Gunny Jones a lesson in front of all of us? Shit, Jones ain't never going to live this one down. I wish my

CO was as cool as yours." He then puts his hand on his mouth and turns around to see Colonel Hardcastle staring at him with laser beams coming out of his eyes. All enlisted men hightail it out of there after that, except for the six Coast Guard enlisted men, including Schuette. They all throw their shoulders back and turn and salute their captain before leaving the gym. Jacob returns the salute and waves them away.

The four men left in the gym stand and look at each other for about ten seconds until Hardcastle breaks the ice. "Gunny, I wanted this to be a gesture of good faith between us and the Coast Guard base, but according to Captain Williams here, you used it to perpetrate some kind of twisted vendetta you have against the Guard. By doing that, you've put mud on all of our faces."

Jones throws both hands in the air in exasperation. "Colonel, I told you I never wanted to train a bunch of puddle pirates—"

Hardcastle gets right back in Jones's face. "If you think for one minute that I give a damn what you want or don't want, you're nuts. Captain Williams here tells me that you're part of the inter-military law enforcement cooperation black ops program that he is the head of. The commandant of the Marine Corps confirmed that for me earlier today. He is the only reason you're not on a bus to Leavenworth, Gunny. He also tells me that Commander Edwards here is a ranking officer in that unit."

Jones slyly eyeballs Jacob and he finally understands what he is dealing with. "I heard about you at the captain's school. No one has topped your ratings yet."

Captain Williams laughs, pats Jacob and Jones on the back and looks at the colonel. "Gunny Jones here is one of the best men I have ever trained; and he's right, Jacob is the best. If you don't mind, Colonel, I need to speak to both these men in private."

The colonel eyeballs all three of them and then says to Captain Williams, "The commandant told me to give you my full cooperation, Captain. I'll leave you with the pleasant task of straightening out this mess." He then looks over at Jacob. "Commander, you were never here, and this never happened. I'll make sure my men know and understand that. I suggest you do the same."

Jacob salutes. "That will not be a problem, Colonel, and thank you, sir." Colonel Hardcastle returns the salute and turns and leaves the gymnasium.

Captain Williams waits until the colonel is gone and then turns to Gunny Jones. "Rick, I've given you almost two years to get over this bullshit. This is your last chance. What are you going to do?"

Gunny Jones stands there for a second, grinding his teeth and sneering at Jacob. He then looks back at the captain. "Sir, I lost half my men waiting for that Coast Guard transport and that candy-ass skipper wouldn't even help me go back and collect my fallen. We still haven't retrieved some of them. I can't even look at some of those widows in the eye. Two of those Marines had kids."

Captain Williams blows out an exasperated huff. "Gunny, we've been through this a dozen times. That transport got there as fast as they could. There is no way in hell anyone would have let you go back into that war zone until it was safe to look for those bodies. It's what happens in war. You know that."

"I don't care, Captain. It never should have taken them that long and no one will explain it."

Jacob interrupts their exchange. "Captain Williams, I have a few documents in the locker room that might help here. Do you mind if I go get them?"

Tommy nods his head, and Jacob runs back to the lockers. When he comes back, he is holding a manila folder that says "Top Secret" on it. He opens it up and pulls out two military personnel photos and some documents and hands them to Gunny Jones.

The Marine takes them and asks, "What's this?"

Jacob points his finger at the first picture and then the second. "This is Seaman John Kaiser, and this is Chief Ralph Maynard. They were killed by enemy fire breaking through a blockade just before their vessel rescued what was left of your platoon that day."

Gunny Jones looks over at Captain Williams. "No one told me that anyone died on that boat!"

Captain Williams ignores Gunny Jones and glares at Jacob. "Commander, that information is classified. How the hell did you get it?"

By this time, all three men are seated on the bleachers at the side of the gym. Jacob chuckles. "I went back to my office last night to find out what happened with Gunny here and that Coast Guard cutter. When I pulled up the records, I saw right away that some info had been blanked out, so I used my security clearance that I got from you to access more. I was still denied. I was about ready to give up when my dad called me on my cell phone to talk. After a while I told him what I was doing, and he said he knows someone that could probably help. He tells me to wait at my desk for a while and hangs up. About an hour later, I get these two files in my email from the Sheridan County Sheriff's Department in Wyoming. The note attached said: 'Tell Jim he's welcome. Lt. Al Freeburger.'"

Gunny Jones grabs the papers and looks at the note. "Is that who I think it is, Captain?"

Captain Williams looks over at the papers and nods his head. "Yup, that would be retired Sergeant Major Al Freeburger of the United States Marine Corps. I was not aware that he was still with the sheriff's department, though. He's almost ninety."

Gunny Jones scrutinizes Jacob. "Commander, how the hell does your dad have a connection with that old warhorse?"

Jacob shrugs. "Dad was a Sheridan County sheriff's deputy back in the early seventies and Lt. Freeburger was his training officer. That's all I know."

Jones looks over to Captain Williams for clarification.

"Don't look at me. All I know is the secretary of the Navy once burned my ass for stepping on the Sergeant Major's toes. Anybody who knows of or has even heard of Freeburger says he's more connected than Verizon and ATT combined."

"I'll let you in on something you probably don't know, Gunny. Seaman Schuette is Freeburger's only grandson."

For the third time that day, Gunny Jones's face turns ashen. He then gets ahold of himself and says, "OK, OK,

I've been a real dickhead lately, sirs. Just tell me what happened on that Coast Guard ship before it rescued us."

Captain Williams grabs the papers out of Gunny's hands. "Well, since Freeburger got permission for Jacob to let you see all of this, I guess I can tell you the rest. But guys, this one's barely in my security clearance rating, so keep it to yourselves. The ship was doing evac of refugees from the war zone when it inadvertently picked up a deep cover CIA operative that had classified intel on some terrorist cells in that area. The enemy did not know who this guy was and no one from their side could ID him, but they knew he got on that ship; so, they sent out a strike force to take that Coast Guard cutter out. Well, the good guys made it and they passed the intel on, but the operative wanted to go back. At first, they denied him because they deemed it too risky. Then the Coast Guard got your distress call. It was Chief Maynard's call to go back and try to retrieve you boys. The CIA operative tagged along. They went back the same way they had come and ended up having to fight their way through the force that had chased them. They fought their way through, dropped off the operative, and picked up what was left of your unit. As far as I know that operative is still functioning in that region today. Now that I told you all this, you probably could ID that guy, couldn't you, Gunny?"

Gunny Jones has both elbows on his knees as he cradles his forehead in his hands. Jacob and Captain Williams can tell how overwhelmed and deeply ashamed the truth makes him feel. He looks up with moisture in the corners of his eyes. "The Coast Guard skipper told me he was a refugee who wanted to see if he could find the rest of his family. I even argued with him that it was too dangerous, but the man jumped ship and waded into shore before I could stop him. The answer to your question is yes, I can identify the man. What now, Captain?"

Captain Williams puts a reassuring hand on Gunny Jones's shoulder. "Now we all keep our mouths shut and pray to God that whoever Freeburger got permission from to give Jacob this info is big enough to keep all three of us out of hot water."

Texas Ranch, Earlier the Same Day

The former president of the United States—who was also the former director of the CIA—sits in in his private office, talking to his favorite Marine on the phone. Al Freeburger does not get out much these days. The doc told him he has lung cancer and can't put too much stress on himself.

"Mr. President, I can't thank you enough for getting me those files. I can't stand to hear about a Marine going bad because he doesn't understand something. Jim's boy just wants to help him, and it looks like that peacock black ops guy, The Living Legend, wants to also."

The president chuckles at Al's reference to Tommy Williams. "What do you have against Captain Williams, Al?"

"Nothing, really. He got uppity with me a few years back trying to dig into Jim Edwards' past, and I had to make a few phone calls and send him a note to back him off."

"Geez, Al, remind me to never get on your bad side, OK?"

"Ain't no commander-in-chief, former or present, ever has to worry about any flak from yours truly. All they will ever get is a salute and a 'yes, sir.'"

"You take care, Sergeant Major, and don't worry about that intel leaking. We've already pulled that asset out of the Middle East and he's back at Langley getting ready for his next assignment."

"Gotcha, Mr. President. Thank you!"

Next Day, Coast Guard Dock, *First Responder* Bay

Jacob is talking to Lt. Commander Phillips on the dock next to the now completely refurbished Coast Guard cutter, *First Responder*. Chief Thompson and Seaman Schuette are standing next to their CO and XO as they discuss how to proceed with their personnel problem in the gunnery department of the ship.

Thompson is standing there with his arm in a sling as he says, "Excuse me, Commander, but the fact is Schuette here is a bright kid and will make a fine gunnery officer someday, but he still has a lot to learn. I'm the only noncommissioned officer in this sector who is fully rated in the operation of the OTO Melara. Broken arm or not, if you want to test it out on maneuvers and target practicing, you're going to have to bring me along. The doc ain't going to like it, but how do we have a choice?"

"Because I'm here to replace you, Chief." All four men turn to see Gunny Jones walking toward them. He steps up to Jacob, salutes, and hands him some papers. "Commander, Gunnery Sergeant Rick Jones reporting for temporary assignment to replace Chief Thompson as gunnery officer for *First Responder*."

Gunny Jones remains at attention as Jacob, Lt. Commander Phillips, and Chief Thompson look over the orders that were just handed to Jacob. Earlier, Thompson was briefed on everything that had happened the previous evening, except for the CIA asset who was involved in the Gulf War incident with Gunny Jones losing half his men waiting for rescue. He holds no grudges toward Gunny and is pretty flabbergasted at what is transpiring.

Jacob reads about four pages then hands the report part of the orders to Phillips and looks over at Gunny. "At ease, Sergeant. This is extraordinary. It says in these orders that you served on an Oliver Hazard Perry-class frigate as a staff sergeant in charge of a Marine security detail. And that you were certified on the OTO Melara, and hold a trainer's status for that weapon with the United States Navy. Care to elaborate, Gunny?"

Gunny Jones can't hold back a slight chuckle as he responds. "Well, sir, during our maneuvers in the Gulf, the gunnery chief and I became friends. I asked if he could put me through the training on that weapon and he did. You know that the Marine Corps is part of the Department of the Navy and such cross-training is not that uncommon. Plus, every bit of certification can only help your career. The chief who trained me was killed in a naval confrontation in the Gulf. The CO asked me to take over, which I did. We ended up taking out three attacking vessels in that fight. It took the navy almost three months to get another gunnery officer to replace me. By then, I had seen a dozen more fights and earned my trainer's status in that weapons system. Colonel Hardcastle called me in this morning and gave me these orders. They have been cleared through the offices of the Marine Corps and Coast Guard commandants. Until Chief Thompson here is cleared to return to full active duty, I am your gunnery replacement officer."

Jacob directs his attention to Chief Thompson. "Chief, you OK with this? The man has combat experience with the OTO Melara, and he is a certified trainer. Schuette here would be in good hands; but if you don't like it, I'll call the commandant myself and request other arrangements."

Chief Thompson glares at Gunny Jones for a second, making everyone think he will object to the man's help, but then he gets a huge grin on his face as he laughs then holds out his good hand and says, "Gunny, I'd be honored for you to take my spot for a few weeks. Hell, my wife is so excited about my paid time off she's already booked a flight to South Padre Island, where she wants to stay in some fancy hotel and lounge on the beach the whole time. Now I don't have to worry about getting a frying pan to my head for telling her to cancel."

Gunny Jones lets out a big sigh of relief. He takes the chief's hand and warmly shakes it. "I can't tell you how sorry I am about the arm, Chief. You really are good at judo and grappling. I started using those wrestling mats when your Coast Guard personnel were invited to join the sessions. They gave me an unfair advantage because of my Taekwondo background. Aerial kicks are our thing. The commander here was the first to figure it out and teach me a lesson. When the colonel checked in with your medical people and found out your arm would heal fine, he told me. That's when he let me in on his plan to offer me as your replacement until you're better. After the little pow-wow last night, and how I got straightened out on some personal issues, I was gung-ho on the idea. Thanks, Chief."

Jacob smiles at Thompson. "Enjoy your time off, Chief, and while you're down in South Padre Island, look up my father-in-law, Chief Garcia, at Brazos. If you're lucky, he'll invite you and the missus over for some BBQ spareribs. Once you eat those, you'll never want to leave."

"Thanks, Commander. I'll do that." He then salutes his superiors and leaves the dock.

Lt. Commander Phillips sees that Gunny Jones wants to talk privately, so he grabs Seaman Schuette and heads back aboard *First Responder*. Once they are gone, Gunny Jones motions Jacob to a bench and they sit down. "Did Captain Williams get ahold of you last night?" he asks.

"No, Gunny. I had my phone turned off all night so I could enjoy my family. What's up?"

"Well, sir, the captain says he caught wind of a terror threat to the major oil rigs in this area of the Caribbean, and he wants us to do reconnaissance, ASAP."

Jacob shakes his head and slaps his knee. "So that's why I got a Marine Corps gunny on my crew. Boy, Captain Williams sure can pull strings, can't he?"

Gunny Jones holds up a forestalling hand. "No, Commander, after you left last night, Colonel Hardcastle called me in to his office. He talked with your new CO, Captain Harrington, and apologized for what I did to Chief Thompson. Captain Harrington is the one who said you did not have a ready gunnery replacement available, and that you were about to go on your shakedown cruise after refit. Hardcastle knows my background and called Marine Corps HQ and got ahold of the commandant, who got the ball rolling for me to be here this morning. I didn't even hear from Captain Williams until I got home. He told me to let you know he'll see you later today to discuss the details of the op."

Jacob sits there shaking his head and chuckling. "You know, they call him The Living Legend, and no one is ever willing to say why he got that rep, but anymore I'm thinking it's because the guy has more luck than seven little green Irish leprechauns."

Jacob and Gunny Jones stand and head toward *First Responder* to board and introduce everyone to the new gunnery officer.

CHAPTER FIVE

MAKE A DEAL WITH THE DEVIL

Same Day, Northern New Jersey

Vice Commandant Admiral Will Harrington never has liked anyone to know his private business, especially that his late father, the famous Senator Harrington, wasted the family fortune. All the Harringtons had left was a small, local bank named Harrington Savings and Loan. James is sure it won't last another decade, and it's really all he will have left when he retires. Some bigger banking chains in the state offered to buy them out for a pittance of what he honestly believed it was worth; but he knows that if anyone buys the institution, certain unsavory details about how his father conducted business would be at risk of being exposed, and to a Harrington, that is unacceptable. It's better to close the operation and liquidate the assets once and for all.

He's about to call a realtor and have the property assessed when he receives an email from some firm called Rasmov-Sebastion Conglomerate. They say they want to form a partnership with a licensed banking institution in New Jersey. James looks up the company and sees that it's a multinational corporation that has its fingers in multiple stratums of the economy, including the automotive wholesaling industry in New York, New Jersey, and Pennsylvania. He gets really excited when he sees that many of the businesses in the conglomerate are Fortune 500 and that the organization's ledgers are very much in the black. He eagerly responds to the inquiry and sets up an appointment for later that day at the bank with a representative of the conglomerate named Boris Rasmov. The name alone shows that the man has some negotiating power for the company, and James is eager to meet him.

As the appointment time with Boris Rasmov draws near, the front door of the savings and loan opens and a distinguished, dark-haired man with a foreign appearance comes in and seems to recognize James right away. He walks up, and with the slightest crease of a smile extends his hand and says, "Admiral James Harrington, Vice Commandant of the United States Coast Guard. It is a pleasure to finally meet you. My name is Boris Rasmov. Is there someplace private we can go to discuss my company's proposal?"

James takes the Russian's hand and shakes it heartily. As he stares into the man's eyes, there is something unsettling about his demeanor that leaves the admiral feeling cold and defenseless. "We can use the back office. Please, Mr. Rasmov, follow me."

As they head through the old bank, they see a picture of a World War I United States Coast Guard captain with a plaque under it that says, "Captain James A. Harrington, Founder of Harrington Savings and Loan."

Boris looks up and says, "Quite a dynamic individual, your grandfather. Very impressive military record. I've wondered why your father chose a career in law and then politics instead of following him into military service like yourself."

James's face turns a little red as he coughs out a response. "Senator Bill Harrington served his country in another way. My grandfather fully supported his career choices and was proud of his accomplishments." He opens the door to the rear office and asks the bank manager to give them some privacy.

Boris checks to make sure that the ousted bank manager closes the door then says, "Ah, but does that explain why he threatened to cut your father off from the family fortune if he did not encourage you to pursue a military career?"

James is visibly shocked by this display of insight into his personal business by someone he has never met before. He plops down in the desk chair and does not ask his guest to take a seat. "I do not know where you get your information from, but the decision to pursue a career in the Coast Guard was mine alone and not my grandfather's or my father's."

Boris takes a seat on a couch in the back part of the office that is somewhat shaded. Then he reveals to James that he knows that his stoic and noteworthy grandfather's plan to keep his father from wasting the family's resources was unsuccessful. It left all of the once-promising set of enterprises he started in this area of New Jersey at risk of being liquidated to pay for the late senator's elaborate campaigns, bribing, and gambling debts. That there are also still several open paternity suits by individuals claiming to be his siblings and wanting a piece of the Harrington pie. Then he brings up the issue with his son, the promising young and newly appointed commander of Sector Corpus Christi in Texas, Captain William Harrington. How he has kept his addiction to painkillers a secret since his football accident at the academy is impressive.

James Harrington does not ever stand for this accusation to freely fly his way, truth or not. No one speaks to him like that. "Now, look here, Mr. Rasmov. I don't know what game you're trying to play, but I'm one of the highest-ranking admirals in the United States military, and my family is well-known and well-connected in Washington political circles. You'll find that trying to blackmail me will be a disastrous endeavor on your part!"

Boris, in an almost fatherly response, tells the admiral to sit down and be quiet. "Admiral, I have no intention of blackmailing you. One look at the remaining Harrington family assets would conclude that an action such as that would yield a somewhat pitiful profit."

James looks like he will respond in force to the subtle jab at his financial malnutrition, but Boris puts up a forestalling hand and continues. "What I am here to propose to you is, how do the Americans put it, making all your dreams come true. You see, Admiral, my organization needs a legitimate American banking entity to funnel our western hemisphere funds through. We would very much like to make Harrington Savings and Loan one of the largest and most powerful banking institutions in the state of New Jersey. We have no desire to take over the management of your institution but will leave you and your family in control as we give it enough business to achieve both of our goals. We are keenly aware of the enormous amount of capital it will take to make this a reality, and we will put up one hundred percent of the corporate rebuilding costs in the form of a loan to you personally. We require only the bank and its license as collateral. The fringe benefit of this proposal is that I will see that it completely takes care of all your other financial and personal problems to your utmost satisfaction. Even your son's addiction to painkillers will no longer be of any concern, because I will make sure he is discreetly supplied by my medical people, who will treat him in a way that will appear legally legitimate."

Boris stops for a few seconds to look at the now very pacified and excited Admiral James Harrington, then reaches down and pulls a black satchel out of his briefcase and hands it to him. "As for any immediate financial needs you may have, take this as a token of our intent to have a long and prosperous relationship with what we would like to call Harrington Enterprises."

James receives the bag with a greedy gleam in his eye and opens it to see several bundles of hundred-dollar bills with paper binders around them that are labeled $10,000. He counts fifty in the bag. He looks up and says, "Half a million dollars is a generous gesture to begin a business relationship."

Boris leans back, pulls out an expensive Italian cigar and lights it. "There will be three more bags just like that delivered here when I leave, if we have a deal."

Harrington eagerly gets on his feet, walks over to Boris and extends his hand. "Mr. Rasmov, you have a deal, and you can count on my full cooperation and discretion in all of our future business deals. Now, where do I sign?"

Boris ignores the extended hand, picks up his briefcase, and as he is turning to leave, he says, "I appreciate your choice of words, Admiral. You will come to find that cooperation and discretion are two qualities I find most necessary in anyone who works for me. My representative will be in touch to set up the legalities and logistics of our new relationship." Boris then stares deep into James's eyes and with ice-cold force says, "And, Admiral, never presume that this is a full partnership. I will always have the last word in any endeavor. Comply, and the rewards will be astronomical, as you can already see. Betray or circumvent me, and the consequences will be equal." With that said, Boris turns and leaves the bank.

Two days later, Boris's nephew, Yuri Sebastion, and two lawyers show up at Harrington Savings and Loan to iron out all the details of the deal. When done, Rasmov-Sebastion Conglomerate holds an eighty percent controlling interest in Harrington Enterprises. It leaves James with twenty percent, five of which he owns outright. The deal accredits the other fifteen percent to him in the form of a loan from Boris's company. James has no problem with this because they mention nothing of the two million Boris had already given him. The contract gives both him and his son an annual salary of $500,000 each as president and vice president of Harrington Enterprises. James has to swallow about a barrel full of blue-blood pride when he learns that Boris's weaselly little nephew, Yuri, is named chairman of the board of his company. But in the next two weeks, he's delighted that all the paternity suits against his father's estate have been dropped and that a Coast Guard-approved doctor's office in Corpus Christi, Texas, has taken over as his son's physicians and are discreetly supplying all of his needs. Most impressive of all are the plans he receives showing the design of the proposed new corporate headquarters of Harrington Enterprises, LLC. Smugly, he sits in his desk chair at Coast Guard Headquarters in Washington DC thinking to himself, *The Harrington name will finally get the respect it deserves. Grandfather will finally be proud of us.*

Port Sulphur, Louisiana

Peter Rasmov has been in a lot of third-world countries in his extensive career as an agent for his uncle Boris. It never ceases to amaze him that a rich and powerful country like the United States can still have areas like Port Sulphur, which sits at the southern tip of the Mississippi

River below New Orleans, Louisiana. It has a definite third world feel to it. When it lost its main benefactor, The Freeport Sulphur Factory, in the late 1990s, it went from a thriving industrial town to a ghost town. But that also makes it the perfect place to set up a staging ground for his and Boris's contributions to making the ambitions of Prince Abuella Hasheen of the Saudi royal family a reality. Peter's major interests in the town are the families of the oil riggers who live there, and the transport boats and helicopters that bring them to and from work. As usual, Uncle Boris has already provided him with names and complete dossiers of individuals he can exploit and coerce.

Peter drives up to a single-wide mobile home situated in the middle of a trailer park just off the main strip in the town. It is white and shabby looking, with half the skirting around the bottom missing. Also, there is a 1993 green Ford Taurus out front that shows considerable sun damage. He pulls out a manila folder and opens it up to look at a picture of a man in his late thirties, with dark hair, an average build, and multiple tattoos. His name is Gustave Landers, and even though he has spent time in the Louisiana State Prison for drug smuggling, he works for Star Oil, the biggest oil producer in the Caribbean. His job is to transport oil rig workers to and from their jobs.

He was an army helicopter pilot during Desert Storm in the early nineties and was honorably discharged. It was when he came home from deployment that the more unsavory elements of his family enlisted his help to smuggle drugs from South America. After spending five years in prison, he came out with no prospects and a lot of slammed doors in his face until he approached his uncle, New Orleans City Councilman Ferdinand Landers, who used his ties to Star Oil to get his nephew a job.

The fact that Gustave makes several trips a week to the three closest oil rigs to New Orleans and one near Galveston, Texas, is what makes him so interesting to Peter.

Peter walks up to the front door. The yard around the trailer is little more than clumps of weeds here and there, with a lot of dried patches of dirt that still have boot prints in them from the last time it rained and turned them into mud patches. The rickety aluminum step and small front porch create enough noise when he steps onto them to make knocking on the front door unnecessary. The noise from his approach already has Gustave waiting there. Peter recognizes the man he sees through the screen door from the pictures in his folder. Gustave is wearing a dirty white tank top and some old Nike running shorts, and he's holding a half-empty bottle of bourbon in his left hand. In his right, he has a .38 caliber revolver that he is loosely pointing at Peter. "You don't look like a cop, and you sure as hell aren't a Jehovah's Witness. Nobody around here wears expensive leather shoes like you're sporting, pal. So, you're either a stupid salesman that got lost or one of my crooked uncle's thugs coming to break my balls and try to get me to smuggle shit for them out to the rigs. I told them I won't do it, and Uncle Ferdinand said I did not have to, so if any of his brothers don't like it, tell them to take it up with him! He's the only one I answer to these days."

Peter is not without a sense of humor and the sight of this Cajun peasant waving a gun at him, which he obviously does not know how to use, hits his funny bone. But Uncle Boris taught him a long time ago that when a man points a gun at you, he must be taught a lesson, sooner or later. Peter chooses sooner. In one fluid movement, he thrusts his open right palm through the screen door mesh, grabs Gustave's hand, and twists it and the gun up and away from pointing at him. Then he grabs Gustave's hand with his left hand and shoots his right hand up and underneath Gustave's armpit. He whips his left leg and hips around and to the left with a powerful jerk. Gustave's body slams into the flimsy screen door, tearing it from the hinges, and propelling Gustave into the railing of the small front porch that is just as flimsy as the screen door. Both Gustave and the door wind up in the front yard with him face-down in the dirt.

Peter retrieves the cheap revolver from Gustave's hand and points it at him. "You should check your voice messages more often. Your uncle called you two hours ago to let you know I was coming and to be sure to give me your full cooperation."

As Gustave picks himself up, Peter walks into the trailer, carrying the bottle of very expensive bourbon he had managed to salvage from Gustave, and makes himself at home in the man's living room.

The inside of Gustave's home tells a different story than the outside. While the exterior gives the impression of trailer-park trash, the inside looks like a downtown luxury high-rise. The bar between the kitchen and living room is dark mahogany with genuine dark leather padding on the lips. The barstools are also mahogany and padded with the same dark leather. The sectional couch and recliner chair, which Peter surmises was just vacated by Gustave from the cigarette burning in the ashtray next to it, are also finely upholstered with the same expensive, dark leather. There is a sixty-six-inch flatscreen TV with a soccer game on, and underneath it is a stereo system that, along with the TV, is hooked up to an eight-speaker-plus-subwoofer home theater system.

Peter walks over to the refrigerator in the kitchen and grabs a glass from the shelf next to it. Then he gets ice from the refrigerator ice dispenser and pours himself a shot of bourbon from the bottle he had confiscated from Gustave, and takes a seat in the recliner. As Gustave walks in, he is using his shirt to wipe the blood from his face and arms. He looks over at Peter sitting in his chair with an unreadable expression on his face. "Please make yourself at home in my humble abode. You must excuse me as I get bandages from my kitchen cabinet."

Peter leisurely stands and points the .38 at him. "Dress your wounds, but if you have another gun up there and you go for it, you'll be dead before you can point it at me."

Gustave stands back and away from the cabinet and holds both hands up in the air. Then he slowly reaches over and pulls a cabinet door open wide enough for Peter to see what is inside. On the middle shelf is a white plastic container with a red cross on the lid. Peter nods his head and Gustave carefully grabs it, cautiously steps into his living room, and sits on a barstool to take care of the scrapes and cuts on his face and shoulder.

Peter sits down at the bar and positions his stool so that he's looking at Gustave. He lays the .38 on the bar, takes a sip of the bourbon, and says, "This is a high-quality bourbon, and your home here is very deceitful. On the outside, it appears that you are just another unemployed vagrant living on American welfare. But inside, it looks more like the kind of place a high-priced oil company helicopter pilot would live in. Why the ruse?"

Gustave shakes his head and laughs as he begins applying a bandage to his shoulder. "I thought you were one of my other uncle's men. I had the gun out because I figured they had found me, and I'd have to do something with him and move again. All my uncles think they own me, and Uncle Ferdinand does not have as much say over them as he would like me to believe. Eight years ago, when the cops caught me smuggling drugs for them from South America, the shipment they confiscated was worth over two million dollars. They think I owe them for it, and they want me to use my job to help them get it back. Oil rig workers can spend a lot of time out in the middle of the ocean and some chemical distraction is appealing."

Peter picks up the glass of bourbon and tips it in Gustave's direction. "When you say, 'do something' with your uncle's man, what exactly did you have in mind? You are not that comfortable with a handgun, although your record shows you were a good military transport pilot. There is no mention of your actually having to use a weapon. I really can't imagine that you would kill him."

Gustave blows out a puff of hot air and just says he probably would have tied the man up and driven him to a beach somewhere this evening, and then quietly leave during the night. As the Cajun man explains his dilemma, Peter laughs. Gustave has moved six times since going to work for Star Oil. Though his Uncle Ferdinand got the local police to help him move to his present home, he knew that his other uncles had way too many connections in the New Orleans Police Department for this to be any kind of permanent arrangement. He tells Peter that he already has plans to disappear from the area permanently as soon as he has a big enough cash roll to do it.

Peter finds the bourbon agreeable and pours another glass. He then gets up and walks over to the couch and helps Gustave finish bandaging his shoulder. Before he takes over the job, he hands the bottle of bourbon back to the owner. He takes the last piece of medical tape and finishes securing the sterile pad to Gustave's shoulder. "I think I'm the answer to all your problems, Gustave. What would you say if I could make your bad uncles leave you alone permanently and make you rich enough to do anything you want?"

Gustave's face contorts into a quizzical smile. He grabs the bourbon, tips it to his lips and takes two huge gulps. Then he pulls it away, and wipes his mouth with the back of his hand. "I would say you don't know who my uncles are and what they are capable of around here. Between the three of them, they control almost all the underworld in New Orleans. They only tolerate their youngest brother, Ferdinand, because he's a popular political figure, and it gives the family a semblance of legitimacy. He likes to think he's beyond their control, but they're just waiting until his power and influence grow enough to be of use to them. When it does, I fear my dear uncle and benefactor will have a vulgar awakening to reality."

Peter is sitting next to Gustave now and the two of them look more like drinking buddies than two guys who were just in a physical altercation a few moments earlier. Peter slaps the man on his good shoulder. "Gustave, I too have a powerful uncle who has taken an interest in not only your enigmatic uncle Ferdinand's affairs, but also yours and that of your three notorious uncles." Peter looks down at the Patek Philippe watch that his cousin Natasha gave him for his twenty-first birthday and notes the time. "Please turn your television to a local news station, Gustave. I think you'll be very interested in the breaking news."

Gustave changes the TV from the soccer game to a local news channel, which is broadcasting a scene outside the New Orleans City Hall, where Gustave's Uncle Ferdinand is standing next to the chief of police and the mayor. The mayor is in the middle of announcing that due to some very incriminating evidence, Councilman Ferdinand Landers had turned over to the police department three of the most notorious underworld bosses in New Orleans— Albin, Emeric, and Zephirin Landers—all of whom were arrested and arraigned earlier that morning. They are being charged with drug trafficking, money laundering, extortion, murder, and corruption. Each of them was incarcerated in the county jail and denied bail, pending their trial date to be set later. The mayor ends by saying, "It is with great humility and pride that we applaud the true courage and civic loyalty shown here today by the youngest brother of these three enemies of our fair city."

With that, the mayor steps back, and Ferdinand steps up to the podium.

With a slight quiver in his voice, Ferdinand addresses the crowd. "It is with the deepest regret that I admit to the fine citizens of our great city that I have waited far too long to perform my civic duty in finally showing the courage to stand up to my family's wrongdoings and make up for the harm they have caused. It was thirty-five years ago when our only sister, Josette, lay on her deathbed, having given birth to my nephew, Gustave. Her only request was that I protect him from our brothers' influence. It is with the deepest of sorrow in my heart that I admit I failed my beloved sister and allowed these evil men to corrupt and almost destroy his life, until today. I stood idly by as they took a fine young man, recently honorably discharged from the army, and made him use his skills as a helicopter pilot to smuggle their drugs and contraband in and out of the United States. For that crime, he spent five years in prison; and when he came out, he had no prospects and no future. I could have helped him then, but my brothers felt he owed them a debt and would not leave him alone when I got him legitimate work transporting oil rig workers to and from their jobs. They were trying to intimidate him into working for them again. I finally found the strength to stand up to them and end their plague on him and our city once and for all."

When councilman Landers finishes, the applause is thunderous and the newsfeed cuts to a reporter across the street from the steps of City Hall. A very attractive young African American woman is holding a microphone with her station's letters on it to her chin. "Councilman Landers's tarnished reputation, plagued with accusations of being involved in underworld dealings and collusion, may just have ended today with his unprecedented move to turn state's evidence and help in the capture of his three notorious brothers, who are now in custody and awaiting their day in court. Some may speculate that this could be a real turning point for the often-embattled councilman. Back to you at the station."

When the report is over, Gustave jumps out of his seat and heads for the back of his trailer. He flails his arms as he exclaims, "Has he lost his mind? We'll both be dead by the end of the day!" Before Peter can respond, the cell phone on the coffee table rings and Gustave turns around and retrieves it. When he answers, he shouts into it with exasperation. "Uncle Ferdinand, how could you be so stupid? Their business associates will kill us both."

He stops and listens for a moment, replies with two yeses and then says, "That is incredible! If you say so. Yes, he is here right now." He disconnects the line on the little flip cell phone and stares at Peter in fascination. "Uncle Ferdinand says there is nothing to be afraid of, that his new benefactor has taken care of all our problems. No crime syndicate business associate of my uncles in the country will dare touch us now. I am to give you whatever you want. Who are you, and who is this uncle of yours who has so much power?"

Peter displays the slightest crease of a smile. "His name is Boris. Now let's discuss your weekly flight itinerary to and from the four oil rigs you service."

CHAPTER SIX

ANCHORS AWAY

First Responder's Shakedown Cruise

Jacob opens his eyes, excitement vibrating through every atom of his body. He jumps out of bed and springs into the bathroom where he quickly shaves, brushes his teeth, and grooms himself for the day. He thinks about how all the months and weeks of preparation are finally coming to a head today. He quickly dons his new commander's uniform, picks up his hat, and adjusts it in the mirror. As he bends down to kiss his wife goodbye, she stirs, looks over at the clock on the nightstand, and exclaims, "Good lord, Jacob. It's three-thirty in the morning! You don't have to be there for another two hours."

Jacob sits down on the edge of the bed and faces his wife while placing a hand on her shoulder and lightly shaking it. "Honey, I can't sleep another wink. *First Responder* is yelling for me so loud I can't hear anything else."

Mary sits up, flings her arms out in a long stretch and a wake-up yawn, and then says, "Well, that ship of yours can wait until its captain has had a good breakfast with his wife and daughter. You go get Danielle up and I'll make us some eggs, bacon, and toast."

At the mention of some good food, Jacob's stomach rumbles and he kisses Mary and then sprints to his nine-year-old's room where he's met with a similar but more juvenile response to waking up so early in the morning. Danielle flings a pillow in his face, and as he peels it away, he laughs, reaches down, picks her up in his arms and carries her into the living room where they wait for Mom to make breakfast.

Ten minutes later, the Edwards trio is sitting around their breakfast table. Mary and Danielle are showing signs of being fully awake and Jacob is telling them what he is about to do on his shakedown cruise now that all the refit is done on his new ship. Danielle wipes her mouth as she swallows a mouthful of eggs and toast. "Daddy, are you going to be gone as long as you were when you went to the North Pole when I was a baby?"

Jacob inwardly cringes at the memory of having to lie to his family about going to Captain Tommy Williams's special training school for six months, then he smiles and pats her on the head. "Heck no, spunky monkey.

Three weeks tops, then I'm back, and we all move back down to South Padre Island near Grandpa Roberto and Grandmother Isabella. We'll be part of Sector Corpus Christi then, and *First Responder* will patrol that part of the Gulf of Mexico and the Caribbean."

Danielle claps her hands with glee. "I was talking to Grandpa Roberto last night, and he said the junior championships are in two months. Does that mean you'll be there as my sensei, Daddy?"

Before Jacob can respond with a yes, Mary pipes in and says, "Not only is he going to be there for that, but he won't miss your winter ballet recital of the Nutcracker, either. Will you, Jacob?"

Jacob laughs, puts his hat on, and kisses his wife and daughter goodbye. "Wouldn't miss either for the world," he says as he leaves the apartment. "You two are always first in my book. Danielle, mind your mother and keep up your practicing. Honey, I'll contact you once we're underway. Love you girls!"

At 5:30 a.m. Commander Jacob Edwards, captain of the refurbished Coast Guard Hamilton-class cutter *First Responder,* steps aboard to start her shakedown cruise. He's immediately met by his XO, Lt. Commander Larry Phillips, Chief of Security Lt. Alex Maelstrom, and the new temporary gunnery officer, Marine Gunnery Sergeant Rick Jones.

Phillips steps forward. "Commander, all stations report ready, and Sector Command New Orleans has given the OK to launch. What is our heading, sir?"

Jacob smiles as he tries to keep the quiver out of his voice. "Set your heading for Event Horizon. We'll patrol all three of the closest oil rigs to New Orleans and then move to Sector Corpus Christi, where we'll receive the rest of our itinerary from our new command."

Phillips responds with an "Aye aye, sir," and turns to the navigator to lay in the course.

Jacob smiles and turns to Gunny Jones. Seaman Marvin Schuette is standing back and to one side at attention, waiting for Gunny. "Well, Gunny, here we are. I think this is a first for both of us. I never had a Marine on a crew before, and I'll bet you never thought you'd be serving on a Coast Guard ship, either."

Gunny Jones laughs and shakes his head. "You have a flair for understatement, Commander. But I'm honored to be here and I promise you that when we're done, Schuette here will know more about that OTO Melara than he does about his own mother, and he'll be able to operate it in his sleep because that's all he'll be dreaming about, sir."

"Sounds good, Gunny. Looks like Seaman Schuette is in good hands. Carry on."

Jacob turns to his new security chief. He comes to attention and says, "Commander, Lt. Alex Maelstrom reporting for duty, sir."

Jacob inspects the officer before him. *Good officer* is the first thought that comes to his mind. "At ease, Lieutenant. I read your file, Alex. I'm very impressed. You're a fully qualified diesel mechanic engineer with a bachelor's degree in that field, but you chose security after you saw combat in the Gulf just after 9/11. Your last CO said you're command material, and he recommended you to this post. I'm glad we get to keep you from Admiral Billings's old crew."

Maelstrom remains straight as a board, but Jacob looks closely and sees a definite twinkle in the man's eye after receiving the compliment. "Carry on, Lieutenant."

Alex salutes and says, "Thank you, Commander," and then heads back to his post. Jacob takes a deep breath, mentally going over his checklist of all his department heads to make sure he has checked in with each of them in the last twelve hours and has them all caught up and ready for this cruise. Satisfied that all his i's are dotted, and t's are crossed, he approaches the helm. As he enters the main cabin, Lt. Commander Phillips sees him and announces, "Captain on deck!"

Jacob holds up a calming hand and says, "I'll take her out, Larry." The helmsman steps away as Jacob puts his left hand on the throttle and the right on the steering bar, looks up into the watcher's tube, and asks for an all-clear from the lookout deck. Then he eases the throttle slightly back. He can feel the Fairbanks Morse diesel engines power up the aft propeller, putting the 378-foot-long, 3,250-ton vessel into forward motion. The completely refurbished *First Responder* purrs like a kitten under Commander Edwards's firmly competent control as it leaves the dock in New Orleans to head out on its first mission under its new captain. *First Responder's* top speed is twenty-eight knots, or roughly thirty-two miles per hour, but that is while engaging the extra gas-turbine booster engines that use much more fuel. Jacob knows that he is not in any real hurry, so he sets the speed at thirteen knots and calculates that they will be at the first oil rig, Event Horizon, in roughly ten hours. When he clears the bay and makes open water, Jacob turns to his XO Phillips. "OK, I've had my fun. You can let the helmsman take over now."

Phillips looks over to the corner. "OK, O'Brien, you're up."

Jacob turns and sees a young woman with deep red hair and bright green eyes in her early twenties wearing the rank and striker of a seaman helmsman. She steps up to Jacob and salutes. "Seaman Barbara O'Brien, helmsman third class. Commander, permission to relieve you, sir."

Jacob steps away from the helm and returns the salute. "Permission granted. Carry on, seaman." He smirks and looks over at Phillips. "Lieutenant Commander, let's tone it down a couple of notches with the military protocol. This isn't an academy training cruise, OK?"

The tension in the room immediately dissipates and Phillips's shoulders relax as he responds, "You got it, Commander. OK, everybody back to work."

As Jacob walks out to go look at some other sections of the ship, Phillips comes up behind him as he makes his way out onto the open deck. "Commander?"

He swings his head around. "Yes, Phillips, anything else?"

Phillips holds out both hands in a "let me explain" gesture. "I'm sorry, Commander. It's just that with you being one of the first two men to get the Coast Guard Cross, plus being one of the youngest officers to assume a command like this, and then there's what you did for Schuette and Chief Thompson...the whole crew is a little awestruck and frankly nervous to boot."

Jacob sighs, then looks at his XO with a slight smile in his eyes. "We're all just getting to know one another, Larry. Give it a little time. We'll get into our own groove and be the best team any of us has ever been on. Don't worry, they'll find out soon enough how human I am, and reality will replace this so-called awe you're talking about. Just take it one step at a time. Help everybody do their job right, and we'll all get it together. OK, Lieutenant Commander?"

Larry gives Jacob a casual salute. "You got it, Commander. Oh, Gunny Jones asked to speak with you when you get a minute. He and Schuette are over doing maintenance checks on the OTO Melara right now."

Jacob makes his way down to the gunnery station and finds Jones and Schuette stocking in several types of loads for the ship's armaments. When he gets closer, he notices that Gunny Jones is grinning from ear to ear. He is obviously pleased with the huge inventory of ammunition they are stocking in. But Schuette looks more flabbergasted as he moves the crates to their proper locations.

"How's it going, Gunny?"

Jones looks up and smiles. "Fantastic, Commander. We have a full payload of every type of ammo this baby can handle. HE, MOM, PFF antimissile projectiles, SAPOM armor piercers, DART antiaircraft, and even VULCANOS guided long-range projectiles. Schuette here almost soiled his pants when he saw all of this because he thinks we're going to war or something. I haven't told him about the target practice you want to do later in the cruise."

Jacob sees that this new info causes Schuette to relax a little, and he laughs. "Seaman, I want no one outside *First Responder's* senior officers and Jones's gunnery crew to know how well armed we really are, and that includes any sector brass. I have my orders straight from Coast Guard command and the commandant himself. Gunny Jones is right. We'll use some of this up in target practice maneuvers later, but that order also authorizes us to carry a much heavier payload of ammo than the other Hamiltons. Our new patrol will be South Texas, Mexico, and Central America. We're part of the president's new War on Drugs Initiative, and Mexico and a lot of Central American countries have signed on, so we'll be part of a joint task force in those areas. Gunny Jones here has already worked in that task force in a Marine Corps detachment, so his knowledge will be invaluable in helping us know what we are up against."

Schuette looks over at Gunny Jones and nods his head, acknowledging the new info, and then turns back to Jacob. "Aye aye, sir."

Jacob tells him to carry on and then directs Jones outside to talk.

Once they get out beside the gun platform in the ship's bow, Jacob has to yell to be heard over the noise of the engines, the wind, and the waves splashing up against his ship. "Jones, have you heard anything from Captain Williams? I haven't checked my satellite phone yet and

I know he wanted us to take recon pictures of the three drilling platforms we'll be cruising to in the next week."

Jones, holding his hand to his head to keep his cap from blowing off, yells, "Yes, Commander! I talked to him this morning. He had the special camera equipment sent to your cabin before we launched. Said you knew how to use it. Also, he wants to know why you're not answering that expensive phone he gave you."

Jacob turns sideways so that he is speaking right in Jones's ear. "I've been a little busy assuming this new command. Besides, it's not the kind of thing you want to go around talking on in front of everyone. It looks like a miniature flat-screen TV set and it's touchscreen-controlled. It's like something right out of Star Trek. Captain Williams calls it a smartphone. Civilians don't even have them yet. What am I supposed to do if that thing rings in a crowd?"

Gunny Jones laughs. "Commander, you know those things have a vibrating option you can activate with a switch on the side? Also, you can check them anytime for text messages. The screen will bring up a full keyboard for you to communicate back with."

Jacob puts his hand on Jones's shoulder and shakes his head. "OK, I'll check it when I go look at the camera equipment. Williams told me we can even do a video call with those damn things. Boy, my daughter will lose her mind when these things go public."

He motions for them to head back to the gun compartment area. Once inside the outer hatch, Jones stops. "Commander, what was all that stuff about me being such an asset to Schuette for? You're the one who has been on umpteen missions down south of the border working cartel activity. I went on one reconnaissance mission down to Honduras three months ago. Besides that, they've grounded me at the base in New Orleans. Captain Williams sent me on that one only because he said his assets at Falcon Lake were indisposed, and he needed to call me up from a temporary suspension to go on an intel hunt."

Jacob stops and motions Jones to the side as he checks around the door to make sure Schuette and the others can't hear him. "Phillips told me the crew is a little jumpy about how I got this command, the promotion, and the medal all at the same time. Plus, when I stuck up for them with you that was kind of like the straw that broke the camel's back. I told him to help the crew tone it down a notch so we can get the job done. I figured I needed Schuette to see you in a different light, so I gave him something to look up to in you. Gunny, we need this whole arrangement to work on this ship, or we won't get anything done. I don't need hero worship, and you don't need everyone hating you if we're going to make this work. It's like you and I have two sets of orders and one can't hinder the other. They have to work together."

"Not a problem, Commander," Jones says.

Jacob grabs his shoulder lightly. "One more thing, Gunny. The safety of this ship and her crew is my top priority. First and foremost, we're here to protect our country and its citizens, and that's the only reason I'll put her or her crew at risk, orders or no orders. Are we clear?"

"As a bell, sir. I'm with you one hundred percent, sir."

CHAPTER SEVEN
SNEAKING AROUND

Star Oil Personnel Transport Helicopter, Event Horizon Drilling Platform

Gustave has never been this nervous in his life. It was one thing to sneak down to Central America, pick up a load of drugs, and drop it off in the Louisiana swamp somewhere for pickup. He made dozens of those runs before they caught him. But smuggling an international terrorist saboteur onto a federally protected oil drilling rig in the middle of United States waters is about the dumbest, riskiest, and scariest thing he's ever done, and that includes his tour in the Gulf War.

As he lands his Airbus transport copter on the platform, his twelve passengers prepare to disembark by grabbing their gear. Among them is Peter Rasmov, who assumed the identity of a newly hired roughneck last week. Gustave can only guess what happened to the real Adrian Barlow, who was hired by Star Oil six weeks ago to handle this new shift. But when Peter showed up with the proper ID and designation papers to be transported to Event Horizon, he could not help but marvel at how perfectly the Russian assumed the identity of the Texas oil rig worker in appearance and mannerisms. Everything from the standard Texas drawl in his speech to the goatee facial hair, and even the way he walked and held himself. No one would ever figure out that he was anyone else but an eight-year veteran of Gulf oil rigs from Houston.

As he passes the pilot's seat, Peter looks over at Gustave. "I'll see you in one week. Make sure all else is arranged for your part in the next phase. My uncle Boris will be in contact with you to brief you on the details. You're about to become a free, rich man, Gustave. Don't screw up this opportunity."

Gustave nods and waits for this enigma of a man who has so radically changed his life in the last few weeks to disembark. He closes the hatch and gets back in the pilot's seat of his Super Puma EC225 long-range helicopter, and waits for clearance to take off after the last of his passengers have left the landing platform. When the clearance is given, he lifts off and proceeds back to the Star Oil helicopter port in New Orleans. When he gets there, he fully intends to head back to the apartment he rented and drown himself in the very expensive bottle of bourbon his uncle Ferdinand bought him last Christmas.

Peter watches the helicopter take off and makes a mental note of the erratic behavior Gustave is displaying. The man is not just afraid but has moral scruples about what they are doing. That will make him a liability once this is over, and Uncle Boris does not tolerate liabilities. He'll have to kill the pilot and maybe his uncle. He picks up his duffel bag and heads to the check-in table where he is supposed to receive his housing assignment and work shift orders. He stands in line behind the eleven other passengers who all look like they would rather be somewhere else. A large, hairy Latino man is standing directly in front of him as they wait. He slept during the whole ride out to the rig, so Peter never caught his name. He turns his head and stares at Peter with a sideways glance. "Hombre, I don't know if I can handle another twelve weeks without a drink." He lightly elbows Peter in the midsection and laughs. "I tried to drink enough last night to last me, but this hangover isn't worth it. Now I can't even fix it with two shots, so it'll be hell for the next couple of days."

Peter opens his duffel bag and points to a small case of carbonated water bottles and then shows him a prescription from a doctor, telling the man that he needs to be supplied with them consistently for his stomach condition. He leans in and whispers, "There is nothing wrong with my stomach, and these are full of carbonated, 190-proof Everclear grain alcohol. Let's see if we can bunk together, and I'll work out a deal with you. Sound good?"

Peter puts his hand out, and the man heartily shakes it. "My name is Raphio Cortez, and you got a deal, my friend." They both pat each other on the back, and then Raphio steps up to the check-in table. As the roughneck manager is checking Raphio in he says, "This is my good friend, Adrian Barlow, from Houston, Texas. He's new to this rig. How about you let us bunk together?"

The roughneck manager looks up at Peter then down at his notes and compares the picture he has on record. "Lost a little weight there, huh, Barlow? Looks like you have some good credentials, but the first time that ulcer of yours causes you problems, we'll ship you out on the next transport."

Peter musters up some redneck bravado. "Shit, boss, I can hold my own against any other roughneck you have here, ulcer or no. Just let me keep my meds and water close by and I'll be fine." He then hands his paperwork over to the man and watches closely while he studies it.

The manager finally looks up. "Looks like you have a certification in hydraulic systems maintenance, Adrian. Well, today is your lucky day, because Raphio here is one of our drill technicians, so you two can work together on the same shift. I'm assigning you both to the swing shift, so you report in three hours. Here's your quarters assignment." He hands back their papers and key cards, then he looks sternly at Peter. "Adrian, our nurse is still off the platform and is not due back until next week, but as soon as he's back, you report for a checkup. You got it?"

"No problem, boss." Both men pick up their things and walk to the stairwell to head to their housing.

Raphio shows Peter where they are bunking. To his surprise, the accommodations are not unlike a four-star hotel room—two queen-size beds, a desk, two chairs, and a full bathroom and refrigerator. As soon as they close the door, Raphio grabs Peter's shoulder. "OK, how much for a bottle of that stuff, buddy?"

Peter reaches in his duffel bag, grabs one of the twelve-ounce bottles and hands it to him. "First one is free. Just don't overdo it. I don't want to get thrown off this rig on my first day."

Raphio grabs the bottle, twists off the cap, and takes two gulps, then puts it in his side of the dresser next to the desk. He throws his duffel bag in the corner and lies down on the bed farthest from the door. "No problem, hombre. Just needed something to calm the pounding in my head. Just make sure I'm up in two and a half hours for our first shift."

Peter turns off the light and quietly leaves the room. The first place he goes to is the galley, which to his surprise is also very modern-looking. They have set the food up buffet style, and there are two pool tables and one air hockey table on the other side of the room. He recognizes the man who checked him in earlier and walks up to him. "Excuse me, boss, is it OK if I walk around the rig to get a feel for my way around?"

The man looks up from his newspaper. "Adrian, isn't it?" Peter nods. "Yeah, that's fine. Just make sure you wear the ID badge I gave you when you're walking around. Our security guys are pretty laid back, but they're sticklers on those badges."

Peter pulls the badge out of his front shirt pocket, clips it on, and heads for the service elevator that will take him to his intended location. He has studied schematics of this facility for weeks, and he's confident that he can find his way around with no help, but to strengthen the ruse that he is a brand-new roughneck to the rig, he stops and asks several people along the way for directions. His first destination is new equipment storage, which sits directly under the helicopter landing deck. It can be accessed either by a platform elevator lift to the side of the landing pad or a large, double-wide stairwell where workers can load and unload equipment. He descends the latter.

The first person he runs into is a dark-haired, voluptuous forty-something woman wearing a security uniform that looks a size and a half too small for her. She looks up from the book she is holding and immediately looks for the employee badge that Peter is wearing. When she spots it, she puts the book down and leans in to read it more carefully. "Adrian Barlow, hydraulics maintenance." She then looks up to get a closer look at him and continues. "Well, you're a nice new addition to our little family here. What can I do for you, sweetie?"

"Someone told me we have a shipment of hydraulic oils and seals that I'm supposed to check. Could you point me in the right direction?"

She puts a seductive hand on his shoulder. "Sure, Adrian. That shipment is right over there. Follow me." She takes his hand and leads him around the corner of some big crates and shows him a pallet full of one-gallon buckets marked Hydraulic Oil; a crate the size of a foot locker that is labeled Hydraulic Pump; and two boxes that are marked Seals, one labeled A and the other labeled B1.

He exclaims "damn it", then bends down and picks up the one marked B1 and turns to her. "They sent the wrong seals. I need the regular B size. These might work, but I need to check them with the equipment specs down in pumping. Do you mind if I take this? I'll bring it right back."

The security guard gives Peter a big sideways smile and winks. "Well, sweetie, I'm supposed to get management approval for that, but if you promise to bring it right back, I'll let it slide this time."

Peter sees that the woman is a little more interested in him than what he wants and decides to exploit the opportunity. "Thanks, this means a lot, Miss...?"

She steps in a little closer and puts her hand on his chest. "It's Mrs., but don't worry, I'm divorced. The name is Sally Crabtree."

Peter puts his hand over hers and strokes it. "Well, Sally Crabtree, I sure appreciate you trusting me like this. My shift starts in about two hours. You security people do twelve on and twelve off, right? So, we'll probably be off at the same time. Want to meet for a cup of coffee after our shifts are done?"

Sally laughs and leans in close enough to talk right into Peter's ear. "Honey, I have ten years seniority with Star Oil, which means I get a cabin all to my little ole self. How about you join me there? I have a nice, big shower we can both fit into, and then a luscious king-size bed to rest our weary bones. What do you say, roughneck?"

Peter leans in and kisses Sally on the lips, which she returns eagerly, reaching around with her free hand and cupping his butt in her palm. After she releases him, he steps back, picks up the box and turns to walk away. From behind he hears, "How old are you, Adrian?"

"Twenty-eight," he replies.

"Well, don't keep momma waiting, young man."

"Oh, you don't have to worry about that. I'll be there before you are."

"I like your attitude," he hears as he closes the doors at the top of the stairs.

He rounds the corner and heads for his room. When he gets there, Raphio is still asleep, so he opens the box and retrieves the hi-tech radio transponder uncle Boris had shipped in the box of supplies. He hides it in his duffel bag, and shakes Raphio awake. "Hey, buddy, we are on duty in forty-five minutes. Better get up."

Raphio stirs and sits up. Peter looks over at the bottle of alcohol and sees that he did not drink any more of it, which shows at least some discipline. Raphio notices and says, "You don't have to worry about me, my friend. Showing up drunk my first day back on the job, especially on this alcohol-dry rig, is something I don't need on my record."

Peter laughs. "Well, it's good that stuff has no scent. I have enough to last about a week and more coming. Keep it under control and for fifty a bottle, you can have all you want."

Peter tells him he has to return the box of seals back to equipment storage and he will meet Raphio at the pumphouse. Raphio winks at Peter. "You must've met Sally already, huh? Hombre, that is one hot cougar, and she loves them young and tough like you. Be warned, my friend. She can do a number on a man that can leave him more strung out than ten of those little joy bottles you have in that duffel bag. Pace yourself, boy."

He makes a quick stop at Sally's post to drop off the box and tells her it needs to be returned. She tries to coax him back behind the crates again, but he tells her that his shift starts in a few minutes and he doesn't want to be late. One thing he learned from the encounter is that behind those crates none of the security cameras have a direct view. He logs that info for future use. Before checking in to his workstation, he looks down at his watch and notes the time he gave Raphio the drink. He was hoping the man would have at least taken a few more swigs, but he's still fairly confident the delayed-reaction drug in the drink will kick in nicely within the next three hours. He makes a mental note to grab, dispose of, and replace the bottle in their room with another that has nothing but alcohol in it.

Raphio shows up at their workstation a few minutes late, but no worse for wear. Both men settle in and work on their separate areas. Raphio's is simple maintenance of the main petroleum pump. Peter's is to check and maintain all hydraulic components in the area. After about an hour, a security guard walks through and waves at both men from the other end of the room. Peter notes the time and watches for his reappearance, which happens exactly one hour later. About three hours into their shift, he sees that the drug is affecting Raphio, and the man sits down on the floor, leans up against a wall, and goes to sleep. Peter checks his watch and surmises that he has about forty minutes before Raphio wakes up, and ten minutes after that the security guard will swing by.

He goes to the duffel bag he brought with him and pulls out some dark clothing, a face mask, and light rappelling gear. He grabs the micro transponder, puts it in a utility pouch on his belt, and goes to the hatch leading outside over by Raphio's station. Then he secures his line on some pipes, opens the hatch and hops out on the side of the oil rig just above the main pipe. With all his gear in place, he rappels down the side of the rig until he is almost all the way down the pipe to where it descends into the ocean. He reaches inside his pocket, pulls out two straps and uses them to fasten his feet to the nylon rope. He then hangs upside down so he can take the transponder and fasten it to the pipe just below the surface of the water. Once done, he reverses his position so that he is right-side up again and ascends the rope.

Peter's upper-body strength has always been impressive, and he easily climbs the rope. Halfway back to the hatch he came out of earlier, he looks out over the large waves silhouetted on the moonlit sea and is stunned to see the outline of a Coast Guard ship passing by the oil rig. He knows all the Coast Guard patrol times for this area, and none of the boats were supposed to be in this area until the following morning. This wasn't one of those smaller patrol boats, either, but a full-size Hamilton cutter. He checks his watch to note the time, and rapidly makes his way toward the hatch. Once inside, he takes off his wet clothing and gear, stuffs them back into his duffel bag and goes over to Raphio and shakes him. Raphio's blurred vision focuses as the face of his new roommate becomes clear. "Raphio, for crying out loud, you have to wake up! The security guard will be here any second."

Raphio reaches out his hand, and Peter helps him stand. He reaches over, places the other hand on Peter's shoulder and shakes his head, purses his lips, and blows out air, trying to shake off the drowsy feeling. Finally, he looks up at the man he knows as Adrian and says, "Hombre, I don't know what happened. That drink really did a number on me. Do you think it had something to do with it being carbonated?"

Peter shakes his head and taps Raphio on the back. "Buddy, I think it had everything to do with you trying to get twelve weeks of drinking into one night when you went out last night. You need to go on the wagon for a while."

As they are talking, the security guard comes around the corner and sees the two men standing over by the pump station. He yells out, "You guys get a twenty-minute break in another hour! Get back to work. I don't want to have to report you to your boss."

Peter and Raphio wave back at the guy and go back to work.

Same Time, Communications Station Command Deck of *First Responder*

Seaman Striker John Bliss sits at the communication console going through his standard checklist for the evening.

This assignment is a paved road to promotion, and he couldn't be more excited. He served on a Hamilton once before, and his crew chief saw he had an aptitude for organization and technical equipment, so he recommended the then-seventeen-year-old recruit for specialty training. Now, at nineteen, he proudly wears the communications technician insignia above his rank, showing he is a certified communications officer for Hamilton and Ice Breaker cutters. Wearing his headphones and engaged in his duties, he does not notice a man come up behind him and place a hand on his shoulder. John turns around and rockets out of his seat, coming to attention and giving a brisk salute. "Commander, Seaman Striker Bliss, sir."

Jacob smiles inwardly. "At ease, Bliss. I have a project I need your help with."

Bliss smiles from ear to ear. "You bet, Commander. What is it?" His face turns beet red and he pulls off another hasty salute and says, "I mean, aye aye, Commander."

Jacob holds up a specialized HD camera and hands it to Bliss. "The Navy wants me to take photos of the rig we just passed, Event Horizon, and forward the images to their intelligence division. This has one of those new USB connectors." He reaches in his pocket and pulls out a 3x5 card with some handwritten numbers on it and hands it to Bliss. "This is the designation and access code to the internet link for Naval Intelligence. Upload everything on the camera onto that site, securely store the access info in our system, destroy the card, and report when it's finished."

Bliss is vibrating with excitement because he's been on his new assignment for only one day and he's already doing special projects for his CO. "Aye aye, Commander. I'll get right on it." He grabs the card and the camera and heads over to a computer terminal hooked into their satellite network. As he is connecting the USB cable to the camera, he feels the same hand on his shoulder. He looks up and sees the commander. When he tries to stand up, Jacob gently holds him down and says, "Bliss, I'm going to my cabin now. Just buzz me when you're done, OK?"

"Uh, yes sir."

Jacob heads out of the command deck to his cabin and runs into Gunny Jones. "Jones, I finished taking those pictures of the first rig. Seaman Bliss is uploading them now to Captain Williams's site. When he's done, go get the camera, and you take the pictures of the next rig in the morning. I'm heading to my cabin."

"Sure thing, Commander. Good night, sir," he says as he heads back to the gunnery station.

Jacob walks over to his private quarters thinking, *here is a guy who is basically here on a reprimand and has more reason to be uptight than anyone on the crew but is more chill than the rest of them.* As he opens the door to his small captain's quarters, he hears the slight hum of a cell phone on vibrate mode. He goes over to his dresser and opens the top drawer. In it he sees his smartphone—the one from Captain Williams—activated with the large initials *TW* on the display. He swipes his finger across the screen and immediately sees Captain Williams's face staring back at him. "Hello, Captain. Geez! I don't know if I'll ever get used to doing a video call on a cell phone. It's like Captain Kirk on Star Trek or something."

Tommy laughs. "Jacob, you have to keep up with the latest stuff in this game. Did you get those pictures taken yet?"

"Sure did. My communications man should be uploading them as we speak. What makes that camera so special, anyway? We have plenty of photography equipment on board," Jacob says as he takes a seat at his little desk next to his bed and props the smartphone up against the lamp.

"For starters, that is a state-of-the-art, long-range, full-spectrum lens camera that will record things you and I can't see with our naked eyes. My people back at Naval Intelligence will take those pictures, squeeze every atom of info out of them and report back to me in about a week. We're expecting a type of terrorist attack on oil production in the Gulf of Mexico within the next thirty days; we just don't know where or when. What you're doing now is giving us a picture of what it's supposed to look like at those rigs during normal working operations. The president has allowed several of our best surveillance satellites to be trained on that region of the world to monitor the oil rigs you're photographing. You're giving us a baseline to compare with what they pick up." He laughs at Jacob struggling to keep his phone upright so that the mini camera is pointed at his face. "By the way, kid, if you look in your duffel bag, you'll find a stand that you can put the phone on that'll let you use it without holding it. It'll also charge the phone if you plug it in," Tommy says.

Jacob reaches into his duffel bag on the floor, finds the stand Tommy is talking about, sets it up on his desk and plugs the smartphone into it.

DAN E. HENDRICKSON

"Charge that every night, kid. They aren't like the regular cell phones we use where the battery can last a couple of days on normal use. That's why we don't take them with us when we're out on ops. But since you and Jones are on *First Responder,* I thought it'd be nice if I could see your smiling faces when I talked to you."

Jacob can't help but jive Tommy. "Bullshit. You want to know if we beat the hell out of each other again and wanted to use these to do it."

"No one ever accused you of being stupid, kid. But actually, I talked with Jones earlier and he said you and he are getting along famously. I think you'll find he's one hell of an operative, and he won't let you down in a pinch. Get some rest. I see you're due to report to your new sector command in Corpus Christi in eight days. Get those pictures of the other two rigs uploaded to me before you get there. Once you pull into port, they monitor all your transmissions. It's not that I don't trust Captain Harrington, but his dad is a little too political for my taste, and if Junior found out about us and told his dad, your commandant would string me up by my entrails and feed me to the sharks."

"Captain, I don't think that Captain Harrington is much of a fan of his old man. He seemed like a straight-shooter to me. You know, he was the XO on this ship before its refit. Billings wouldn't have anyone as his second who could not pull their weight, no matter who their dad is."

"On that point, I agree. Billings is one of the best. He recommended Harrington for an administrational

108

command because he knows what *First Responder* will do after refit, and neither he nor the commandant thought Will had enough experience in combat and cartel activity to handle that kind of command."

Jacob leans back against the chair and rubs his temples with the heels of his hands. "This is quite a tightrope you and the commandant are making me walk, Captain. I'll never disobey a direct order from a superior officer, especially if they are my commanding officer. So, you guys better be ready for that and have a way around it."

"We do, kid, and we wouldn't trust you if you thought any other way. Get some sleep, you look tired. I'll talk to you later."

"Good night, Captain Williams."

"Good night, Jacob."

Next Morning, Event Horizon Oil Rig

Peter wakes up to Sally Crabtree lying across his chest wearing nothing but a smile as she lightly snores. He has to admit to himself that for an older woman, she is attractive and boisterously energetic. Their lovemaking last night was something between a wrestling match and a dance-off. She polished off a bottle of his special carbonated Everclear, so he knows she won't be awake for at least another three hours. Getting her to drink the whole thing by herself was a lot easier than he thought it would be. He had another bottle of carbonated water that looked exactly like hers and pretended to get drunk with her. He gently moves her to the other side of her cabin bed and slips out at the bottom, grabs her security keys and the card from the dresser, and gets dressed.

After he quietly closes her cabin door, he heads to Sally's station down in storage. He has already memorized the security shift and knows that Sally's more lethargic counterpart would have the area all locked up and would be lounging in the rig's galley right now, watching a movie. Stealthily, he approaches the entrance and uses Sally's keys to unlock the door. He makes sure no one is around, opens the door, and makes his way back to the same pallet he and Sally were at the previous day. Then he reaches down, picks up a box labeled Hydraulic Gears and pulls out a square, leather pouch about six inches wide and a foot high. He opens it, extends an antenna, and reaches in to pull out a high-powered satellite telephone. He punches in a code and hears the phone begin to ring. After the third ring, a familiar voice answers. "Yes, Peter. Are you finished with stage one?"

"I am, Uncle Boris. The transponder is in place and will continue to send out an intermittent pulse signal for the next two weeks. If the drone does not reach it within that time frame, it'll detach and fall to the bottom of the ocean where it and the drone will self-destruct, leaving no trace."

"Very thorough as always, Nephew. We have no reason to believe the drone will not make it in time, but the precaution is both wise and appreciated. Albeit, the collateral damage the explosion would cause could bring down a small battleship. In one day, you must ingest the potion the doctor gave you. You'll become pretty ill with what will appear as your ulcer flaring up. The medical personnel on that rig will be forced to have you airlifted out. I'll plan to have Gustave pick you up. Once he has administered the antidote, you two can proceed to the next stage of the operation."

"Uncle Boris, regarding small battleships; at the time of my activities last night, a United States Coast Guard cutter cruised by the rig. I'm positive they did not see me because I was behind the pipe and out of their view. There were no patrols scheduled at the time and certainly not one by a ship of that class. Should we be concerned?"

There is a five-second pause before Boris replies. "All unforeseen events are to be taken with grave seriousness, Nephew. Regulations require the Coast Guard to let all oil rigs know when they are doing any maneuvers close to their vicinity. Our contacts both in Star Oil and that branch of the military should have alerted me to the occurrence. I'll have to check both of those sources and see if information is purposely being held from my attention. If so, I may need to divert you to take care of that problem."

"You might use Natasha for that, if the need arises. She's expressed a desire to use what you've taught her in a real-life scenario. She has progressed beyond all of our expectations and may prove to be our most formidable operative in your organization, Uncle."

"I share your optimism, Peter. I'll take your suggestion under advisement. Let's proceed as planned for now. One more thing, Peter."

"Yes, Uncle?"

"I'll bring Dominik up from Central America to help with the final stage of the plan at the South Texas location. Not to worry—he'll not set foot on United States soil and will aid only in the capture of the cruise ship carrying the choir children. They're scheduled to cruise by the oil rig in that area. His brand of terror should make the ship's personnel compliant to our wishes."

"Understood, Uncle. I'll contact you as soon as I'm able after taking the antidote from Gustave."

Peter disconnects the line and returns the receiver to the pouch. He takes the pouch and hangs it over his shoulder using the strap. As he leaves the cargo area, he makes his way to his workstation area, which he knows will be empty at this early hour. He waits for the on-duty security guard to make his rounds past that area and goes over to the door he used the day before to descend to the ocean surface; once there, he scans the immediate area and then throws the pouch containing the satellite phone into the ocean and watches it sink below the surface. Confident that the pouch is gone, he closes the door and heads back to Sally's cabin. She does in fact wake up precisely when he thought she would; but much to his amusement, he finds that her hunger for his companionship is not yet satisfied. They spend the rest of the morning and early afternoon having a repeat of the past night's activities, minus the alcohol and knockout drug.

Late that evening, immediately after his shift is done, Peter hurries to his room before his roommate, Raphio, gets there. He goes directly to his duffel bag to retrieve the potion Uncle Boris referred to earlier. He takes one look at the vial filled with the auburn, transparent liquid inside, and with a slight hesitation swallows it and then flushes the vial down the toilet. Three hours later, Raphio calls the ship's medic to their room. He examines Peter and then has him taken to the infirmary. After a thorough examination, he calls the mainland and arranges for Peter to be airlifted off the platform and taken to a hospital as soon as possible.

CHAPTER EIGHT

LIKE FATHER LIKE SON, KIND OF

Coast Guard Sector Command, Corpus Christi, Texas, Private Quarters of Captain William Harrington

William hates the mornings because that's when the pain is the worst. It has been almost twenty years since the rugby accident at the Coast Guard Academy, but the intense throbbing pain from having his shoulder dislocated is as real today as it has ever been.

It helped that his dad, the vice commandant of the Coast Guard, helped him get his medication in the discreet way he did. But still, how he ever kept it a secret that long from a man like Billings was quite the phenomenon.

Now it seems like he has won the lottery. Although a promotion was inevitable, along with a possible command of *First Responder*, he never in his wildest dreams thought he would be the youngest sector commander in the Coast Guard. How his dad got him under a doctor's care who gave him all the meds he would ever need and made it completely kosher with the military is like icing on the best cake he has ever eaten.

He sits up, grabs a water glass and the bottle of prescription meds from the nightstand next to his bed, and takes two of the pills that he knows will dull the incessant throbbing in his shoulder. The night before, his father called him to let him know about this new foreign investor named Boris, and explain that Harrington Savings and Loan in northern New Jersey is being restructured into a financial institution now called Harrington Enterprises.

He was flabbergasted to learn that all the paternity suits against his grandfather's estate had been dropped. A few months ago, the family attorneys had told Will and his father that several of the suits against the family came with iron-clad DNA tests that showed the plaintiffs had legitimate claims against what was left of the dwindling Harrington estate. He thought for sure that by the time he was ready to retire from the Coast Guard, nothing would be left. Now it looks like the family holdings will grow. He gets up, stretches his shoulder, and dresses while whistling a tune and thinking about how the Harrington family is headed for great things again.

As he heads to the bathroom to shave and brush his teeth, his cell phone rings. He looks down and immediately recognizes the number. "Hi, Dad. Did you call to give me more good news?"

There is a brief silence, and then James's raspy voice manifests itself on the activated loudspeaker on Will's phone that is lying on the kitchen counter. "Why is *First Responder* patrolling the Event Horizon oil rig off Port New Orleans? That's not on her itinerary!"

Will rolls his eyes. "Geez, Dad, someone from your Washington office called me last night and told me that Naval Intelligence asked the commandant to have her go by the rig to set up good satellite pings for heavier monitoring in that area."

Another brief silence, then his dad responds. "They only do that if there is a terror threat increase in an area. I've gotten no such notifications."

"Dad, you took paid time off and have been in New Jersey for the last two weeks setting up the new business. You probably just haven't checked your Coast Guard emails or faxes lately. And if that's true, then how do you know what *First Responder* is doing anyway?"

There is a longer silence. Will hears something like clicking on a computer keyboard and papers shuffling. "OK, now I see the terror threat notification. Came straight from Naval Intelligence. Looks like they base it on reports of suspicious activity in Prince Hasheen's camp in Saudi Arabia. He's the biggest of the oil sheiks over there. Some spook in naval intel thinks he'll try to sabotage the Gulf of Mexico oil production so he can corner the market."

Will switches off the speaker on his phone, picks it up and puts it to his ear, and with the opposite hand rubs his forehead. "Well, Dad, that sounds like a good reason to divert *First Responder* to that area. Commander Edwards knows how to ping satellites and set up coordinates for surveillance monitoring. His ship is the only one in the area capable of linking up with those satellites. Why are you upset about this? It came straight from the commandant."

There is a long pause on the phone. Will thinks he hears his dad talking with someone in the room while his hand is covering the receiver. "OK, Will. You and Edwards did your duty. But from here on out, you let me know about any changes going on down there in ship itineraries or anything else in your sector. If the commandant thinks he can circumvent my financial oversight of the Coast Guard, he's got another think coming. I have to account for every dime of fuel that every ship in our fleet burns up. We are not the CIA that can just say it's top secret in the interests of national security. Those Senate military oversight committees can be ruthless, and when I give my report, I don't want to be caught with my pants down. Do you understand, Captain Harrington?"

Will gulps as he processes the reprimand. "Yes, Dad, I mean Admiral, uh, sir." The line goes dead and Will finishes brushing his teeth and shaving. He slaps some Old Spice cologne on his face, then walks back over to his nightstand, grabs his bottle of meds, and pops another pill in his mouth, washing it down with a swig of water. Then he heads out to his office.

Executive Office of the Newly Refurbished Harrington Enterprises Building in Northern Virginia

Admiral James Harrington sets his cell phone down on his desk and looks over to the corner of his new office, where a very attractive young woman lounges in an auburn Corinthian leather recliner, lightly toying with a nickel-plated Walther PPK semiautomatic pistol. He gulps and then holds both hands out in a pleading gesture. "I didn't understand that there was a change in itineraries with our cutter. I have been so busy getting the business set up here, according to your father's instructions, that I have not had time to keep up on all my emails."

The woman leans forward and, while still toying with the pistol, purses her full red lips, then flashes her perfectly white teeth at James and answers in a deeply seductive Russian accent. "That is precisely the reason you can still breathe the free air, Admiral." She gets up from the chair and walks toward the door. The sway of her hips as she walks does not go unnoticed by the very nervous vice commandant of the Coast Guard. She reaches for the door, and then turns. "Never forget, James Harrington, that my father and I now own you and all that you have. That includes your opioid addict of a son, even if he does not know it yet."

James takes a handkerchief and wipes his forehead. "I understand, Miss Rasmov, and I will from this point on inform you of any more deviations of itineraries in the Gulf. I promise!"

"Please, James, call me Natasha. I am sure that now that we understand one another, our working relationship will be exemplary. Goodbye."

Natasha leaves his office on the top floor of the five-story complex and heads for the elevators. She marvels at the vastness of her father's empire, both legitimate and not; and though his name is not on any document of ownership or partnership in the world, he maintains an iron-clad control over all of it. To the outside world, Boris Rasmov is just a retired financial investor who is helping his nephew, Yuri Sebastion, build an auto trucking and wholesaling business in New York City. But to the elite and powerful underworld, he is an emperor with his tentacles reaching multi layers of wealth and power all over the world.

She has completed her first field assignment for him, which in her opinion was a one-hundred-percent success. As she enters the elevator, she feels the vibration of her cell phone and reaches in her hip pocket to retrieve it. As she suspected, it is her father. "Father, I was just about to call you. James Harrington is compliant with our needs and is also adequately terrified of any repercussions for not obeying your every word. He did, however, inform me of some alarming details that could adversely affect your and Peter's operations in the Gulf. The Office of Naval Intelligence has advised their commander in chief to raise the terror alert level in the Gulf. Someone ordered *First Responder* to cruise by Event Horizon to help line up satellite surveillance in that area. They suspect Prince Hasheen to be the most likely instigator of any acts of terror that are perpetrated, as he is the one most likely to benefit from a Gulf of Mexico oil production slowdown."

"Your cousin and I expected this from the beginning," Natasha's father responds. "Our contributions to the good prince's operation will remain transparent no matter the outcome. This whole plan has only a minimal chance at success in truly bringing oil production in that part of the world to a halt. The true profit will be in the public relations disaster for Star Oil, and the political pressure it will provide to put a moratorium on future drilling and expanded production in that region. Hasheen has chosen an all-or-nothing strategy toward achieving his goal of world market dominance. If he fails, his own people will eat him alive. If he succeeds, he will depose his own king and be the next superpower of the Middle East. Either way, my daughter, they have paid us for our part in his plan and will gain much profit, no matter the outcome."

"What would you like me to do next, Father?"

"Your cousin Peter has been airlifted off the oil rig and will be at the hospital in New Orleans within the hour. Fly out there, check on him, and then proceed to Corpus Christi. It's time we let Captain Harrington know who his true benefactors are and that we now own him."

She listens carefully and her forehead crinkles as her eyes squint while she processes the new information. "Do you believe the opioids we are providing for him are sufficient for this or is a more intimate strategy also needed?" She says this a little more sternly than she should have.

"What I believe, Daughter, is that I need you to go there and assess him thoroughly and then proceed with a strategy that will be the most advantageous to my organization and our needs. Is that understood, Natasha?"

"Of course, Father. Forgive my rashness." She hears a bit of amusement in her father's voice when he assures her that everyone in his organization is called on to make sacrifices that do not agree with their natures; and at those times they must focus on the outcome and not the procedure. He then disconnects the line and leaves her to settle her own demons.

CHAPTER NINE
NO TURNING BACK

Aboard *First Responder,* Five Hours from Docking at Sector Corpus Christi Coast Guard Command

Lt. Commander Larry Phillips steps up to Jacob on the command deck. "Commander, that phone call you were waiting for from your wife just came through."

Jacob smiles and turns to leave. "Thanks, Larry, uh, Lieutenant Commander. I'll take it in my quarters." When he gets to his desk, he grabs the phone receiver and pushes the button with the flashing light. "How are the two most beautiful girls in the world handling moving day?"

"We're doing just fine, darling. I always find it interesting how you are away every time I have to move this household to your new assignment location. Hold on, here comes Danielle. I'll put us on speaker."

"Hi, Daddy!"

Chills go up and down Jacob's spine at the sound of his daughter's voice. "Hey there, spunky monkey. You helping your mother out and staying on her good side? You know how she gets when it's moving day."

Jacob can hear his wife give an exasperated sigh as Danielle giggles and replies, "Yes, Daddy, I am helping. She hasn't scolded me once. But those poor military movers are getting their heads kicked in. I don't know what you guys pay those poor people, but it should be more. After the first hour, they started bubble wrapping everything before they would move it for fear of damaging it somehow."

There is a slight shuffling sound on Jacob's mic and then Mary's voice comes through. "Jacob, they are all very nice boys and they are doing a fine job, but when they came into our room, they tried to pick up the vanity my grandmother gave me by its legs and carry it out sideways. That piece is over a hundred years old and has belonged to four generations of women in my family. I took the time to instruct them on how to handle our furniture with more care and respect," she says.

Jacob laughs heartily. "Honey, it's a good thing we only brought a few of our things to New Orleans. Have your dad and mom been able to move the rest of our stuff to the new house yet?"

"Yes, it is so wonderful that we will live just a few blocks from their house. Mama even got Willito to help with the moving. Getting a high school senior to help with that kind of thing on a Saturday is quite an accomplishment." Mary says this with a smile in her voice.

"Has he decided what he's doing when he graduates yet?" Jacob asks.

"As a matter of fact, yes. He will enlist in the Marine Corps. Mama wasn't too happy, but Daddy backed him up and that was that," she answers.

"I still support that idea. Willito is a warrior and needs discipline. The Marine Corps will be a good fit for him. Plus, when he's done, if he wants to go to college, he'll have funds available." Jacob looks down at a flashing red light on his phone. "Honey, Danielle, I have to go. We are a few hours out from Corpus Christi, and it looks like my CO is calling."

Before he can hang up, Danielle pipes in, "Daddy, Grandpa Roberto bought that old Buick Skylark of Miguel's and wants us to help him restore it when we're moved in and you have time."

"That's great news, sweetie. You tell him we're in. I'll talk to you both soon. I love you girls." As Jacob reaches down to switch lines, he hears them say "We love you too!" before he disconnects.

"Commander Edwards."

"Jacob, it's Will Harrington."

"Yes, sir, Captain. What's up?"

"Everything is fine, commander. It's just that my dad, Admiral Harrington, got all bent out of shape about your itinerary changes. Being the vice commandant, he's the designated bean-counter for the Coast Guard, and he hates having to document unplanned use of fuel and resources without having a good reason that he can put on the regular report—meaning a reason that does not end up endangering national security."

Jacob sighs. "Boy, Captain, I don't know how we could have handled that any better. I got the orders after we left dock. They informed me that the commandant's office was advising you, so I assumed that accounting would already be aware."

"To tell you the truth, Jacob, Dad's in New Jersey looking after some family business and he just checked his emails this morning. He's probably just nervous about our unprecedented promotions and being assigned these commands, and he wants nothing looking fishy on our starting blocks, you know what I mean?"

"Sure, Captain. How about from now on I will inform you of any orders I receive that don't come directly from you?"

"Sounds good, Jacob, but you and I both know that a ship like *First Responder* answers to the commandant first and foremost. So, let me clarify that I am not ordering you to betray that line of command; but helping me keep my old man off my back by keeping me informed when you can, sure would be nice."

Jacob gives a sigh of relief. "Thanks, Captain, I'll do my best."

"Thanks, Jacob, and when it's just you and me, let's keep it on a first-name basis. We've both served under Billings, and when at sea on deck it was like that."

"You bet, Will. Edwards out." Jacob hangs up his cabin phone and thinks to himself that he will like his new CO a lot.

Jacob steps out of his cabin and pays his gunnery officer and his trainee a visit. He walks around to the front of the ship where the OTO Melara gun is mounted, and steps into the gunner's area. Gunny Jones sees him enter and calls "Attention!" to Seaman Schuette, and they salute. "At ease, guys. I just came by to see how the training is going, Gunny."

"I'm glad you asked, Commander, because Schuette here is a quick study. He's ready for live-fire exercise any time you want to try this bad boy out," Gunny Jones says as he has one hand on Schuette's shoulder and uses the other to pat the controller handles of the OTO Melara gun.

"That's good to hear, Gunny. We'll be docking at Corpus Christi in about four hours. I'll get clearance and location where we can test Schuette and the weapon out from sector command. Then we'll head out in two days for our war maneuvers. Carry on, gentlemen."

Jacob leaves the station and heads for the communication room. Seaman Bliss is busy doing radio checks with Corpus Christi and does not see him come through the door right away; but when he does, he jumps out of his seat, knocking a clipboard onto the deck, and gives a hasty salute.

"At ease, Bliss," Jacob says with a jovial smile. He reaches in his front pocket and pulls out the SIM card from the special camera equipment Captain Williams sent him, and hands it to the seaman. "Bliss, upload this to the same source you did at Event Horizon, ASAP. Naval Intelligence wants those images, stat."

"Aye aye, Commander. Anything else, sir?"

"Yes, kid. Learn how to chill a little. I want efficiency and respect on my ship, but erratic nervousness doesn't help you or me." Jacob pauses for a second and softens his gaze, because he sees that Bliss is turning beet red. "Look, John. You're doing a fine job, and I like you. You'll make a great petty officer someday. Just give yourself a chance to grow. You'll get it, kid."

Bliss's shoulders relax slightly, and he gives Jacob his best Nebraska cornhusker smile. "Thanks, Commander, I'll give it my best. It's just that I never had to deal with so many officers in my last assignment, and never directly with the captain."

Jacob listens thoughtfully and then gets an idea. "Bliss, you ever do any piloting on your last tour?"

"No, sir. I was basically on kitchen duty the whole time. Chief Rogers, my superior, checked my records and saw that I had put down IT and communication equipment experience from high school on my Coast Guard application, and recommended me for radio/radar training when my first tour was up. I graduated at the top of my class. That's why I got this assignment."

Jacob already knew this about Bliss's training and previous assignment, but hearing the seaman explain it gives him an idea. "OK, Bliss, this is what I want you to do. Most new enlisted men and women get a shot at piloting if they are on deck. I will not pull you out of the radio room, but I want you to pull a couple shifts up on the command deck piloting *First Responder*. Lt. Commander Phillips is in charge of training the seamen for that, and I think it will give you the perfect opportunity to rub shoulders with the senior officers. That way, you'll figure out we're all human and then you'll settle down into your job."

Bliss's eyes light up and he jumps out of his seat and salutes. "Aye aye, Commander. Thank you. I have always wanted to pilot but never got the chance when I worked the KP shift."

Jacob winks, returns the salute, and turns to leave. Seaman Bliss sits back down and grabs the SIM card Jacob gave him to upload the info to Naval Intelligence. When he is sure that his captain is gone, he closes his eyes and says, "Thanks, God, for giving me the best CO in the Guard."

Four hours later, *First Responder* is docking at Coast Guard Sector Command Corpus Christi. Lt. Commander Phillips walks up to Jacob and hands him a note. "Sir, this just came from the communication room. Lt. Commander Chuck Yeager just requested to see you and Gunny Jones after you report to Captain Harrington. Isn't he the one who helped you take down that drug-smuggling ring on Falcon Lake last year?"

Jacob takes the note and looks at it. "Yes, we both commissioned into the Guard from Kings Point together. This is my first assignment without him. He's supposed to be moving to DC and enrolling in Quantico next month. I don't have a clue what he's doing here. Tell Gunny Jones to meet up with him at the location on the note and I'll be there after I report in."

"Yes sir, Commander."

Jacob begins to turn and then remembers something. "Larry, my wife Mary and my daughter Danielle will be here tomorrow night. We'd love to have you and your wife, Tina, join us for dinner somewhere."

"I'll talk to Tina, and that would be great, sir. We've been here for six months now, so why don't you bring your family to our place? I'm known to whip up some wicked good steaks."

"Sounds good. I'll bring the wine. Any preferences?" Phillips gives him a brand name he's never heard of, but he commits it to memory and excuses himself from the command deck.

Thirty minutes later, Jacob is sitting in Captain Harrington's office, discussing business. He looks around the room and notices that the only pictures on display are those of Harrington's now institutionalized mother; his father, the vice commandant; his grandfather, the former senator; and his famous great-grandfather, the World War I Coast Guard captain. "Sir, I don't mean to impose, but is there a Mrs. Harrington?"

Will squirms in his seat. "No. I'm forty-one years old and still single, much to my dad's dismay. Had a few close calls through the years, but no one has bagged this Harrington yet."

"I am sorry, Captain. I didn't mean to pry; it's just that my wife wanted to make sure I invited you and your wife to have dinner with us sometime when I'm in port. That invitation still stands, and if you want to bring a friend, that would be great."

"Well, thanks, Jacob. That'd be wonderful. After you and the Mrs. get settled in, let me know and we'll work something out."

Jacob stands up and waits to be dismissed. Captain Harrington tells him he will have the coordinates for the live-fire exercise with *First Responder's* OTO Melara gun by the end of the day and will forward them to him by email. Jacob salutes and leaves.

As Jacob rounds the corner, heading toward the lounge at Sector Corpus Christi, he sees Chuck sitting in a chair drinking a cup of coffee and talking to Gunny Jones. Chuck gives Jacob his best "gotcha" smile, grabs his hand to shake it, and then gives his old buddy a man hug. Jacob returns the hug and nods at Gunny Jones, then looks back at Chuck. "What the hell are you doing here? You're supposed to be at Quantico getting ready to be a G-man."

Chuck shakes his head. "When Tommy calls…well, you know."

"Yeah, I know. What's up and why are you here?"

Chuck and Gunny Jones explain to Jacob that for the next four weeks, Captain Williams wants his top operatives in the Gulf of Mexico and the Caribbean coordinated under Jacob, and to be ready for anything. He got Chuck's admission to Quantico postponed until the heightened terror alert level is over, and Chuck is now the chief special investigator for Coast Guard Sector Corpus Christi. Jacob looks over at Chuck. "So, besides the three of us, who else is in this group?"

"The Legend said you're in charge, so he didn't tell me anything else. Maybe your secret command is on a need-to-know basis, and right now you don't need to know."

Jacob lightly punches his friend in the shoulder. "Yeah, that makes about as much sense as another hole in the head. OK, guys. If the Legend needs us, I'm sure he'll call."

The three say goodbye and head in different directions. Jacob is dying to see his new house, so he heads over to the motor pool and requisitions a vehicle, then drives out to South Padre Island to meet up with his family.

Will Harrington thinks he will like Jacob Edwards, but he sure hates it when someone asks him if he is married or not. Seeing his mother and father's marriage fall apart, and then his mother institutionalized with a severe nervous breakdown over the whole thing, has left him with a real hole in his soul. He knew that his father was more to blame than the old man would ever admit. Will vowed he would never make his father's mistakes. Nothing would please him more than to have a wife and family, but he knows that his opioid addiction would ruin it. Being single is the only way he has hidden it so far. The girlfriends he has had in the past have been wonderful women, but as soon as they sensed something was up with him, he would break off the relationship.

He reaches up and rubs his shoulder. The doctors told him a long time ago that the pain is now more mental than physical. They called it ghost pain. All he knows is that when it was at its worst, he could not tolerate it without the drugs. He reaches in his desk and finds his pill bottle hidden behind the files there and pops a couple in his mouth. *Funny,* he thinks, *the act of just taking them makes me feel better.* He chides himself for still hiding his medication. After he moved to Corpus Christi, his dad arranged for him to be under the care of a military-approved doctor, who prescribes all the pills he wants. Life was definitely looking up. Maybe now, under a doctor's care, he could meet someone and not have to worry about being caught. Maybe. He feels a spark of excitement because now that *First Responder* is docked and Edwards is in port for a couple of days, he can take time off and go up to Houston and do some clubbing and maybe meet someone who can save him from himself. He reaches over to the intercom on his desk and buzzes his assistant to come in. A minute later, a thirty-something female chief petty officer named Patty Rosenburg comes in with a pad. "Captain, may I help you?"

"Yes, Chief Rosenburg. I'm taking four paid days off and heading to Houston for the weekend. Forward *First Responder's* live-fire practice coordinates to them, and when I'm gone, call Commander Edwards and tell him he's in charge until I get back."

Rosenburg has a slight smirk on her face and she squints her eyes a little. "Captain, Commander Edwards requested the time off to get his family settled at Station Brazos over near South Padre Island."

Will waves his hand dismissively. "Brazos is still part of our sector. Tell him to just keep his phone handy. If there's an emergency, he can coordinate from there. Otherwise, it'll be like neither of us was ever gone."

Captain Harrington grabs a few things from his desk, puts his cell phone in his pocket, and heads out the door, whistling a tune as he leaves.

Chief Patty Rosenburg closes the captain's door and locks it, then goes to her desk and finds her cell phone in her purse. She looks around, making sure no one else is nearby, and then dials a number she had recently been given. "Hello, Natasha. The captain will not be staying in the area this weekend. He has decided that since *First Responder* is docked and Commander Edwards is here, he can take a weekend off. He's headed to Houston for some, uh, R&R."

There is a ten-second pause on the line and beads of cold sweat form on Patty's forehead. She nervously switches the phone from one ear to the other, and Natasha finally responds.

"Please find out and forward to me his hotel reservation and the most likely places he will do this rest and relaxation at. And Patty..."

"Yes, ma'am?"

"We have removed your son's inappropriate actions from the school files. No colleges will ever hear about his extracurricular locker room activity with that high school cheerleader he molested. But let me remind you that I can put them back in the system and no institute of higher learning will ever take a chance on him."

"I understand, Natasha, and I am deeply grateful. What else do you want me to do?"

"Just get me that hotel information as quickly as you can and keep your phone on, in case I need you again."

One Hour Later, Luxury Hotel Suite in Houston

Natasha purrs to herself as she remembers the phrase her father drilled into her from her youth: "Chance favors the prepared mind." Now that she does not have to set things up in Corpus Christi for Will Harington's recruitment/ enslavement into her father's organization, things will go much more smoothly. With the meager availability of resources in Corpus Christi no longer being a problem, she can now do a much better job of entrapping the captain. She sits down and looks up an underworld contact of her father's who operates in Houston and calls her. "Vivian, dear, it's Natasha Rasmov. My father and I have a need in Houston this weekend and your special resources will do nicely to meet that need."

The raspy voice of a fifty-something woman who smokes too much answers. "Natasha, your father has not called me for years. The last time I saw you almost ten years ago, your cousin Yuri and you were at the hospital here in Houston."

Natasha closes her eyes and smiles at the memory of raking a knife across Yuri's stomach when he tried to force her sexually. He was supposed to be watching Natasha while they waited in a hotel room for her father to come back from a business deal. Back then, Boris was establishing a network of businesses under Yuri Sebastion's name, who is also an American citizen and Boris's nephew through his only sister. Yuri was always way too stupid to be put in charge of anything, but his citizenship made him the perfect patsy to front her father's operation.

That night, while getting out of the shower, she thought she would tease him a little, so she let her towel drop a little too low below her ample cleavage. Yuri thought with the wrong head as usual and took that as a sign that his fifteen-year-old cousin was inviting him to have taboo sex with her. When he grabbed her, she backhanded him across the face and told him to control himself, but he then attacked her. He pushed her onto the bed where she slept. While he was taking his shirt off, she found the knife she always kept under her pillow, and she raked it across his belly. She was careful not to seriously injure him, but the cut was deep enough that he needed stitches. Not wanting to incur her father's wrath, she made up a story of how Yuri let her practice her knife fighting on him and she accidently cut him.

It was then that Boris called Vivian Narcellas and had her meet Natasha and Yuri at the hospital to fill out a statement that Yuri was a relative visiting from back East, and how he was out in the garage helping his aunt gut a deer that one of her brothers had shot recently while out hunting. Yuri was inexperienced, and when the guts spilled out on the floor of the garage where the deer was hanging, he lost his footing and fell on the knife he was still holding. They accepted the story and the emergency room doctor gave him fifteen stitches. Every time Natasha thinks of that scar across Yuri's belly, it brings a smile to her face.

"Yes, Vivian, be assured that neither I nor my father have forgotten how valuable an asset you can be. I trust you are still enjoying our monthly installments of the retainer fees we send you?"

Vivian laughs and then hacks a little as she spits the phlegm from her throat into a cup. "Being loyal to Boris Rasmov, no matter how little he communicates, is always the healthiest option one can choose. How can I be of help to you, Natasha?"

"I need one of your most attractive girls—full-figured, blonde, and between fourteen and sixteen—to be available Saturday night. They must be new recruits who have not been in any published media. She also must be willing to be a surrogate mother if asked. The target is a high-ranking and well-connected Coast Guard sector commander who is coming to Houston this weekend to blow off steam and sow some wild oats. He is also an opioid addict, so his manipulation has already begun. We are just completing the trap this weekend."

"I will have everything ready when you need it, Natasha."

With everything in place, all she needs now is the hotel location Will Harrington will be staying at, and then to find out where his first stop will be in his adventure to enjoy Houston's nightlife.

Later that Evening, Houston's Premier Night Club

Will goes back to his apartment, throws together a few things, gets in his new Jaguar and heads to Houston as fast as he can. After six months of shadowing the admiral at New Orleans and then being cooped up at Sector Corpus Christi Command for another four weeks, he is ready to get out of Dodge. He knows Commander Edwards can handle anything that might come up over the weekend, and his being in port is the perfect opportunity to bolt.

After checking in at the luxurious Marriott Suites, he dumps his things, freshens up and heads right to the night club. A few of his friends from prep school recommended this place. It was always filled with gold-digging women looking for a sugar daddy like Will to solve all their problems. The nice thing about gold diggers is that they are always ready to show a man a good time when he looks like a promising prospect. Being a single man in his early forties, the youngest Coast Guard sector commander, the son of the vice commandant, and the heir to a now-promising banking institution, makes him a very promising prospect.

He stands at the bar sipping his vodka martini and getting the lay of the land. He spots a very voluptuous, red-headed girl wearing a slinky, black mini-dress with a bare back and cut low enough in the front so one does not have to guess about her breast size. She is giving him looks from the edge of the dance floor. As he pushes away from the bar to go introduce himself, he feels a hand touch his shoulder and he turns around. What he sees as he turns almost makes him fall over backward. She is at least a head taller than the girl he was going to talk to, and she looks like something out of a Greek goddess movie—long, dark hair with blonde highlights that softly fall around her shoulders; the most intense green eyes he has ever seen surrounded by long, luscious eyelashes. Her lips are full, and the gleam from her sparkling white smile almost blinds him with its brilliance.

The gown she is wearing has a hypnotic effect on him. It is also black, but full length with an erotically provocative slit up the left side that exposes a very muscular and tanned thigh.

Before Will can say a word, Natasha leans in close, puts her lips right up to his ear and says, "Seeing you standing there all alone was almost unbearable. But then you were going to talk to that little tramp over there, and I knew you had not seen me yet, so I decided to let you know what you would miss if you did. Why don't you put that drink down and take me onto the dance floor? They are playing something slow, and you and I can talk and get to know one another."

As she speaks, Will knows he's captured. The thick, sexy, Russian accent is almost too much for him to bear. She seems to instinctively know what he's feeling and leans in and kisses him on the lips just long enough for him to want more, then pulls away and takes his hand and leads him to the floor. Will does his best to maintain his composure as he follows this goddess.

He sets his drink down on an empty table next to the same red-headed girl he had wanted to talk to. Oddly, she picks up the drink and takes it back to a darker part of the bar, puts something in it, and then brings it back and leaves. Will and Natasha are dancing in the direct center of the floor as the sparkle of the disco globe rolls across both their forms, and Will doesn't notice her actions. But Natasha sees that her operative had successfully spiked Will's drink. She had a powerful prescription-strength aphrodisiac put into his drink, because she knew that the evening was young, and with him being an opioid addict mixed with all the alcohol he would consume tonight, she still needed him virile for later to ensure her plans would work. After her red-headed operative leaves the room, she pulls back slightly from their dancing embrace, then softly brushes the side of his head above the ear with her right hand. "So, what is your name?"

To her delight, Will needs no more coaxing than that. He enthusiastically tells her his name, what his job is, who his father is, and what kind of business his family is in—all before they leave the dance floor and occupy the table where he had put down his drink down earlier. When he finally stops to catch his breath, she orders a drink for herself. She then reaches inside her little purse and pulls out a prescription bottle labeled as painkillers and pops one in her mouth, washing it down with her drink.

Will squints at her and says, "That's not recommended, you know. Alcohol and opioids don't mix well together."

Natasha leans into Will and speaks into his ear. "I was a gymnast in Russia while growing up. I tore my ACL when I was fifteen. These are the only things that help me deal with the pain." She holds up the bottle in one hand and her drink in the other. "These, together, make it so I can enjoy a good time with a man like you. I plan to enjoy you very much, Captain Will Harrington."

At first, what she says stuns him, but then a devious smile slowly crosses his face as it dawns on him how very fortuitous this chance encounter is. He then reaches in his jacket pocket, pulls out his own bottle, takes a pill out and says, "Rugby accident at the academy. Tore a tendon in my shoulder when it was dislocated." He picks up his spiked drink and washes the pill down with the whole drink.

As they sit and talk, she begins to see that Will has scooted closer to her and has rested his hand on her shoulders as he lightly caresses her hair. Natasha gives a sultry laugh and pulls Will's head to hers until their lips meet. The kiss is long and passionate, and to her delight she can see that the aphrodisiac is kicking in with full force. She releases herself from the kiss and stands while holding his hand. "I think we should take this back to your place, Captain. What do you say?"

Will finds it erotic that she called him captain and quickly stands up and puts his arm around her back, strategically positioning his hand under her arm and high enough that the tips of his fingers are touching the side of her breast. Natasha uses her arm to hold his hand in place and subtly move it forward so he can feel more of the prize he is after.

As the couple leaves the room, a lone figure stands up at the far end of the ballroom, and with his high-powered mini camera, he takes one more shot of the couple as they leave. He then feels the vibration of his cell phone in his pocket and flips it open. "Uncle Boris, Natasha just left with Will Harrington. I got several photographs of them drinking and taking the opioids while they were sitting at their table."

"Nicely done, Peter. Get to a computer and a secure line as soon as you can and upload what you have to my server, then meet the rest of the crew at his hotel and be ready to send me the rest of the photographs. Oh, and Peter…"

"Yes, Uncle?"

"Vivian's doctor confirmed that the young girl she is bringing is at a good stage of the month to be impregnated. Her appearance is close to Natasha's so she believes our deception will work. Of course, Natasha will have to get him drunk enough not to know the switch and aroused enough to perform properly."

Peter sighs, "Uncle Boris, perhaps I was a little premature in recommending that Natasha was ready for full field activity. How she will pull off having Harrington impregnate that girl this evening when he thinks he is only with her is still beyond my ability to see."

Boris laughs lightly. "Peter, do not let family and sentimentalities interfere with our business. Natasha only misjudged considering caution. As to the night's maneuvers, the good captain has over five hundred milligrams of medical-grade Viagra in his system, and combined with the alcohol and opioids, he will hardly know who or what he is romping with. In the morning we will own him, and Natasha will be no worse for the wear."

"Yes, Uncle Boris. I will get these photos to you shortly and then proceed to the hotel." The line goes dead and Peter takes a calming breath and buries the urge to rush out to the parking lot and kill Captain William Harrington with his bare hands. He had to deal with his demons concerning his cousin Natasha long ago. Unlike their mutual cousin, Yuri, Peter never acted on any of those impulses. But he has always known that his passion for her is his one driving force; and if he could never have her as his, he could at least give her his complete loyalty and follow her as he does her father. With that thought, the old, cold, calculating aura settles through him and he proceeds on to his next task.

Next Morning, Will Harrington's Hotel Suite

Will opens his eyes to the blinding sunlight coming in through the open window at the foot of the king-size bed he is in. The throbbing hangover pulsing through every fiber of his being is something beyond anything he has ever experienced. He puts one hand up to block out the sun coming through as he takes the other to rub his eyes and forehead—a feeble attempt to assuage the pain, but he has to do something. Before he loses control and barfs all over his sheets, he jumps out of his now empty bed and dashes into the bathroom to relieve himself. As he finishes and goes to the sink to wash and gargle, a hand protrudes through the door with a white hotel bathrobe in it. A Russian-accented male voice reaches his ears. "Clothe yourself and then take these."

Will finishes wiping his face after he spits out the water in his mouth and grabs the robe. Once he has it on, he takes the pills and does not even look at them but puts them in his mouth and swallows. The man whom he still cannot focus on then says, "Captain Harrington, once you have adjusted yourself, please join me in the living room. We have much to discuss."

When Will's eyes are finally focusing, he sees an older, very distinguished-looking man wearing a dark suit, deep black Italian boots, and a very expensive Rolex watch on his wrist. But the most noteworthy item in the man's wardrobe is the most exotic cane he had ever seen, made of dark mahogany and capped with a silver handle. The man does not look or walk like he needs the cane, but somehow it looks as much a part of him as his arms and legs do.

Finally, fully awake and cognizant of his surroundings, Will steps out into the living room and sees the same man seated at the dining table with several folders and some photographs on it. Before looking closer at the contents on the table, he points his finger and says, "Who are you and where is the lady who was with me last night? If this is a kidnapping, I need to tell you that I am a high-ranking officer in the United States Coast Guard."

Boris looks up and considers the pathetic man before him like he would a piece of meat he brought home from the market and is trying to decide whether he wants to barbecue it or broil it. "Yes, you are Captain William Harrington, commander of the United States Coast Guard Sector Corpus Christi. Your father is Admiral James Harrington, vice commandant of the same Coast Guard, who has also recently become a junior partner of mine in the banking industry. My name is Boris Rasmov."

Stunned and a little dizzy by the words he just heard, Will sits down at the table and looks at this man with a bewildered gaze that is so comical it makes Boris show the slightest crease of a smile. "You're the new investor Dad told me about," he says.

Boris reaches down, opens a manila folder, and pulls out several large photographs and hands them to Will. Among them there are pictures of him and the ravishing woman, Natasha, who he met last night, at their table drinking liquor and taking their opioids. He remembers that, but the next couple of pictures are of him in this hotel room with another women, and they show him having sex with her; but to his deep panic, he cannot recall having ever seen her before. Upon closer examination, the panic becomes a full-blown anxiety attack when he realizes the woman is not a woman at all but a teenage girl, and probably under the age of sixteen. "What is the meaning of this? I made love with a woman last night, but it wasn't this girl. I remember bringing her to my room, undressing her, lying down with her and…"

Like a lightning bolt, Boris jumps out of his seat and grabs his cane. While holding it with his left hand, he pulls the silver handle with his right hand, draws out a thin, steel blade and places the razor-sharp edge against Will's neck. "That is enough. Say another word about her and you will have breathed your last breath." While Boris's eyes are boring into Will's with a ferocity that communicates death is but a heartbeat away, the outer door opens and in walks the beautiful woman that Will brought back to his room last night. She quietly walks up to Boris and gently pulls his sword hand away, relieving Will of the immediate threat of having his throat sliced open.

"Yes, Will Harrington, I allowed you to enjoy me last night for a moment. It was really nice, I have to admit. But in your drunken, opioid-affected condition, you were not aware of when I left, and this girl entered your room. As you can see…"

Boris reaches over and places a hand on his daughter's shoulder and says, "I can continue, Natasha. Forgive me for my momentary loss of judgment."

She smiles and backs away and takes a seat on the couch to let her father continue. Boris nods to her and then refocuses on Will. "As you can see, Captain, the female you slept with last night is underage, and we have already uploaded these pictures to our own private server, and had our operative at Corpus Christi download them to several of your own computers. Incidentally, though it is too soon to tell, we believe she has conceived by you and will in time produce offspring that could legitimately be tied to you and your father's estate. Having spent most of your life hearing about and dealing with your grandfather's improprieties and paternal lawsuits, I am sure you can appreciate the significance of what I am saying to you, can't you, Captain Harrington?"

Will feels so dizzy that he has a hard time standing. He drops on the couch next to Natasha and says to her, "Do you even have an ACL injury, or was that a lie too?"

Natasha purses her lips and looks to her father for permission. He gives it with a nod, and she answers his question. "Captain Harrington, I have had many injuries in my life, including a torn ACL; but he"—she looks at Boris— "would never allow me to be so weak as to become addicted to painkillers."

Boris clears his throat and says, "The gist of the matter is that you and your father work for me now.

145

You will do whatever I say and feed me with any intel I need. In return, I will restore the Harrington name and fortune to its former glory. If you defy me, the least of the consequences will be the release of these photos and the identity of your bastard offspring, if any progeny results from last night. The worst will be you and your father's deaths. Are we clear, Captain?"

Will puts his palms to his forehead and leans forward, resting his elbows on his knees, and says, "Clear, Boris. I will do whatever you say."

Natasha reaches over and lightly pats Captain Will Harrington's back. Boris smiles and says, "That is good, very good."

Natasha quickly grabs the folders on the table, puts them in a briefcase and takes her father's arm as they leave the suite. Once out in the parking lot, Peter walks up and says, "So everything worked out precisely as you expected, Cousin. You are your father's daughter and we are stronger with you."

Boris allows himself to smile as he looks at the two before him. "I am pleased with your performances of late. We still must pursue Prince Hasheen's objective and finish the operation. With Captain Will Harrington under our control, the prince's chances of success just rose considerably. Barring unforeseen rogue elements interfering with the operation, Hasheen may well be the next king of his country."

CHAPTER TEN
UNFORESEEN ROGUE ELEMENTS

Coast Guard Station Brazos, South Padre Island, Texas

Jacob and Danielle drive over to see his father-in-law at work. Chief Roberto Garcia is the ranking noncommissioned officer at Station Brazos, Texas, and is in command of the swim rescue division there. Though Jacob did not go there on any official mission, because of his rank and command of *First Responder,* he and his daughter are immediately allowed through the checkpoint gate at the station. When they pull up to the parking lot, two enlisted security personnel are waiting for him at the door. One steps forward and salutes.

"Commander Edwards, welcome to Brazos, sir. The chief is in the communication room and he told me to let you know there is a priority message for you from Corpus Christi command."

Jacob returns the salute. "Thank you, seaman. I know the way." He looks down at Danielle. "Come on, spunky monkey, let's go see what's up."

They go through a couple more doors and enter a room that looks out over the south bay at the tip of South Padre Island. There are four more enlisted men in the room, but Danielle breaks away and runs to the one she knows as her *abuelo*. Chief Roberto Garcia reaches out and enfolds his granddaughter in his arms and kisses her on the top of the head. "Danielle, I was hoping you and your dad would visit me. How is the move going?"

Danielle rolls her eyes. "Mom is 'Sergeant Slaughtering' those poor military movers to death. By the time Daddy got home, he really didn't have to do much. After a while she kicked both of us out and said she wanted to handle the rest herself."

Roberto rolls his eyes the same way his granddaughter just did and exclaims, "Ay yi yi, she is just like her mother. Neither of those women can stand to have anyone else do anything to help setup a house." He winks at both Danielle and Jacob. "It's good you both left when you did. I have inside intelligence that your grandmother is heading over there right now to help. Neither of you want to be around for that."

Jacob and Danielle both burst out in laughter, and Jacob says, "So, Pops, how about the three of us go out for supper when your shift is up and then have a look at that '72 Buick Skylark you want to restore?"

Before Roberto can answer, another chief comes up to them. "Commander, we have a priority one message for you from Sector Command."

Jacob stops laughing, a little embarrassed that he forgot. "Sure, Chief, what is it?"

The man hands him a fax from Captain Harrington's assistant, Chief Patty Rosenburg. It reads: "Please inform Commander Edwards that Captain Harrington is taking a long weekend of paid time off, and since he is the ranking officer in the sector, he will be in command until the captain returns. P.S. Just tell him to keep his phone handy and check in from time to time. Everything is pretty quiet right now."

Jacob blows out a puff of air out of frustration and hands the paper to his father-in-law. "Geez, Pops, and I was just starting to like this guy. Go figure. He knew I was moving my family in this weekend."

Roberto grabs the paper and reads it. "It's not that bad, Jacob. He's been in training for this post for almost six months now with no time off. It's just over the weekend. What could happen?"

Jacob stares at Chief Roberto for a moment with a *Yeah, right* look on his face and grabs the paper. "Chief Roberto, I am assuming command of Station Brazos while I get on top of some details. Please take care of my daughter until I'm done."

Jacob looks over at Danielle. "I'm sorry, honey, but look at the bright side. You get to hang with *abuelo* at work for a while."

Roberto and Danielle stare at each other for a second, and then she smiles. "Works for me, Daddy. Do what you got to do." Roberto and Danielle then head out to the station's dock and Jacob heads to Roberto's office to make phone calls and check on schedules, current orders, and ongoing itineraries in the sector.

Six hours later, a very weary Commander Jacob Edwards stands up from his father-in-law's desk and stretches. He's been working on trying to get a final understanding of this temporary command that someone has put him into. His biggest concern for the seriousness of the situation is the raised terror alert level that he knows is over the whole Gulf of Mexico. He's relieved to find out that his "heads up" from Captain Tommy Williams about said level was not released to law enforcement and military entities until that afternoon. So Captain Harrington did not leave his command knowing that his sector could be at more risk. He reaches for the phone on the desk to make a call to Will's hotel in Houston to let him know about the raised terror alert level and that he should probably cut short his long weekend, when he feels his own cell phone vibrate in his pocket. He looks down and recognizes the contact number immediately. "Hi, Captain. What's up?"

Tommy Williams answers. "Sorry to bug you on your move-in day, kid, but we have an emergency brewing over at Event Horizon. Are you somewhere where you can talk privately?"

"As a matter of fact, my CO took the weekend off and left me a message telling me that I was in command of Sector Corpus Christi until he got back. I am at Station Brazos in my father-in-law's office trying to get on top of what I'm supposed to do."

Tommy listens and understands what that kind of shift in schedule and lack of prudence could do to a man like Jacob. "So how long have you been there trying to learn that whole job? You know it took Harrington almost seven months to prepare for that post."

Jacob rolls his eyes. "I've been here about six hours trying to get up to speed on what's going on today."

"Well, Jacob, if you had a whole week I am sure you could tackle the job, but I just got off the phone from briefing Commandant Rogers and he wants you on *First Responder* yesterday, hightailing it back to Event Horizon. Harrington has to cut his party short by forty-eight hours and come home."

"Well, I was just about to call his hotel and try to get in touch with him about the terror alert level increase when you called, Captain."

"OK, Jacob. You get hold of Harrington, and I'll activate all our Gulf of Mexico assets. Once you're on your ship and out to sea, I'll brief you on what's going on. Let me know when Harrington is back in his office. The commandant wants to brief him personally."

"OK, Captain. I can be back to *First Responder* in about four hours. We should be able to launch two hours after that. I'll have Lt. Commander Phillips round up the crew."

Jacob picks up the desk phone and dials the number for the Captain Harrington's hotel in Houston. He introduces himself as Commander Jacob Edwards of the

United States Coast Guard and asks for Harrington's room. The receptionist replies, "I am sorry, Commander Edwards, but Captain Harrington checked out about two hours ago. His father called us and said there was a family emergency and Captain Harrington had to leave suddenly. He handled the checkout and asked us to pack up his son's belongings and save them for when he could pick them up later. Even his Jaguar is still in our parking garage. He seemed very distraught when some people came in and took him out to his cab."

"Did you hear anything about what happened?" Jacob asks. The receptionist coughs and mutters that they really did not know but thought they heard something about Captain Harrington's mother dying.

Four Hours Earlier, Houston Hotel

Will has been sitting on his bed in the hotel suite for two hours now. He found a bottle of vodka left over from the previous evening and drank it straight down. He still can't believe how easily he was manipulated. Now it seemed they have trapped him with no way out. They involved even his own dad in this sting operation that now made him a slave to this man, Boris. How could this happen? He was a good officer. Sure, his dad was a little whiny, like his grandpa, but Will always thought he himself favored his great-grandfather, the first Captain Harrington, hero of World War I. Now he owes everything to a Russian crime lord and his daughter. He looks over at the full bottle of prescription opioid pills on the dresser and rubs his shoulder a little. He stands up and walks over to grab the bottle. When he opens it, a new thought hits his mind— *Here is a way out. Betrayed by everyone, including myself, why not?* He takes the whole bottle, empties it into his mouth, and washes it down with the remaining vodka. He lies down on the bed and waits for the inevitable.

Boris is about to get out of Peter's car at the airport when he feels his cell phone vibrate in his breast pocket. He retrieves it and sees it is a Houston number belonging to one of his contacts. "Vivian, my dear, I wanted to call you when my plane touched down in New Orleans. Your recent contributions to our latest operation were exemplary. Much more lucrative business will be forthcoming."

"Thank you, Boris, but you asked me to monitor Will Harrington with the surveillance cameras we installed. He tried to commit suicide. We saw him take the whole bottle of his opioids and wash it down with what was left of a bottle of vodka that he has been working on all morning."

Boris holds up his hand to Peter indicating that he should not leave the terminal drop-off area yet, and says into his phone, "No one has called an ambulance yet, have they, Vivian?"

There is a sarcastic huff on the other end. "Please, Boris, I've been at this game for almost as long as you have. My people forced their way into his suite within minutes of him taking the pills, and my medical people are setting him up right now to have his stomach pumped in the same suite. Once they finish, we will move him to a safe location. What do you want us to tell the hotel people?"

Boris has contingency plans for all his operations, and the Harringtons are no exception. He looks over at Peter and waves him on as he grabs his things and proceeds to the ticketing area. "Tell them that Captain Harrington has checked out because of a family emergency. And, Vivian..."

"Yes, Boris?"

"Let someone hear your people say that his mother has suddenly passed away." He then steps through the airport terminal doors and sees his daughter, Natasha, standing by the closest kiosk for his airline, waiting for him with their tickets. He walks up and receives his ticket for first-class passage to New Orleans. "You will accompany me to New Orleans, but then you must buy a ticket to Denver, Colorado, from there. I need you to go to a sanatorium in that area that houses people who are diagnosed with chronic depression and psychosis." Natasha stares at her father for clarification. "Natasha, Will Harrington tried to take his own life after we left. Vivian remedied the situation by having his stomach pumped while he was still in his hotel room, but he will be worthless for at least two weeks. We have to provide a suitable alibi for the Corpus Christi Coast Guard Sector Commander not to return to his command right away."

Natasha's expression is still unreadable. "What is it you want me to do, Father?"

Boris matches the intensity of her stare and replies. "They house Will's mother in that institution. I need you to go there and kill her, but make it look like a stroke. That is the most common way her family tends to die, and she has had small strokes in the past. My people will meet you at the Denver airport and provide you with everything you need."

She nods her head. "Yes, Father."

Boris puts a hand on her lower back. "This is how we stay ahead of the competition, Natasha. James and Will Harrington are much more important to the future of our western world ambitions than they could possibly understand. It is paramount that both of them be compliant to our wishes, and at this point that means both of them must be alive and functioning in their present positions. We'll contact Will's father and have him get things moving. I'll have Will flown to Denver, where he and his father will attend the memorial service together. After you assassinate the mother, your sole responsibility will be to nurse the captain back to full-functioning composure. Do you understand, Natasha?"

Natasha smiles wickedly as she strokes her father's arm and leads him to the security check-in at the airport. "Of course, Father."

Six hours later, Natasha finds herself at the Denver International Airport. Immediately upon exiting the 727 aircraft, she retrieves her things and proceeds to the adjacent parking lot where she's met by two men driving a dark Ford Taurus sedan. They properly identify themselves and take her to the mental hospital a few miles away. She is met with no resistance at the check-in and is given leave to proceed to the target's room. Once in the room, she sees that Mrs. Harrington is unconscious. Natasha reaches inside her purse and pulls out a small syringe filled with methyl iodide—a poison that mimics a stroke—and injects it into the unconscious woman's foot between her toes. She puts the syringe back in her purse, leaves the room, and proceeds outside where she is swiftly driven away. Her father, upon taking an interest in the Harringtons over a year ago, had already had several operatives working in the facility monitoring Mrs. Harrington's condition. Subsequently they were prepared for something like this to happen, and all video surveillance of the facility during Natasha's maneuvers there are wiped clean and replaced with doctored looped footage that tells quite a different story than what happened. The coroner's report will state that Louise Ann Harrington died of complications from having a stroke. Her time of death will be recorded as eighteen hours earlier than it really occurred.

Sector Corpus Christi Coast Guard Dock, *First Responder* Command Deck

Jacob and Lt. Commander Phillips go over their final check before launching *First Responder* and heading for New Orleans. As Jacob is about ready to give the order to launch, Seaman Bliss comes running into the command deck out of breath, panting, and beet red, like an overexcited puppy. "Commander Edwards! Commandant Rogers is on the secure line in the communication room and wants to speak with you, stat."

Jacob looks over at Phillips. "Take her out, Lieutenant Commander. I'll be right back." He looks at Bliss. "Seaman, let's go." When they get out on deck and around the corner to the communication room, Jacob stops and puts his hand on Bliss's shoulder. "John, you didn't stumble once delivering that message. Taking a call from the commandant could rattle anyone's cage. Good job! Wait out here for me."

Bliss gives Jacob a brisk salute and says, "Aye aye, Commander. Thank you, sir."

Jacob walks into the communication room, closes the door, and sits down next to the communication equipment console. He grabs the headphone and mic that Bliss uses and connects to the priority line. "Commandant Rogers, Commander Edwards here, sir."

"Jacob, good. Are you in private so we can talk?"

"Yes, sir, I am alone in the communication room, and I have a headset on so no one can hear you anyway."

"Good thinking, Commander. The president just raised the terror alert level to orange. He did it on Tommy Williams's recommendation. We don't know what's coming, but we have a good idea where and when. That's why *First Responder* is ordered to Event Horizon. We need you to go there and neutralize any attack you can uncover. We are sure that oil rig isn't the only target, but it's definitely the biggest. Tommy has some intel he wants to brief you and Gunny Jones on later. He says you both know how he wants you to contact him. There's one more little problem we have to deal with, Jacob."

"What's that, sir?"

157

There is a slight pause as Commandant Rogers clears his throat. "Will Harrington's mother has di ed of a stroke yesterday in a sanatorium hospital near Denver, Colorado. She and James got a divorce ten years ago, and she had a nervous breakdown over the ordeal. Will had her put there when she was proving suicidal. In the last couple of years, she's had a few minor strokes, but yesterday's was massive and she died almost instantly. The captain and Admiral Harrington will be on grievance leave for the next two weeks."

"Well, I am sorry to hear that, sir, but at least I know now why Captain Harrington hasn't returned any of my calls. He took a long weekend as soon as I docked and then had his office assistant forward a memo to me at Brazos telling me that I was in command of Sector Corpus Christi while he was gone. It was overwhelming trying to catch up on exactly what that meant, but I did my best, sir."

He hears a chuckle on the other end and the commandant replies, "Geez, Jacob, anyone else would have just followed his CO's suggestion and kept his phone handy for the weekend. You take command of Brazos, kick your father-in-law out of his office, and spend the rest of the day driving the whole sector crazy trying to figure out what you're supposed to be in charge of. But I guess that just confirms why Tommy and I have so much faith in you, son. You do nothing half-assed. You will remain in command of Sector Corpus Christi until Will returns. No one out there understands this terrorism threat more than those on your and Tommy's team, and now you guys don't have to tip-toe around our command structure to get things done."

Jacob leans back in his chair and lets out an exasperated huff, but then gets an idea and a huge grin breaks out across his face. "Sir, Lt. Commander Yeager is temporarily assigned to Corpus Christi. He's there to help Tommy and me figure out what is going down with the threat, but I could also use his help to stay on top of the sector. Can you make him my second, so I can command through him?"

Jacob waits for a few seconds and the dead silence on the other end of the line makes him squirm in his seat. Then the silence breaks as he hears two men laughing. The commandant finally says, "Sorry, Jacob, I have Tommy sitting in front of me in my office, and you made both of us feel like a couple of idiots."

"I'm sorry, sir, I don't understand."

Captain Tommy Williams replies. "What the commandant means, kid, is that neither of us thought about that obvious solution to a whole mess of problems that you just gave us."

Commandant Rogers continues. "Jacob, there is another lieutenant commander with seniority in Corpus Christi who is over in accounting. He's a good officer but really not qualified to handle a terrorism emergency. Yeager is perfect, and he is actually assigned there as chief investigator. We just didn't think of him."

Jacob rubs his temples and gives a kind of half-smile. "Sir, I looked at all the officers' files in Sector Corpus Christi yesterday and decided that no one really had the experience or training to help me with a real terrorism threat. They are all good officers and will support with the right direction, but not being there and not having Captain Harrington in command was scaring the hell out of me until I thought about Lt. Commander Yeager."

"It's a done deal, Commander. I'll send the orders to Corpus Christi as soon as we sign off. Good luck, Jacob," says the commandant.

"Thank you, sir. Captain Williams, when do you want Gunny Jones and me to call you?"

"Fourteen hundred hours, and make sure it's private. This stuff is sensitive."

"You got it, sir. Edwards out."

Jacob takes the headset off, checks his watch and sees he has enough time to check in with Chuck Yeager after he receives his new orders from the commandant, and then he will prep his crew on the raised terror alert level and where they are going. He must wait for the briefing from Captain Williams before he can tell them very much about the reason and what else to expect.

CHAPTER ELEVEN
BAD GUYS

Tampico Dock, Mexico

Dominik waits for the driver to open his door to let him out of the shuttle car that picked him up at the helipad near the local airport that morning. The driver's hands are shaking as he closes the door and steps back. He forces a smile and asks if everything was to his liking, and says he hopes Dominik enjoyed his trip from Mexico City. Dominik sneers at the man and turns to walk toward the dock entrance. He loves the fear and worship people load on him wherever he goes. His mother told him that his father had the same effect on people. He daydreams about how wonderful it would have been to maraud, rape, pillage, and ride with his father, the famous Pack Leader of the Wild Wolves biker gang. It infuriates him that Boris won't let him go to the United States to get payment for his father's death. He knows that if he could just get into the northwest part of the country, he could find out who killed his father back in the early '70s, and finally get his vengeance. He can still hear Boris's response to his asking to go: "Dominik, your appetites and methods are too savage for you to operate effectively in that country. You are my most prized operative in this region of the world, and it is in Mexico, South America, and the Caribbean that your aptitudes serve me best."

He knows that ever since that day back in '96 on the yacht of the Mexican finance minister, when he wanted to ravage the tugboat captain's beautiful daughter, and Boris put a blade to his throat and stopped him, he would never defy the man again. Not even Anthony Santiago or Maximillian Manerez, the two most powerful cartel leaders in the Americas, could infuse such total loyalty in the deepest core of his psyche. Boris was more than human to him, and he would always obey his master. He shakes the reverie from his conscience and looks up to see Peter Rasmov waiting for him on one of Boris's infamous stealth yachts. Dominik steadies himself and lifts his chin to acknowledge his most capable and accomplished protégé. When he gets closer to the man, he looks him up and down. "I see you have recovered from that poison. I trust you're up to the next phase of our mission."

Peter comes down the plank and immediately grabs his bag. "It's good to be back with you, boss. I believe I'm at one hundred percent, but you are to be the judge of that, and I only pray I live up to your expectations."

Dominik throws his head back with a hearty laugh and slaps Peter on the back with enough power to knock a normal man on his face. Peter has worked under Dominik long enough to know how to absorb his frequent over-the-top back slaps. He also, in the depth of his heart, prefers the man. Dominik encourages Peter's baser appetites and allows him to have fun whenever the opportunity presents itself. Dominik says, "You seem to be back to yourself." He laughs again, puts a big hand on Peter's back and walks with him up the plank to the deck of the yacht. "Your uncle has ordered me to capture a ship carrying choir children on some cruise off the coast of Houston. Sounds like our type of mission. What do you say, Peter?"

"Yes, boss. That sounds like something right up our alley."

Waiting for both men on the upper deck of the stealth yacht is Francisco Sanchez. Next to Peter Rasmov, Francisco is Dominik's closest lieutenant. Both he and Peter began their careers with Dominik years ago, when they helped him capture the Mexican finance minister's yacht off the coast of Honduras.

When Dominik and Peter get to the command deck, they acknowledge Francisco with a nod. He smiles at Peter and winks, then turns to Dominik. "I stowed everything Boris wanted us to pick up below deck. He said Peter would know what to do with it all. What are your orders, boss?"

Dominik rolls his eyes and then laughs. "Tell me where the captain's cabin is and get me some rum. I had to get up way too early this morning. Peter will tell you what to do and where to go. Once we're ready to bash heads in, wake me up. Leave me alone until then."

Peter says, "I know all these yachts like the back of my hand, boss. I'll show you to the captain's quarters and get you the rum." He then turns to Francisco. "I already set the coordinates for our next destination into the navigational computer. Just press the data button and it'll show you what to punch in. I know you've wanted to pilot one of these for a while, so go for it."

Peter leads Dominik off the command deck and out the door to his cabin, where he had already made sure there were two bottles of his favorite Jamaican rum in the liquor cabinet.

Peter walks back to his cabin, musing about how he enjoys working for the mighty Dominik Thrace. For many years now, Dominik has been training Peter in several of the most lethal martial arts known. Dominik was the epitome of what an ancient champion gladiator was. With over one hundred kills to his credit at Maximillian Manerez's famous underworld cage fights, and then countless others while working for his Uncle Boris, Peter has a special reverence for the man. Boris is the only man whom Dominik truly obeyed, but that same Boris made it clear to Peter that he would hold his nephew personally responsible for any mishaps in the operations he would assign to the Jamaican's team. So, for his tenure with Dominic, Peter has learned the delicate balance of being the brains behind Dominik's crew without ever letting the man feel anything other than that he was in total control.

In return, Dominik rewarded his lieutenant in two ways; he gave him access and training with his vast knowledge of martial combat; and he let the young Russian indulge in his wildest epicurean appetites. Peter found the relationship to be symbiotically superb and wanted it to go on indefinitely. Having been called away from the crew recently and finding himself once again under the direct control of his uncle only reinforces that desire. Deep down, he truly wishes Natasha would rise to become Boris's second-in-command, leaving him to enjoy life under Dominik's umbrella.

Peter opens the door to his cabin, sits at his desk, boots up his laptop, and calls up a file he has been working on: "Fluoroantimonic Acid Deployment Drone." He scrolls down and looks at the schematics. It's a picture of a small, submarine-type drone that has a sophisticated electronic propulsion system and two cargo chambers; one labeled "Acid Containment" and the other labeled "Explosives." In the front part is an underwater receiver antenna attached to the navigational and helm section. Its original design was for sabotage warfare. The operation is simple—a passive beacon tag is attached to a target that will, when activated, send out sporadic pulse signals under water that the drone will pick up on and follow. The signal will pulse at infrequent times and for only a few seconds at a time. The drone is programmed to follow the last pulse signal it receives until it hits the intended target. If it receives no more pulse signals, it will continue to follow its last signal until it finds something solid to attach itself to. When attached, it is designed to explode.

Boris's engineers have changed the one Peter is looking at. Plastic explosive fills one holding chamber, but the other is filled with a modified and highly concentrated dose of the fluoroantimonic acid. The acid becomes volatile when mixed with water, and this modified version is especially sensitive to saltwater. The drone is carrying enough acid to eat through a solid foot of steel under water within a few minutes. While looking at the specs, Peter takes note that the hole caused by the acid should be somewhere between four and six feet in diameter. One of the nice features of the construction and acid deployment is that the drone itself will be completely engulfed and disintegrate along with the metal as it is burning through, thus leaving no evidence or remains of the drone for the authorities to inspect. And since the acid is so sensitive to saltwater, it will quickly dissipate in the ocean, leaving no real evidence regarding what caused the hole.

The target of this drone is the Event Horizon oil rig that Peter was on a short time ago. He is sure that after they contain the massive oil spills and they conclude the investigation, they will determine that faulty equipment and bad management caused the disaster. That will fuel Prince Hasheen's plan to force the United States president to put a moratorium on all oil production in the Gulf of Mexico. Peter reaches inside his desk drawer, pulls out his own high-powered satellite cell phone and pulls up a contact in New Orleans.

"Hello, Peter. I hope you're feeling better than the last time I saw you."

"Gustave, it is kind of you to ask, and yes, I have fully recovered. I am calling to be sure we're on schedule and that you will take your helicopter out and deploy our drone two hundred miles northwest of Event Horizon this afternoon."

"I was loading up when you called, and we're on schedule. The drop-off will happen within twenty minutes of the next pulse signal you said will come out at that time of day."

"Excellent. That pulse will activate the drone and it should hit its target within twelve hours after you deploy it. You'll then need to immediately head to Houston where you'll stand by to pick us up after our exercise in that area is done."

Gustave gulps. "Geez, Peter, it's one thing to cause a major oil spill and risk a bunch of oil rig workers' lives, but using a bunch of choir kids on a cruise ship to cause another oil spill is nasty stuff."

"We're paying you handsomely, and your uncle is in good shape to be the mayor of New Orleans. I suggest you focus on those positive realities. Or you could also consider your other uncles and how being on the wrong side of Boris can adversely affect your quality of life."

"Say no more. I'll be where you want me and when."

"I expected nothing less from you, Gustave. Cheer up. My uncle knows how to take care of his own. Goodbye."

Chapter Twelve
Second Thoughts

Heliport Southwest of New Orleans

Gustave puts his cell phone back in his pocket and goes through his checklist for takeoff. He has to admit that since he began working for Peter and subsequently his uncle Boris, things like dealing with the red tape of getting an itinerary approved were a lot easier. As soon as he asked for the change to let him divert to Houston after his rendezvous with Event Horizon that day, it was immediately approved. The drone is hooked up to the bottom of his transport copter, and since he is only bringing supplies to the rig this time, no passenger is there to ask him any questions when he takes the copter down to hover over the surface of the ocean as he cuts the drone loose into the water. Then he has to fly faster to make up for the lost time and be on schedule landing on the rig.

After unloading his gear, he sees a familiar face waving at him from off to the side of the helipad and he goes over to talk with her. Gustave feels a pang of guilt as he talks to Sally Crabtree and she asks how Adrian Barlow is doing and when he is coming back to work.

Gustave tries to put his guilty conscience on hold as he takes off to proceed to his next destination in Houston. After leaving the rig, he cannot shake the feeling that he might not see Sally again. Peter said there would definitely be casualties once the oil spill started, and he knows that her station in storage was dangerously close to the main oil pipe coming up from the ocean floor. About halfway to Houston, he spots a Coast Guard Hamilton-class cutter speeding in the direction he had just come from. He doesn't know how or why, but his gut just assures him that he is the reason it is sailing toward Event Horizon. He closes his eyes for a second, takes a deep breath, and then decides to turn around and go back toward the oil rig. He then slows his copter down, makes a huge turn in the air, and follows the cutter. He gets on a universal military frequency and hails the cutter.

Three Hours Earlier, Aboard *First Responder* after Leaving Corpus Christi

Jacob leaves Bliss in the communication room and heads straight for his cabin. When he gets there, he finds the new smartphone Captain Williams had given him, then finds Yeager's contact info and calls him. The phone rings about ten times before someone answers it. A very puzzled Lt. Commander Chuck Yeager appears on the screen. "Jacob, geez, I was eating breakfast in the cafeteria. I had to duck into the bathroom and lock the door so no one could see me talking on this thing. What's up?"

"Before I answer you, tell me how your investigations are going."

Chuck leans sideways on the wall next to the toilet and brushes his hair back with his free hand. "Well, something is definitely up with the personnel roster on Event Horizon. Houston PD discovered the body of an Adrian Barlow in a dumpster over by the docks yesterday morning, but that same Barlow reported to work on the rig two weeks ago and then was emergency airlifted out for a severe ulcer flare-up about a week later. The pilot who brought him to the rig was the same one who picked him up. Nothing strange there, but get this—the pilot is a Desert Storm war veteran named Gustave Landers. He is also an ex-con. He did time for smuggling drugs for his uncles, who just happen to be the major mob bosses in New Orleans."

"Wait a minute, I read that story. That's about Councilman Ferdinand Landers who turned state's evidence against his brothers. He's a local hero, and everyone's saying he could be the next mayor. That's a lot of noise going on around that family all of a sudden."

"Yeah, and you and I both know that when it comes to crooks, a lot of noise means—"

"Something big is about to happen," Jacob finishes. He rubs his chin and leans back in his chair. "So, this fake Barlow is probably our terrorist, and whatever he did, it's a done deal. We're headed there right now. You think we should get a bomb squad out to that rig, Chuck?"

"I don't know yet. It doesn't feel like someone will blow the whole rig up. My guess is sabotage."

"Why is that?"

"Well, for one thing, Prince Hasheen of the Saudi royal family just checked into the Hotel Diana in Mexico City two nights ago. The story is that he is here for some art show display of ancient Arabic artifacts. But I think he's here because he knows about or has orchestrated something big that will be going down related to the Gulf of Mexico oil production. A conventional terrorist attack wouldn't benefit him much there, but a sabotage could."

"I'm kind of following you, Chuck. What do you think a sabotage could accomplish that an outright terrorist attack could not?"

"Well, for starters, if your goal is not to make a terrorism statement but instead own the oil industry, then making a huge oil rig disaster look like faulty equipment and bad management could go a long way to forcing our government to shut down oil production in this region."

"And let me guess," Jacob replies. "This Hasheen is the head oil guy over there in Saudi Arabia, right?"

"You got it, Jacob."

"OK, Chuck, this is what I need from you. Find our fake Barlow, if you can. Figure out what he did on Event Horizon, and figure out what else these guys, whoever they are, are up to next. Something tells me Event Horizon is not their only target. Oh, and you will get orders from the commandant stating you are now the number two man at Corpus Christi. I assume you already know about Will Harrington's mother and that I was put in charge. So, you'll be my eyes, ears, and mouth on that end for a while. OK, buddy?"

Chuck shakes his head and laughs. "I guess some things were just destined to be. You better come up with one hell of a best man's toast next month, Commander. That is, if we make it through this."

Jacob smiles and holds both hands out in front of him, makes two fists, and then points his thumbs up in front of his face. "It's what we do, Chuck. We get the bad guy—"

"Before he gets us," Chuck interjects. "Yeah, yeah, I know. I'll go get my orders and report back officially after that. Talk to you soon. Be careful out there, sir."

"You, too, Chuck." Jacob slips the smartphone back into his pocket and heads over to the OTO Melara gunner station. When he enters, Seaman Schuette comes to attention and throws him a smart salute.

"At ease, Schuette, Where's Gunny Jones?"

Before Schuette can answer, Jones's head pops out from under the gun's mounting platform. "I'm down here, Commander. Checking the gun mounts and making ready for combat operations, considering the live-fire exercises tomorrow."

Jacob almost forgot about the live-fire training scheduled for the next day, but quickly decides he does not want Schuette expecting anything different just yet.

He looks back over at the seaman. "How you going to do on that test, Schuette?"

"Commander, Gunny Jones here has had me do over a hundred simulations just this morning and my average is 98.7 percent in all five ammunition loads. I believe I'll do great, sir. But Gunny says there is nothing like the real thing. So, we'll see tomorrow, sir."

Jacob thinks the real thing might just happen much quicker than this kid could ever imagine. "Seaman, I need to speak with Gunny Jones in private. Take your scores up to Lt. Commander Phillips and have him put them into your progress training log."

Seaman Schuette throws another salute and heads out to the command deck.

Gunny Jones pulls himself out from under the gun mounting platform and stands up. "What's up, Commander?" he says as he brushes the dirt off his uniform.

Jacob reaches in his pocket and pulls out the newfangled smartphone and stand he got from Captain Williams. "The Legend wants to brief both of us together. Grab a seat while I get him on the line."

Jones sits in front of the workbench where Jacob just set up the phone. Jacob touches the contact icon for Captain Tommy Williams and steps back behind Jones so that both of them can be viewed on the screen of the smartphone.

After three buzzes, Captain Williams's face appears on the two-by-three-inch screen. "Glad to see you two made time to talk. How is it going on your end?"

Jacob is the first to reply. "We're sailing toward Event Horizon at top speed and should be there in eighteen hours if the seas are calm. Isn't there anyone else who can respond faster, Captain?"

"Yes, but the president wants no one else involved until we're sure. With the Gulf War going on, oil production is a hot topic, and the chief wants this kept under wraps."

"A lot can happen in the next eighteen hours, Captain. Are you sure it's worth the risk?" Jacob asks.

Tommy rolls his eyes. "No, Jacob, I'm not sure it's worth it, but I'm not the commander-in-chief."

In the background on Tommy's end, someone interrupts him and hands him a folder. He opens it and looks at the contents for a few seconds. "OK, Commander, Gunny, I got the analysis back from those photos you took while passing the two rigs last week. Nothing out of the ordinary about the one off the port of Houston, but Event Horizon definitely has a problem."

He holds up a black and white photograph of the rig and points to it. "This one shows light and heat. You can see the upper part of the rig where the machinery and personnel are. The area is highly lit. But as you go lower, it keeps getting darker and darker." He points at a slight illumination on the main pipe right at the ocean's surface. "Except for right here. It says here that this is the heat signature of a human hidden on the back side of the pipe from where you took the picture. That's why it's so faint. Now, you took these pictures just before midnight, so we know this isn't a maintenance worker out there."

"I'll bet my next vacation pay that's our fake Barlow, whom Chuck Yeager just told me about. What the hell is he doing out there?"

Tommy takes the folder and thumbs through to find another copy of the same picture, but this one shows a dark silhouette of the oil rig with a tight, little green light at the same place on the pipe but just below the ocean's surface. Rippling out from that light is a sporadic signal, vibrating like a submarine sonar pulse. "My guys say this is some kind of low- frequency homing beacon used to call underwater drones. Looks like we have a case of industrial sabotage going on here. What do you guys think?"

Gunny Jones leans forward and looks at the tiny screen. "Captain, we dealt with those over in the Mediterranean. They're hard as hell to detect because the beacon only activates sporadically. The drones with the explosive will catch the signal and maneuver toward it. When the next signal is pulsed, the drone uses it to adjust its course. We are damn lucky the commander took those pictures when he did. Who knows when the next pulse is coming? I've seen them wait as long as twelve hours to send another signal. Those drones can move close to the ocean floor and crawl along as slow as five knots. We don't know when it was deployed, or whether it even has been deployed yet. Captain, you need to get somebody there ASAP. You can't wait for us." Gunny Jones looks pleadingly at Captain Williams's image on the phone and then at Jacob.

Jacob nods his head. "I agree, Captain. This can't wait. You need to get someone there, stat, and they need to be ready to evacuate, and they need to have a bomb squad, emergency medical personnel, and firefighters deployed."

Tommy leans back in his chair and rubs his temples with both hands. "OK, Commander. I can't disobey a presidential directive, but I have an idea. I'm going to leave it to you to get those resources to Event Horizon under Commandant Rogers's authority, but you'll be in command of anything sent. I'll leave it to Rogers to figure out how to explain it to the president and Admiral Bishop at New Orleans. The president wants this kept in my circle right now, and that means you and your team have to control everything. Am I understood— Commander, Gunny?"

Jacob and Jones reply in unison, "Yes, sir."

Tommy chuckles. "And to think a month ago you two almost killed each other. Now the future of Gulf oil production and a lot of lives depends on how well you two can work together. I have to go to the White House now and brief the president. There's no telling how long I'll be, so I'll call Commandant Rogers on the way. He'll smooth things over for you guys." Tommy clears his throat. "Listen, guys, I haven't asked either of you to be politicians before, but this whole thing could really ruffle a lot of brass feathers. Play this close to the vest and still get the job done. Commander, you'll be the Gulf oil production terrorism task force leader on this one. And do it as quietly as possible. Best scenario is that you stop this thing from happening and no one ever knows you've done a damn thing."

Jacob and Jones both laugh. "Captain, anything we have ever done for you has always been top secret," Jacob says. "Why should this be any different? We'll figure things out as they come, sir. Gunny and I will keep our smartphones on us until all of this is over, if you need to talk. Good luck with the president."

"Thanks, kid. Until I get back to you, if you need direction contact Commandant Rogers."

Tommy disconnects the line, and Jacob looks at Gunny Jones. "Tell me everything you know about those drones and what they're capable of."

Chapter Thirteen
Game Changers

Same Day, Marriott Hotel Presidential Suite, Denver, Colorado

The last thing Will Harrington remembers is taking the rest of his opioids and washing them down with vodka. He did not expect to see the light of day again, but it's glaring in his eyes as he tries to sit up in what now is obviously a very unfamiliar bed in an equally unfamiliar room. If that weren't enough to deal with, he feels a leg draped over his hip and a hand lying on his chest. He rubs both eyes with his left hand and turns to see Natasha lying in bed next to him. As his senses clear, he can also tell that she is naked.

Natasha demurely leans in and puts her chin on his chest. "Will, how could you scare me like that? We could barely save your life. You do not understand what danger you put me in with that stunt. My father wanted to blame me for everything."

Will sits up a little more as she leans back on her pillow. He feels exasperated. "What do you mean? You pick me up at a bar, then seduce me. You trick me into making love to a minor, videotape me doing it, and then your father shows up in the morning and tells me I am his property, blackmailing me with the video and the threat of making it and my opioid addiction public. I'm a military officer. I took an oath to serve and protect my country. A bunch of criminals can't own me!" Will is shaking and crying.

Natasha snuggles in close to him, lays her head on his chest and pretends to cry with him. "Oh, darling, didn't you see how angry my father became when you mentioned our lovemaking? He would have killed you if I didn't intercede. I was never supposed to sleep with you that night, only get you aroused. And then in your drunken state I was to sneak the girl in." She then props herself up on one elbow and looks Will straight in the eyes, with her full, plump breasts in plain view. "But I couldn't bear the thought of anyone having you when I haven't. I don't care that my father does not approve of us. I've been his property for much longer than you, and being with you was the most liberating experience I have ever known. We might never be free of his tyranny over our lives, but maybe we can help each other cope with it."

She then leans in and passionately kisses him. Will resists at first but then he succumbs to her bewitching seduction once more.

After they are finished, Natasha waits until they are both dressed and in the dining room section of the suite to tell him about his mother. She steps in close and puts her hands on his shoulders. "Will, your mother died of a stroke yesterday afternoon. That is why I had you flown to Colorado. Your father is staying in this same hotel across the hall. He has already made all the arrangements, but you are the designated executor of her estate, and he needs you to approve all the details for her memorial service."

Will takes a deep breath and sighs. "This has been coming for some time. I'm sure my father is very irritated that he has to be involved in this. I can hardly believe I'm saying this, but Natasha..." He grabs her hands and pulls her closer to him. "If I had never met you, I don't know if I could have handled this at all." He wipes the beginnings of a tear from his eyes and continues. "Now I see how you are a blessing to me and my father. The Harrington name and legacy are preserved because of all that you and even your father have done. If I know that you will be with me through all this, I can do it. I'll obey your father and give him whatever he wants; only please be there for me."

Natasha turns her head to the side and wipes her eye, pretending she is also crying. In reality, she is doing everything in her power not to laugh at this absurd romantic cripple in front of her. Then she gets ahold of herself and looks up with soft, damp eyes. "Will, I will always be there for you. I have to go now to meet up with my father in Texas. Promise me you will be OK and take care of your mother's business. I'll be back in a week, and we can figure out our relationship then. OK, darling?"

She leans in and kisses him passionately on the lips, which he returns in kind. He nods his head, and she turns and walks out the door.

Five minutes later, Will's father, James Harrington, comes in. Both men stoically stare at one another for a few moments and then the admiral finally breaks the silence. "Son, I had no choice. As soon as I made the deal with Boris to go into partnership with him with the family bank, he took over everything. Then all my father's paternity suits were dropped, and we got that brand-new facility in New Jersey. He almost immediately started laundering mob finances through us; and then one day while I was setting up our offices, that vixen who just left you shows up and threatens to blow my head off over intel they were receiving from their planted agents in the Coast Guard that I did not even know about. I'm committed, Son. If this goes down, I go down with it. I am told they got to you, too. Did she threaten you with her little silver gun as well?"

Will stares at his dad for a few seconds. "Not quite, Dad. But yes, they got to me, too."

James and Will Harrington spend the rest of the morning and afternoon going through the myriad of details concerning Will's mom's estate and funeral arrangements. When they are done, Will is astonished to find that his mother had enough wealth in her estate to solve all the Harrington problems—a fact that neither

Will nor his father find very encouraging, having both surmised that no amount of money will ever free them or keep them safe from a man like Boris. The irony of the situation almost brings Will to another breakdown, but his father produces a bottle of Will's prescription opioids and gives him his dose. The effect is almost immediate, and Will's mood brightens.

As father and son prepare to leave the room to meet an estate attorney in the hotel's lobby, James's cell phone vibrates, and he immediately recognizes the phone number. He turns on the speaker so his son can hear and then answers. "Boris, you'll be happy to know that my son Will is onboard with our arrangement and will make himself available to you in any way he can."

Boris's thick Russian accent comes through the speaker. "That is good to hear, James. Now, tell me, what is the name of the Hamilton-class cutter assigned under Sector Corpus Christi at this present moment, and who is its captain?"

"Why, that would be *First Responder,* captained by Commander Jacob Edwards, Boris. Why do you ask?"

"That ship is causing me a considerable amount of difficulty with an operation I have going on in the Gulf of Mexico right now. I need you and your son to call it back to Corpus Christi and make its captain stop interfering with my plans."

Father and son look at one another, astonished. Will grabs the phone. "Boris, my father and I are both on grievance leave. That means that all our command access is very limited right now. If we try anything too aggressive from here, we will definitely blow any cover you have set up for us and then we'll be useless to you."

James adds, "Boris, the president just issued an imminent terror alert warning for that region. That means that there is a whole set of emergency protocols in place that if anyone— including us—tries to circumvent, it will look very suspicious."

They hear a low, guttural growl come over the speaker. Then the bell showing that the elevator has reached the lobby of the hotel rings. Boris responds. "You two are to do absolutely nothing. I'll try to salvage this situation with my own operatives in place. And Will…"

"Yes, Boris?"

"If you ever test me again with a suicide attempt, I'll let you succeed. And be assured that your father will join you in the grave. Am I understood, Captain Harrington?"

"Perfectly, Boris," he says as the elevator doors open, and he and his father step out into the lobby to look for their estate attorney.

Four Hours Earlier, Halfway Point Between Corpus Christi and Event Horizon, Off the Port of New Orleans

Gustave Landers can hardly control the desperate beating in his chest as he attempts to contact the Coast Guard Hamilton-class cutter he had spotted. He punches in a standard military frequency that he knows from his days in Desert Storm, and transmits. "This is Gustave Landers of Star Oil to the Hamilton-class cutter below me. I have vital information concerning an imminent attack on the oil rig Event Horizon that will be happening today." He sends it out three times before he gets a response.

"This is Commander Jacob Edwards, captain of the United States Coast Guard ship, *First Responder.* We know who you are and that you are a person of interest in an investigation into a terrorism threat in this region. What do you want to tell us?"

Gustave takes a calming breath. "I deployed an underwater drone fifty miles west of here that is headed for the oil rig at about fifteen knots. Once it is there, it is set to cause the biggest oil spill this region has ever seen. You won't be able to track the drone with your sonar, but I have the homing frequencies and access codes with me. I can help you destroy it before it can do any damage. Be warned, though—this drone is carrying enough plastic explosive to sink your ship, and it is programmed to explode if someone interferes with it. You don't want to get any closer than twenty-five yards or it will self-destruct. Also, it is carrying one hundred gallons of a highly concentrated and modified version of fluoroantimonic acid that is ignited by contact with saltwater. That could also sink you if it comes into contact with your hull."

"Why are you trying to help us now, Gustave? We know you helped the fake Barlow onto Event Horizon two weeks ago and then got him out of there a week later," Commander Edwards says.

"Commander, I was a military officer once. I took an oath to defend and protect my country. After Desert

Storm, I let family and pressure force me to do bad things. I recently have had the same thing happen, but I can't go through with it. I am ready to accept the consequences for my actions. All I want to do is stop this disaster before it starts."

There is a long pause over the line as Gustave waits for a response. Finally, the radio crackles and Commander Edwards gets back on. "Gustave, we see in your records that you did several sea landings on naval ships in the Gulf. Do you think you can land that thing on our helicopter landing pad safely?"

Gustave knows he is one of the best military helicopter pilots alive. But he also knows that his copter is a little bigger than the ones the Hamilton-class cutters usually carry, but then he decides it's worth the risk. "Commander, I can, but you need to come to a full stop and weigh anchor before I land. My copter is too big to try it any other way."

"OK, but it'll take us about forty-five minutes to an hour to do that, Gustave. Just stay on our tail and I'll let you know when we're ready."

"OK, Commander. I'll be ready."

Forty-seven Minutes Later, *First Responder's* Helicopter Landing Pad

Jacob is standing on the deck watching Gustave Landers land his Star Oil transport helicopter on the deck of his ship. With the commander is Gunny Jones, Lt. Commander Phillips, Lt. Alex Maelstrom, and five fully armed

185

security seamen. Jacob knows he's already broken about a dozen Coast Guard protocols and more laws to boot by allowing the pilot to land his civilian aircraft on *First Responder,* but he has a gut feeling about this guy and he wants to let it play out. The copter powers down, and Lt. Maelstrom plus two of his detail draw their weapons and go to the door to wait for the pilot to exit the craft. When Gustave exits, he sees all the guns pointed at him and immediately puts his hands in the air. As he steps down, Lt. Maelstrom walks up and checks him for weapons, then turns him around and handcuffs his hands behind his back. He looks over to Jacob for direction. "Put him in the detention area and check this chopper out for anything that could help or hurt us."

"Aye aye, Commander," Maelstrom says as he hands the prisoner off to his chief and begins his inspection of the Star Oil helicopter.

Before Maelstrom can begin his search, Jacob walks over to him and says, "Lieutenant, make sure there are no tracking devices on this helicopter. I want no one knowing where we are going. If you find anything that even looks like it might harm the ship and you can't take care of it right away, use the crane and throw this overboard. It will give Gunny Jones and Schuette something to target practice on."

"Aye aye, Commander. Anything else, sir?"

Jacob puts a hand on his chief of security's shoulder. "Yes, Alex, you be careful. Nothing we can learn from this damn thing is worth you or your men's lives."

"You can count on it, Commander, and thanks."

Jacob turns and follows the security detail to the holding cell in the lower level of the ship where they will have deposited Gustave. He muses that his head of security, Lt. Maelstrom, is one hell of an addition to his crew. The man not only has a degree in mechanical engineering but is also a certified explosives expert and has gone through the Coast Guard bomb squad training. One hell of a handy guy to have around.

Jacob makes his way down to the holding cell area, walks up to a seaman on guard duty and asks him to open the door. Jacob walks in and sits down in front of Gustave, who is sitting on the bed with his back propped up against the wall.

Gustave straightens up when he sees the Coast Guard commander come into the cell. Jacob looks the man over carefully and surmises that he is more upset than afraid. "So, tell me again, Mr. Landers, what made you change your mind about sabotaging Event Horizon?"

Gustave closes his eyes and shakes his head. Jacob sees the beginning of a tear forming in his left eye. "I wanted nothing to do with any of this. This young Russian guy showed up at my trailer about two months ago and beat the hell out of me and then told me how he controls my uncle Ferdinand now. Ferdinand is the only one who could ever keep my other uncles from forcing me back into smuggling drugs for them. Then he showed me how Ferdinand put all three of his brothers in jail and that they can never touch me or him again. I knew right away that Uncle Ferdinand did not have the juice it would take to pull off something like that, so I figured that whoever this

Russian is, he's bigger than anyone Ferdinand or I have ever dealt with. He tells me he wants me to use my job as a cargo and personnel helicopter transport pilot for Star Oil to help set up operations in the Gulf of Mexico that will cripple oil production in this region. So, over the last few months I've been smuggling equipment and personnel to Event Horizon and one of the largest ports closest to their next biggest rig off the port of Houston. I only went to the port in Houston because my chopper was never scheduled to go directly to that rig. I just brought supplies from New Orleans to Houston."

Jacob holds up a hand to stop Gustave. "Mr. Landers, I want to hear every detail of this later. You need to tell me everything you know about that drone you deployed that is headed to Event Horizon."

"It's a deep-water drone used to sabotage ships, docks, or anything in the water. It has two storage containers that can hold up to one hundred gallons of material apiece, so it is a lot bigger than a full-size torpedo. It's powered electrically and has a top speed of fifteen knots. It carries a high-grade, long-range lithium battery pack that can last up to three days at that speed. The tracking device controls the navigation system. It locks onto the intermittent signals that pulse out from Event Horizon, navigates in that direction, and proceeds with that course until it sends the next signal, at which time it will readjust its course if needed."

"What exactly is that thing going to do once it reaches Event Horizon?"

"Well," Gustave replies, "once it attaches itself to the main pipe where the homing beacon signal is coming from, it will deploy the acid, which will eat through and cause a huge oil spill. The acid will also destroy the drone and the plastic explosive in it, leaving no trace that it was there. The hole will look like it's a result of corrosion and faulty maintenance. Because they planned the acid to go super volatile in saltwater, it will dissipate quickly. That coupled with the oil spilling out into the ocean in that area will make it next to impossible to detect any acid at all. It's designed to make the whole thing look like Star Oil is doing shoddy maintenance and using substandard parts. The goal is to spook the government into slowing down or stopping oil drilling, pumping, or production in the Gulf."

"What happens if it runs into something or someone tries to detain it?" Jacob asks.

"That's the kicker, Commander, because if anyone or anything messes with that thing before it reaches the source of its homing signal, it will self-destruct. That could blow up something even as big as this ship, and it will also dump a hundred gallons of that highly volatile acid in saltwater. It's equipped with stealth hull plating that makes it almost impossible to track with sonar; plus, it won't come to the surface until it's within twenty-five yards of its target, which is its blast radius. So, if you see it and try to blow it out of the water it will—"

"Most likely cause considerable damage to whoever is attacking it," Jacob finishes the statement. "So, you're telling me there is no way to track this thing?"

Gustave leans forward. "There is one way. If you have the proper signal frequency, you could pinpoint its location the next time the homing beacon sends out a pulse. You could then connect the signal to the recipient drone and for that moment know where it is. If you could destroy it while it's still in deep water, it would cause minimal damage down there. Even the acid would dissipate quickly in all that water, with nothing to attack but more water."

Jacob sits there for a few seconds pondering what Gustave has just told him, then he gets a gleam in his eye as a beautifully dangerous idea pops into his head. "Gustave, does that thing know it is attacking an oil rig, or is it programmed to go off when it hits the source of its homing signal?"

"It's engineered like an electronic remote control. Only the signal pulls the drone toward itself as the drone's onboard GPS figures out how to get there. The trigger is making contact with the structure that the homing beacon is attached to," Gustave says.

"So, if I could send out the same signal, say from *First Responder,* it would think my ship is its destination, right?"

"Well, yes, but that would be one hell of a risk you'd be taking with your own ship, Commander."

"That's why we're out here, Gustave. You were a military pilot; you know the score. God knows what kind of damage to property and lives that thing will do if someone does not stop it. Now, you filled me in on the first attack, Gustave. What about the other one? What else does this Russian have up his sleeve?"

Gustave holds up his hand to stop Jacob. "Before I get into that, Commander, you better get people out to Event Horizon right away. Tell them to check the cargo area where the fake Barlow had his stuff stowed. He didn't tell me anything specific, but he also didn't strike me as the kind of person who would not have a backup plan. He had a lot of stuff brought onto that rig and it all got on with fake inspection passes, so no one really looked at it."

Jacob pulls out his shipboard radio and calls Lt. Commander Phillips. "Yes, Commander?"

"Phillips, I need you to contact the New Orleans Coast Guard HQ and tell them we need two patrol cutters sent to Event Horizon with a full bomb squad contingent. Tell them to contact Star Oil and have them institute an emergency evacuation of that rig right away," Jacob orders.

"Commander, New Orleans is where Admiral Bishop is, and he's over this whole territory. That includes Sector Corpus Christi and this ship. Are you sure you want me to call his station with orders from you?"

Jacob doesn't blink an eye as he responds. "Just tell whoever answers that *First Responder* is dealing with multiple priority-level terrorist attacks and that we are acting under the direct command of Commandant Rogers and Naval Intelligence. If the admiral has any questions, ask him to please contact the commandant." Jacob then turns back to Gustave. "Now tell me about what's going on in Houston."

CHAPTER FOURTEEN

TAKING COMMAND

Coast Guard Territory Command, Sector New Orleans

Admiral Ryan Bishop sits at his desk going over reports. The most troubling news he has to deal with is that of the death of Captain Harrington's mother. He had just finished training the young man to assume Sector Corpus Christi a few months ago. He was really quite impressed with Captain Harrington. Will's father, Admiral Harrington, is also a close friend of Ryan's and had offered him some help in finding a position with the State Department when he retires next year. He had assured the Vice Commandant that he would make sure Will had every bit of his support in his command at Corpus Christi. Now both Will—his new sector commander—and his friend, Admiral Harrington, are on grievance leave in Colorado, taking care of Mrs. Harrington's affairs.

To make matters more complicated, the commandant's office has just sent him orders telling him that a captain of one of the Hamilton-class cutters out of Corpus Christi, a Commander Jacob Edwards, was assuming command of Corpus Christi, and a Lt. Commander Chuck Yeager will be second-in-command until Will returns to his post. Then he gets an alert from the White House this morning stating that the president has raised the terror alert level to Red, imminent right here in his own region. While he mulls all this over, there is a knock on his door. His assistant comes in and salutes. "Admiral, we got a priority one order from *First Responder…*"

Ryan holds up a hand. "Wait a minute, Chief, you mean *request,* don't you?"

The chief looks nervously from side to side and then back at the admiral and says, "No sir, it was an *order* from Commander Edwards. He wants us to send two security patrol boats with a full bomb squad unit to Event Horizon to look for explosives in the cargo hold. He also told us to contact Star Oil and start emergency evacuation procedures immediately."

The admiral's face turns beet red. He jumps up from his chair and yells, "Who the hell does that punk think he is? Get him on the line now!"

The chief, about ready to have a panic attack, replies, "Sir, they said *First Responder* is handling several imminent

terrorist attacks and that if you had questions to please
direct them specifically to Commandant Rogers, and that
they are acting under his direct command and working
with Naval Intelligence."

Ryan's face relaxes a little as he sits back down. He
lets out a huff of air, reaches over and takes a swig of
water from a bottle on his desk, and then looks at the
very nervous chief in front of him. "Call Captain Puells
over at Sector Command New Orleans and have him get
everything *First Responder's* captain asked for, and then get
me the commandant on the line, stat!"

Five minutes later, Admiral Bishop is on the line with
the commandant. "Harry, I don't understand why I was
not in the loop on this one."

Harry had no clue that Jacob would request anything
of Bishop, but he has just gotten the message that Tommy
Williams has left for the White House to brief the
president, and he knows by experience that there is no
better team to rely on in an emergency than Tommy's,
and Jacob is Tommy's best man in the field.

"Ryan, please settle down. Look, you are one year
away from retiring and transferring over to the State
Department, so you'll know what I am about to tell you
soon enough. Commander Edwards is part of a joint law
enforcement and military task force that is headed by
Tommy Williams, and these days Tommy answers directly
to the president. The threat going on in your area is as
real as it comes, and as far as the president is concerned,
Tommy's in charge. He is briefing the president right
now and we are waiting for more direction. The only one

who has the go-ahead to make any moves is Commander Edwards. So, like it or not, he's in charge of the whole terrorism response for the moment. Now, Tommy has already told me he wants as few people as possible knowing what Commander Edwards is doing out there; and the best scenario for the aftermath is that he receives no attention or credit for anything they accomplish outside of being the commander of one of the ships responding to the threat," the commandant says.

"What exactly are you saying, Harry? That this is all top-secret, and no one is to know what's really going on?"

"Exactly, Ryan. But if the public gets wind of this, and they probably will, we will need a high-ranking officer to take credit for stopping the threat."

"Or take the fall if it all blows up," Bishop adds.

Harry chuckles. "Not quite, Ryan. If this all goes south, I have already told Tommy to tell the president I will assume all responsibility for the consequences. If it goes well, which I think it will, then you will be the man who stopped the terrorism threat in the Gulf of Mexico."

"What makes you so sure this is going our way, Harry?"

"For starters, Ryan, we don't call Tommy Williams 'The Living Legend' for nothing. And if there is any man alive who is as good as Tommy, it's our own Commander Jacob Edwards. If anyone can get the job done out there it's him, and I'll bet my career on it."

"So just to be clear, Harry, if Commander Edwards is successful in stopping this attack, you want me to take responsibility for the victory? But if he fails, you'll take the fall. Why?"

"Number one—Ryan, you're right. I kept you out of the loop. They ordered me to, but you're my friend and a damn good officer, too. It's the least I could do after blindsiding you like this. And number two—it never hurts to have a good friend in the State Department who knows you'll have his back when he needs it."

"OK, Harry, I appreciate that. Just tell the commander that my office will give him whatever he needs, but to please ask in the form of a request and not an order next time."

"I have to clear the line now because I'm expecting word from the White House any minute. Let's see our people through this, Admiral."

"Understood, Commandant. Bishop out."

A much-relieved Admiral Bishop presses the intercom on his desk and asks his assistant to come into his office. The chief hurries in. "Yes, Admiral?"

"Chief, *First Responder* is spearheading our response to a major terrorist attack in the Gulf. Commander Edwards has operational control of every level of the response. I could not tell you this until right now. The orders he sent were not directed at me so much as at the personnel over the different resources he's asked for. When *First Responder* contacts us again, I want everyone in the region to treat it as a direct order from me and do whatever Commander Edwards tells them to do. Understood, Chief?"

"Yes sir, Admiral." The man gives a smart salute and hurries out to spread the Admiral's directions throughout the region.

Ryan Bishop leans back in his chair and thinks to himself, *Well, Harry, maybe the world will never know what*

Commander Jacob Edwards will accomplish here, but there is no way in hell we will ever keep the rest of the Coast Guard from hearing about it.

First Responder Holding Cell

Gustave's eyes dart back and forth as he fidgets in his seat. With a definite quiver in his voice, he answers Jacob's question. "The Russian's strategy is twofold; one, cause outrage toward Star Oil for shoddy maintenance and using substandard parts that caused the biggest oil spill in history; and two, terrorize the world by making a ship full of school children collide into another oil rig, killing many of them and causing another major oil spill in the Caribbean."

Jacob sits straight up in his chair and grabs Gustave by the shoulders. He pulls the man to him until his nose is right in Gustave's face and says, "Just exactly when and where is that attack happening?"

"I don't know how they will get a bunch of children on a boat big enough to do that much damage to a rig like that. My instructions were to meet up with my Houston contact and wait for further instructions. The Russian figured that all the attention would be on the Event Horizon oil rig, and that the first attack would keep most of the government's attention around New Orleans, and that will make the second one easier."

Jacob leans back in his chair and takes a second to calm down so he can think. "So, let me get this straight, Gustave. It sounds like you don't know which oil rig is being targeted in the Houston area, and you don't know what cruise ship, and what set of children will be rammed into it. Is that correct?"

Gustave nods his head. "I am so sorry, Commander!" he cries. "That is why I turned around and followed your ship to warn you. I don't know who those kids are or where they are coming from. As soon as I deployed the drone, I was supposed to head to Houston and meet up with someone named Vivian Narcellas. Maybe she knows more, but that's all I have."

Jacob pulls out his shipboard radio and activates it. "Lt. Commander Phillips, call Admiral Bishop and 'request' that we lock down the east coast of Texas immediately. No ships are to leave port until further notice, and especially any with a large group of children on board. Then contact Sector Corpus Christi and tell Lt. Commander Yeager to call my private line in fifteen minutes. He'll know what you're talking about."

"Aye aye, Commander."

Jacob takes a deep breath. "Larry, when you're done with that, go get Lt. Maelstrom and Gunny Jones and meet me at the holding cell. I'll fill you all in on what's going on and why."

"Aye aye, Commander. Phillips out."

Ten minutes later Jacob is standing outside of Gustave's cell in the security office with Lt. Commander Phillips, Lt. Maelstrom, and Gunny Jones. He looks directly at Phillips and says, "As my XO you have a right to know this." Then he looks at Maelstrom. "And as my head of security you need to know this." He pauses, takes a deep breath, and then continues. "The commandant asked

Gunny Jones and me to spearhead a task force effort to quell multiple terrorist attacks that are going on in the Caribbean near Sector New Orleans and Houston right now. This assignment has a presidential approval and priority on it, so right now under Commandant Rogers, I am coordinating the whole operation. There are two targets: one is Event Horizon, which is being targeted by a drone that is carrying enough explosive and lethal acid to bring down this ship if it gets close enough. The drone, if successful, will attach itself to the main pipe and deploy its payload of f louroantimonic acid, thus causing the biggest oil spill in history. We need to stop it before it gets there. The second target is an undesignated oil rig off the port of Houston. The plan is to ram it with a cruise ship full of children. Admiral Bishop is locking down that whole section of Texas as we speak, but we need more intel before we can stop that attack."

Phillips gets red-faced and points at Gunny Jones. "Wait a minute, Commander. You mean to tell me that what happened to Chief Thompson was a setup just to get this guy on the ship?"

Gunny Jones interrupts. "Lt. Commander, the first time I ever laid eyes on the commander here is when he showed up at my class and kicked my ass, pretending to be an enlisted man. My colonel made me take this post to cover for Thompson while he recovers. When this terrorism threat hit, my superiors forwarded my records from the Gulf War to your commandant that show I've had several black op assignments dealing with terrorists over there. The commander then came and enlisted me into his task force. Neither of us really knew any of this until after *First Responder* launched on its shakedown cruise two weeks ago."

Phillips stares at Gunny Jones for a moment, trying to decide what to do with what he just heard, and then he looks back over at Jacob. "So, am I supposed to believe that this is all just some big, lucky coincidence that this black op spook ended up on our ship right when we needed him?"

Jacob stares back at Phillips with mixed emotions. He knows his XO has every right to be mad, but he also knows that he needs his crew functioning at better than one hundred percent and he has to quell this right away. With an edge in his voice that communicates he will tolerate nothing but obedience, he says, "Lt. Commander Phillips, I understand your misgivings about this man, and at one time I was as angry with him as you obviously still are. But we have a job to do and lives are at stake. I need you focused on the 'here and now.' Am I understood?"

"Aye aye, Commander, understood," Phillips says with a beet-red face and anger in his eyes that Jacob ignores.

"Good. Now, Gunny Jones is not staying on the ship anyway. I need someone to go with Gustave and meet his contact in Houston so we can figure out where the cruise ship is and what oil rig it's supposed to hit. I cannot trust Gustave to go alone, and from what I understand, Jones here has had a fair amount of experience with stuff like this. Gunny!"

"Yes, Commander?"

"You and Gustave leave in the next quarter hour. We refilled his fuel tanks so he can go top speed. You should be able to keep his rendezvous. You gather all the intel you can and then report it to Lt. Commander Chuck Yeager at Sector Corpus Christi."

Lt. Maelstrom has been silent, listening to everyone until now. "Commander, what if we need the OTO Melara? Schuette has completed all the training and passed with flying colors, but he has had no live-fire experience yet."

Gunny Jones answers. "Lieutenant, I'll let you in on a little secret. The first time I fired one of those things in live combat was while being trained even before I passed any tests. Schuette is a natural. He'll get the job done if you need him to. You can count on it."

Maelstrom briefly looks at Gunny Jones. "Thank you, Sergeant." Then he looks back at Jacob. "Commander, I found the schematics for the drone and its navigation system in the helicopter's storage unit. I think I figured out a way we can track the drone using our own sonar tied into the OTO's targeting computer. When you asked me to work on duplicating the homing beacon's signal so it would target the ship instead of the oil rig, I saw how this could work. The signal piggybacks on a sonar pulse. We tie our communication equipment into our sonar and match the signal. When the signal reaches the drone, the drone will then alter its course to follow the signal's coordinates. The pulses can be no closer than five minutes apart or the drone will abandon that course and go back to its most frequently pinged course. But it will only show up in incremental blips, and only when it is within a five-hundred-yard radius of the ship. That is when it will show up on the targeting computer of the gun for only a few seconds. We will know when the drone receives our blips, but we won't be able to get a fix on it until it is in the five-hundred-yard perimeter. This will take some very precise shooting to take it out. The helm, navigation, and gunnery are all going to have to be precisely manned and operated simultaneously for us to pull this off."

Jacob turns to Jones. "Gunny, what do you think? Is Schuette up for this or not?" Gunny Jones stares back at Jacob and then bursts out laughing, which makes Phillips and Maelstrom very irritated.

Phillips turns toward Jones. "What the hell is so funny, Gunny? Let us in on the joke."

Jones finally gets control of his mirth and wipes his eyes. "I'm sorry. It's just that for the last two weeks I have been drilling into that kid that all the computer-generated images in the world will not replace him seeing the real thing and shooting at it. I never totally relied on those little blips when I fired the OTO in combat. I used my viewport and aimed the thing the old-fashioned way and pulled the damn trigger. I used the aiming computer to help; but like I said, I wanted to see for real what I was shooting at and then take it out. That kid grew up on video games. That's one reason his simulated scores were so high. Now you're telling me that the computer is all he will have to get a good shot at that drone. What I am saying is, Schuette's more qualified for this job than I am."

Twenty minutes later, Gustave's Star Oil transport helicopter lifts off from *First Responder's* helipad, turns west, and proceeds at top speed toward Houston.

Jacob turns around and faces Lt. Commander Phillips and Lt. Maelstrom. "Gentlemen, let's go find that damn drone and blow it out of the water. Maelstrom, you're with Schuette on the OTO; Phillips you're with Bliss in communications. I'll be on the bridge at the helm. Godspeed, guys. Let's get this done!" Both men salute and hurry off to their assignments.

Jacob makes his way up to the bridge and relieves the seaman at the helm. He straps on his headgear and does a radio check-in with all his department heads. He tells the engine room to be ready to give him everything *First Responder* has in maneuvering power. He then contacts Lt. Maelstrom's people and has all the deck-mounted 50-caliber machine gun stations manned. He tells them that if the drone gets past the OTO, they are going to have to shoot it out of the water. Hopefully, they can see it before it gets too close and the explosion and acid won't cause too much damage. Lt. Maelstrom had previously installed extra monitors at the helm, communications, and gunnery. The display shows a digital representation of the ship and a five-hundred-yard perimeter surrounding it.

Jacob knows that is how they will track the drone when its navigation computer pings with the signal that Phillips and Bliss will start in communications. Jacob's job will be to maneuver the ship to give the gunners the best shot. Maelstrom's and Schuette's job will be to shoot the drone and blow it up far enough away from the ship that it causes no damage. All three stations will have to work precisely together for this to work.

Jacob reaches over and presses the button that allows him to talk to everyone at once. "All right guys, here we go. Gustave deployed the drone about a hundred miles east of us and it has been traveling at fifteen knots for the last four hours, which means it has come about sixty-five nautical miles. That means that the drone is about thirty to thirty-five nautical miles ahead of us. We'll proceed toward its general direction at a pace of twenty knots, which means we should run into it in the next twenty-five minutes. Communications will send out a ping every five minutes and monitor it on their modified sonar until they get a fix on the drone. If the homing beacon on Event Horizon pings it, we will have to wait five more minutes to ping it ourselves to get it back to tracking us. After our first ping, we should be able to calculate when it will come in our five-hundred-yard radius. When it does, Schuette, you and Maelstrom will target it on its very next ping and blow it out of the water. If you need me to maneuver the ship, you must tell me immediately. Engineering, you need to keep all three engines stoked and ready. We might do quick turns out here." Jacob hears an "Aye aye, Commander" over the line from his chief engineer.

Just before he is ready to give the order to proceed, Lt. Maelstrom comes on the line. "Commander, I finished reading all the schematics and details about the drone and the homing beacon, and we have a huge problem."

"What would that be, Lieutenant?"

"Commander, the pulsed signal goes in two directions, forming a triangle. It says here that if the pulse is not pinged, which would mean that someone has destroyed the drone, it will automatically trigger a second device to go off. That means that Gustave is right—the Russian has a backup device in place if the drone fails. I know you have a bomb squad going to Event Horizon right now. But if this is the way this works, then they can't move or touch that device until we destroy the drone, and they will only have about five minutes to do that before that device fails to receive its feedback ping from the drone. Commander, you'll have to have that bomb squad locate the device and figure out how to access its control panel but wait for our signal before disarming it. The only other option is to just evacuate the rig and let their device blow, causing whatever damage they set it to do."

Jacob digests this information and gets a determined look on his face. "Lieutenant, have Phillips and Bliss get you in contact with that bomb squad and tell them everything you just told me, and ask them how far along Star Oil is with the evacuation of the rig. When you know the answer to that question, report back. And Seaman Bliss, are you there?"

"Yes sir, Commander."

"I want to be patched into that bomb squad commander on this line for the entire operation. What we hear and say I want him hearing it, too. Understood?"

"Aye aye, Commander. Understood."

"Lt. Commander Phillips, when Bliss gets him on the line, you brief him on everything we're doing, so he's completely up to speed with us," Jacob adds.

"Aye aye, Commander."

Fifteen minutes later, Phillips says over the line, "Commander, I have Lt. Becker on the line. He's the bomb squad leader on Event Horizon. They're in the cargo hold and have found the device in the fake Barlow's gear. He says the platform is about sixty percent evacuated and will be cleared of all Star Oil personnel within thirty minutes."

"That will make this tight, Phillips. Lt. Becker, can you hear me?"

"Yes sir, Commander. Lt. Tom Becker, Sector New Orleans Coast Guard bomb squad. I read you loud and clear, sir."

"OK, Becker, Phillips already told you the details. This is a level one terrorism response and we're acting directly under the commandant's orders. There will be no communication with any source but me until this is over. Understood, Lieutenant?"

"Yes sir, Commander."

"Good! Lieutenant, are you a praying man?"

"As a matter of fact I am, Commander."

"Well then, throw a couple up the Almighty's way for all of us. We'll need all the help we can get on this one."

Ten minutes later Bliss's voice is on the comm. "Commander, Bliss here. Event Horizon's homing device just sent out a ping. According to our estimation, the drone should be about twelve nautical miles dead ahead of us."

Jacob looks at his tactical display monitor and his controls, and then pulls back the throttle. "OK, engineering, I'm slowing to five knots. Stand by. Schuette, be ready. You'll use the armor-piercing rounds on rapid-fire to cover maximum target proximity, correct, Seaman?"

"Yes sir, Commander. Also, Lt. Maelstrom will watch the ocean with his binoculars in case the drone gets close enough to surface. He can help me aim."

"Good thinking, Maelstrom. Phillips, you take any incoming communications and keep Bliss focused on those pings."

"Aye aye, Commander. As a matter of fact, Lt. Commander Yeager is on the line. He says he needs to speak with you as soon as you're available."

Jacob grins. "Tell him I'll call him as soon as I can."

Bliss cuts Jacob off. "Commander, I'm sending out our first ping now."

The silence on the ship settles like a blanket of snow on a mountain log cabin, as each station waits for Bliss's next report.

The report is so sudden that Jacob almost tears the steering handle from the console when Bliss's voice interrupts the quiet. "Commander, it received our ping. Looks like six miles west of our position."

Before Jacob can respond, Schuette interjects. "Commander, we need to veer five degrees port, right now. And cut our momentum."

"Turning five degrees port now, cutting throttle to the minimum. Bliss, wait twelve minutes until your next ping.

Schuette, when that happens and you fix your target, fire at will. Becker, stand by."

Twelve minutes later, Bliss's voice comes over the comm. "Pinging now, Commander."

Schuette says, "Got it," and fires.

About twenty armor-piercing rounds explode out of the OTO Melara gun, hitting four hundred yards starboard of the ship. None hit the drone.

Jacob yells into the comm. "Maelstrom, you see anything?!"

"Nothing yet, sir. Hold on, there it is! Fifteen degrees off starboard, sixty yards out, coming right at us," Maelstrom says.

"Engineering, all power to port engine only!" Jacob yells. He pushes the throttle to maximum and steers the ship to starboard. *First Responder* jerks right with a riveting jolt as the back of the ship pulls left. Jacob straightens out the helm. "Engineering, full power to the other two engines." *First Responder* almost rockets out of the sea, moving forward like a gigantic white whale breaching the surface.

Maelstrom's voice reports over the comm. "The drone just missed us ten yards astern, Commander. Great maneuvering, sir!"

A cold sweat appears on Jacob's brow, and the pounding of his heart feels like the drumroll of the Barnum and Bailey Circus his dad used to take him to in New York City when he was a boy. He takes a deep, calming breath to collect his thoughts. "Schuette, do you know what you did wrong, and can you fix it next time?"

"Yes sir, I do. I didn't give enough lead to my aiming. I've adjusted my specs. I won't miss it again, Commander."

"Lt. Maelstrom, now you know what that thing looks like in the water. Get out on the deck and see if you can spot it again for our next run. Bliss, I'll get the ship a thousand yards away from that thing and then wait until it's in our five-hundred-yard radius again. When I do, ping it. When that happens, Schuette, keep firing until we run out of ammo or it blows up."

Five minutes later, Jacob throttles down the ship and positions it so that its starboard side is now facing east. "OK, Bliss, ping it."

Ten seconds later the OTO Melara erupts into rapid-fire mode once again. Fifty rounds of armor-piercing projectiles catapult into the sea with an ear-splitting explosion of noise.

Then a huge mushroom of water explodes into the Caribbean horizon, followed by several volcanic eruptions of bubbling, discolored saltwater spouting into the air and gurgling down again as the acid is quickly and violently absorbed by the ocean. Cheers erupt all over *First Responder.*

Jacob yells into the comm, "Becker, get that device disarmed, stat!"

"We're on it, commander!"

While the rest of the people on the ship are still clapping, whistling, and hollering, Jacob and those on the comm wait in stone-cold silence as Lt. Becker and his men disarm the device.

Five painful minutes later, Becker reports back. "Commander Edwards, the device is disarmed. We're taking it off the rig now. My men are also retrieving the homing device from the pipe."

"Good job, Lieutenant! When you get back to New Orleans, the media will have already figured out that Event Horizon was evacuated and might know we sent a bomb squad out there. That's all they're allowed to know until further notice. Inform Admiral Bishop that we need to keep everyone away from that oil rig for the next twelve hours."

"Yes sir, Commander. And sir?"

"Yes, Becker?"

"It was an honor working with you, sir. Godspeed to you and your crew."

"You, too, Lieutenant, you too."

Jacob tells Lt. Commander Phillips to report to the bridge and then sets a course for Galveston Bay, off the port of Houston. He tells the engine room to maintain top speed all the way there. As he relinquishes the helm back to the red-headed female seaman he took it from at the port in New Orleans when they launched, Phillips comes through the hatch. "Commander, Bliss has Lt. Commander Yeager on the line waiting for you."

Jacob smiles at Phillips then looks around at the whole bridge crew. "That was one hell of a ride, Lieutenant Commander. You make sure everyone knows what a fine job this crew did today. I'm proud of every damn one of them. I'll take that call in my quarters. You have the bridge."

"Aye aye, Commander." They give each other a quick salute and Jacob steps out to take that call from his friend.

"Jacob, I don't know which oil rig they targeted in this area. There are three. Two of them are within fifty miles off port and the other is almost one hundred miles southeast of Galveston. Admiral Bishop locked down all the docks, so nothing is going out today. There were only two cruise ships leaving port that would qualify as having school children on them. One was a group of Boy Scouts scheduled to do a three-hour cruise around the area and return, and the other was a charter taking children from two ballet schools to South Padre Island to take part in some kind of big joint recital down there tomorrow."

Jacob jerks his head up and stands. "Chuck, we scheduled Danielle to be a part of that recital tomorrow. Mary is driving her to it in the morning. What are those kids from the Houston area going to do now?"

"Well, they chartered some buses and plan to drive there. They have to leave at 3:00 a.m. to make it on time."

Jacob sits down and rubs his brow with his free hand, trying to relieve a little tension in his eyes. "It seems like we've nipped this in the bud, Chuck. But somehow, I feel like we're missing something. You need to keep digging. If whoever is in charge of this attack does what I'm counting on, they will have already seen that Event Horizon has been evacuated and that we're not letting anyone out there. With any luck, they'll think one of their two plans to sabotage the rig worked and they will either move on to their next target or get out before someone catches them. Gunny Jones is tracking down our only lead with Gustave. He should be reporting to you soon. We'll be there in about seven hours."

CHAPTER FIFTEEN

BAD THINGS

Tampico, Mexico, Main Port

Peter knows Dominik loves this area of the world more than any other. In the Mexican part of the Gulf of Mexico and the Caribbean, he is revered and feared almost as a god. Being Boris's main lieutenant in this section of the world grants him the full protection and support of not only his former boss, Anthony Santiago, but also that of Maximillian Manerez. They own most government and law enforcement officials in this area and control the two largest cartels.

Peter stands on the main dock and watches as the South American Roman Catholic Children's Choir boards the cruise ship they are touring the Caribbean and the Gulf of Mexico in. Their next stop is the port of Galveston, Texas, from where they will be bussed to Houston and will perform at The Winnie Davis Houston Auditorium for the archbishop. Because of his uncle's many connections, he was able to get himself and Dominik assigned as part of the crew. Francisco will follow them in the yacht they came in.

Peter turns to head back to the yacht to get Dominik to begin their assignment when he feels the vibration of his cell phone. His uncle Boris is calling. "Uncle Boris, we are at the docks now, ready to board. I've been watching the ship for two hours. The security is nothing Dominik and I can't handle. Francisco brought all the equipment you sent. We should be able to accomplish this mission with very little difficulty."

"That'd be a nice change, Nephew. We lost the drone and have not yet confirmed that the second device you left in the cargo hold went off. Event Horizon may well be experiencing a much smaller oil spill than the one the drone would have caused. But we won't know for sure for another eight hours at least."

"What happened to the drone, Uncle?"

There is a short pause and then a low, guttural growl from Boris. "A damn cutter tracked it down and destroyed it."

"Uncle Boris, that seems next to impossible. Only Gustave has the tracking information, and he checked in an hour ago. He's on time to land in Galveston and rendezvous with Vivian. And what about the Harringtons? Couldn't they control one rogue ship commander?"

"One would think so, Nephew, but ridiculous circumstances have taken both of them off the playing field for now. Now that I cannot rely on them, I fear Prince Hasheen's ambitions are in peril. However, we must proceed at full force and do what we can to bring it to a successful conclusion. Fear not, though—contingency plans are already set in motion should this operation fail. Whether he becomes the next king or not, we'll still profit from the outcome."

It always amazes Peter that his uncle can stay ahead of almost anything. Even on those rare occasions when a contract fails, Uncle Boris always figures out how to profit from the outcome. "Any other instructions?"

"Yes. Natasha will join Francisco in following you and Dominik in my yacht. Remind him and Dominik that she's my daughter and is to be treated accordingly."

"Of course, Uncle, but might I ask why she is coming? I thought she was handling the Harringtons."

"True, Nephew," Boris growls in frustration. "But the Harringtons are completing the arrangements for Will's mother's memorial service. Because they're on grievance leave, their access to the day-by-day command processes is very limited, making them useless for the present time. Natasha has done all she can with Will Harrington, for now. Her continued presence with him in Colorado would only serve as a distraction to his misguided libido. Besides, I need someone at the helm of my yacht who understands all of its systems and unique capabilities. And that is either you or Natasha. Since you'll be on the cruise ship assisting Dominik, that leaves her. I believe no matter the outcome of this mission, you will need to leave the area much quicker than we originally expected. Any one of you being caught and then questioned by the United States authorities would be intolerable."

Peter and Natasha have spent hundreds of hours training to operate Boris's modified Millennium 140 yachts. They are the envy of the small, elite group of underworld bosses who are privy to Boris's private fleet, which is capable of eighty knots, and equipped with military-grade weaponry, armor, and stealth technology.

"I agree, Uncle. Once she's here, I'll ask her to report to you. I suggest that she take command at that point. Being on the yacht will give her full tactical intelligence and control. Since she's your daughter, Dominik will be properly motivated to listen to her. If things go awry, Dominik tends to start killing and destroying."

"I'll contact Dominik myself and tell him how I want to proceed," Boris replies. "You fill Natasha in. Goodbye."

"Goodbye, Uncle."

Peter puts his cell phone in his pocket and walks back to the yacht. He knows Francisco will be disappointed that someone else will pilot the yacht, but Uncle Boris is right. He and Natasha are the most qualified pilots available. Though it would be nice to take a cruise with his beautiful cousin, letting Dominik and Francisco handle a boatload of school-age children is a recipe for disaster.

As he rounds the corner to walk up the gangplank, he looks up, and at the top standing on the deck is his lovely cousin. "Hello, Natasha. I'm glad you can be on this portion of the mission with us." Peter steps up to his cousin and leans in to kiss her on the cheek, but she subtly turns her chin and for a brief instant their lips touch. Peter immediately pulls away as he endeavors to calm the pounding of his heart.

Natasha laughs. "Oh, Peter, ever the gentleman. I saw how angry it made you when I left the nightclub with Captain Harrington a week ago. You should learn to control your facial expressions. It was only a job that was accomplished well, despite many unforeseen obstacles."

Peter smiles brightly. "You mean, how the man tried to kill himself after you seduced him? What happened? Did you tell him that would be his one and only time, and he could not live with the grief?"

"Oh, Peter, sometimes your compliments make me blush. Now tell me, what are we doing here on my father's yacht? Something about capturing a shipload of school children and running that ship into an oil rig near Houston? Sounds like fun."

"Yes, that's the gist of it. I just got off the phone with your father and we both agree that you should take tactical command of this mission from the yacht. You know Dominik is involved, and I have been under his command for many years now. Trying to usurp his sense of authority is not a good idea. But if we can persuade him to see you as being in the stead of your father, he'll obey your commands."

"Excellent points, Peter. Was this your suggestion or my father's commands?"

"I originally suggested the idea and your father agreed with the logic."

Natasha's smile drains from her face, and she places a hand on Peter's shoulder. "You really do not want to run things after my father is gone, do you, Peter?"

Peter looks her straight in the eyes and shakes his head. "No, Natasha, I do not; but I want to follow you."

Natasha grips Peter's other shoulder and holds both with an uncommonly steel-like strength. "I warn you, cousin. Though I am drawn to you, I'll always look out for my own interests first." She releases Peter's shoulders and nods toward the galley. "Now, I think it's time I met this famous pit bull of my father's. Where is this Dominik?"

Peter steps back and glances from side to side, then back at Natasha. "Be careful, Cousin. Dominik is not to be toyed with. He is, next to your father, the most lethal man I have ever known. The reason you have not met him up until now is that Boris and I both know that you are the kind of woman that Dominik likes, and he is used to taking what he likes and doing whatever he wants with it. Your father considers him one of his most valuable assets, and it would grieve him immeasurably if he had to kill the man for hurting you."

Natasha turns back and flashes Peter her dazzling white teeth, then leans in and kisses him on the lips again and pulls slightly back. "You know as well as I that if I'm truly to lead in my father's stead someday, I must be able to control all of his pets. Please take me to this legendary monster so he may learn to respect me as he does my father."

Peter steps back and blows a puff of air through his lips. "Follow me, Natasha. He and Francisco are in the galley."

Natasha maneuvers in front of Peter and walks up the ladder to the galley entrance. "I know the way, Peter," she says as she steps up to the door and opens it.

When she walks in, both men are sitting at the galley table eating breakfast. Francisco is the first to look up, and he immediately gets a huge, lustful gleam in his eye. But before he can say a word, Peter steps in and silently waves his hand, cautioning the man not to say a word.

Dominik finishes cutting his food and looks up as he is sticking a huge piece of sausage in his mouth. He immediately jumps out of his seat and devours Natasha from head to toe with his hungry, predatory eyes. He steps close, then takes his hand and rubs her shoulder and then places his hand on the side of her face. He turns to the side and focuses on Peter. "Peter, what did you bring me? We have to be on the cruise ship within the hour, and one as exquisite as this would take me all day and all night to exact the pleasure that I see she is capable of giving."

Peter lets out an exasperated huff of air. "Dominik, let me introduce you to Boris's only child, Natasha Rasmov. Boris sent her to oversee the final steps in this operation."

Natasha remains casually quiet as Peter and Francisco stare at Dominik nervously, waiting for his response. Dominik looks back at Natasha and grinds his teeth. "Boris is the only one I take orders from. Daughter or not, I will not be bossed around by some vixen who should pleasure me in my bed."

With eye-confusing speed, Natasha draws two four-inch blades from a concealed holster in the back of her pants and steps into Dominik's perimeter, placing one razor-sharp edge at his throat and the other at his crotch. She leans in close so that her mouth is inches from his ear and, while toying with the blade at his crotch, she says, "My father told me the first time you two met, he introduced you to the sabre he keeps in his cane. I have seen that blade cut through thick tin like it was paper. These blades are made of the same steel." She takes the blade at his crotch and starts to saw at the material of his pants. It cuts through the metal zipper instantly and Dominik feels the sting of the blade against his manhood. He's unable to move as the same metal is now drawing blood from his throat and beads of sweat are forming on his forehead.

Natasha continues. "Now, Dominik, you may apologize for your insolence and submit to my leadership." She wiggles the lower blade a little. "Or I will take away your reason to live."

Dominik looks down and sees Natasha's hand at his crotch and feels the cold, razor-sharp edges of her blades against his skin at both places. With a panic he has not felt since the first time he met Boris, he stutters out, "I am sorry, Natasha. I did not know who you are. Your beauty is beyond compare, and I lost myself for a moment. Your commands are your father's in my eyes. I will do as you say."

Natasha takes the blades away from Dominik's skin and steps back. She flashes all the men in the cabin with her sultry smile and then refocuses on Dominik. "Now,

Dominik, when you throw out compliments like that, how do you expect me to be the ruthless leader my father expects me to be? I am positively blushing."

Her eyes twinkle as she laughs and tells Dominik to go clean up and get ready to board the cruise ship with Peter. All the men leave the galley at that point and Natasha sits down, pulls out her cell phone, and calls her father. "Hello, Father. I am here."

"Good, Natasha. Did Peter tell you we want you to be in tactical command of this operation?"

"Yes, he did, Father, and then he introduced me to the rest of the crew."

There is a brief pause and then Boris asks, "And how did that introduction go over with my men, Daughter?"

"Let's say I introduced Dominik to the blades you gave me on my eighteenth birthday, and everything is moving along nicely now."

Boris allows himself a small laugh. "Disappointment is almost nonexistent with you, my daughter. Make sure Peter has thoroughly briefed you in all aspects of the mission, and then let me know once they have control of the cruise ship."

"I will, Father. Goodbye."

"Goodbye, Natasha."

Twenty minutes later, Natasha and Francisco are out on the deck helping Dominik and Peter collect what remains of the gear they are taking with them. Dominik is silent as he picks up his duffel bag and walks off the ship. Natasha turns and tells Francisco to go prepare the yacht to launch, then waits for him to leave the deck before she quickly steps up to Peter and grabs his arm. "Your pledge of loyalty earlier was received with much gratitude. I had thought that someday I would have to kill you to take over my father's affairs. I know he would perceive your words as weakness, so he will never hear them from me. We are stronger together than apart, Peter. Maybe someday he will see that."

She squeezes his arm and looks him in the eye with almost genuine affection, then releases her grip and walks over to the command deck.

Peter grabs his duffel bag and a large suitcase and hurries off after Dominik. He catches Dominik as he is about to board the cruise ship in the service area. Peter reaches in his pocket and hands the big Jamaican his fake ID and ship employment papers. He had previously gotten them assigned to the ship's security detail. That way, they had access to all the ship's secured areas. As they check in with the personnel coordinator, someone hands them their access cards and uniforms and tells them where to report. The personnel director looks at Dominik. "What is your full name and date of birth?"

Dominik glares at the man. "It is written on my check-in paperwork. Can't you read, man?"

Peter nervously looks at Dominik and then at the personnel director. He notices the man is slightly overweight and has blood-shot eyes and red cheeks. He quickly surmises that the man likes to drink a lot. "I'm sorry, boss. My friend and I were out late last night drinking and we both have some wicked hangovers. He's not used to going through security checks for standard employees."

The director inspects Dominik's paperwork, looking specifically at his work history. Astonished, he looks back at Dominik and says, "I am so sorry, Señor Thrace. A man with your credentials could easily run security for our whole cruise line. Please proceed on."

Dominik grunts and turns to go. Peter didn't need anyone to give him directions because for the last couple of weeks he has been studying schematics of the ship and knows the layout by heart; but in keeping with the facade that they are new to the ship's personnel, he asks for them anyway. When the two of them get to the elevator and step in, Dominik turns to Peter. "Why did you use my real name for this job?"

Peter smiles. "Boss, I know how much you hate stealth missions. After we're done and half of these people are dead, I know you'll enjoy having your name tied to all of it. Your legend will only deepen, and once back in Guatemala, no one can touch you."

Dominik stares at Peter for a few seconds, his countenance unreadable, then he slaps Peter on the back. "That is why I enjoy having you on my crew, Peter. You really understand me. What are we doing next?"

Peter looks down at his watch. "We wait for the cruise ship to launch and then we report to security. There are usually four to five officers in the security office. We'll need to dispose of them, and then we can go to the engine room and begin our sabotage."

Dominik stares straight forward at the elevator door as it opens, then looks sideways at Peter. "I'll handle the security men myself; you go into the engine room and begin. Once I'm done with them, I'll join you."

They both step out of the elevator. Peter points down the hall to a door. "That's the break room next to the security office. If you wait there until the ship is about thirty minutes out to sea, you should be able to take the guards by surprise with no witnesses."

Dominik smirks. "And if someone is still in the break room after that?"

Peter winks. "I guess it's too bad for them, boss. We got a job to do."

Dominik flashes a big, evil smile, slaps Peter on the back again, and heads toward the break room. Peter makes his way to the hatch that leads to the engine room.

When he gets into the engine room, there are two engineers manning the equipment. The room is so loud that neither of them notice Peter entering the room. He knows he has no time to subdue them like Dominik will in the security break room, so he reaches in his bag and pulls out a silenced 9mm pistol and shoots both men in the back of the head. He takes the bodies and puts them in a storage closet, then heads straight to the navigation relay that connects with the bridge's helm. Controlling the ship is a simple matter of cutting the bridge's access to the engines, rudders, and throttle. Everything relays through the junction box that he is in front of.

He opens his duffel bag and takes out a piece of technology that looks like a laptop, and inserts a cable into one of the USB ports, then removes the cover of the junction box and connects the other end of the cable to several circuits. He punches in some codes on the keyboard. "Access granted" displays on the screen; and then the screen displays a virtual image of the helm control of the cruise ship. In the bottom left-hand corner is a digital clock ticking down from four hours. He knows that when that timer runs out, the computer will cut off the helm from the bridge and the device will take over. He hooks up a Bluetooth amplifier to another USB port that will allow him to remotely control the device from anywhere on the ship. He pulls out a mini-computer pad and calls up the same display on the bigger device and tests the controls to make sure he has a connection. He walks over to the anchor-deploying mechanism and finds the chain that connects to the anchor, pulls out a block of plastic explosive material, and connects it to a small detonator device that has a remote-control switch on it that is also hooked up to his mini-computer pad's Bluetooth. He sets the device on the chain at the end closest to the anchor and uses duct tape to hold it in place.

As Peter is putting the rest of his equipment away, he feels a difference in the room, like a door opening. He looks up. There, standing in the doorway in a torn shirt and with several bruises and cuts on his body and face, is Dominik. He has a huge smile on his face.

"Boss, what happened?"

Dominik closes the door and makes his way over to Peter. "The security department for the ship was having a staff meeting when I got there. There were six of them in the break room. I killed three before they could properly react. The remaining three proved to be slightly more of a challenge. But none of them made it out alive."

Peter inspects some of his wounds. "Boss, some of these will need stitches. Do you need help hiding the bodies?"

Dominik takes a breath and sighs. "Peter, always back to business with you. I put them in the office and locked the door. There is a medical kit in the break room. We'll go back there, and you can stitch me up. Then we can work on sealing off this area so the ship's crew cannot get down here. Relax, boy, this will be fun."

CHAPTER SIXTEEN
FIGURING THINGS OUT

Office of Lt. Commander Chuck Yeager, Corpus Christi

Four hours after the last time he talked to Commander Edwards, Chuck Yeager sits at his desk talking to him again on the new smartphone he got from Tommy Williams. "Jacob, that deal with the drone was too close for comfort. If that thing had attached itself to *First Responder*, you'd be at the bottom of the Gulf right now, along with three quarters of your crew."

"I know, Chuck, but we had no choice. There were just too many disasters it could have caused involving civilians, including at Event Horizon. Please tell Admiral

Bishop that I recommend Lt. Becker and his crew for a commendation. Those New Orleans bomb squad guys kept their heads and did their job under some big-time pressure. What did you find out from Jones and Gustave?"

Chuck leans back in his office chair and lets out a heavy sigh. "Gustave led us to a local crime boss named Vivian Narcellas. We had the local FBI office bring her in under the Patriot Act and they have been questioning her for a couple of hours now. She says she was contracted by some people in Central America to provide passage south of the border after they pull off some industrial espionage today. She says she knows nothing about what the target is or why—only that her people were to meet up with their agents at the docks and sneak them inland, hide them, and then get them down south when the pressure cools."

"Is she giving us any names?"

"No, that's the thing—she's clammed up tight. The FBI threatened her with everything short of Guantanamo Bay and she won't budge. Whoever is pulling her strings is scarier than what we can do to her."

"OK, Chuck, now that I know what we don't have, tell me what you do have. I'll take your best guess at this point."

"I don't think the Houston area, or any Gulf state school children are the target. We have all the ports locked down, and when we found Vivian, she was still all set to move ahead with whatever she was supposed to do. I think it's a ship coming in from outside the country."

"Any candidates yet?"

"Yeah, there is one. A cruise ship left Tampico Bay carrying a bunch of South American Roman Catholic choir children scheduled to perform for the archbishop this afternoon, but I can't be sure of the target rig."

Jacob pulls out a map of the Gulf and uses his finger to trace the route a cruise ship would normally take from Tampico, Mexico, to the Galveston, Texas, port. He already knows the three rigs that are the most likely targets and sees that the ship will come closest to the one farthest out to sea before it docks at port. "Chuck, it has to be the one farthest out. What's the name of that one?"

Chuck looks down at a list on his desk. "That one's called Deep Star. We've already been in contact with all three rigs, and they're on standby to begin evacuation as soon as we give the word. But we only have the resources to get one of them evacuated, and Deep Star will take the longest because it's the farthest out. We might not make it in time. Captain Williams called me before you did. He says the president wants as little noise as possible about this second threat, so calling in too much help from the Navy isn't an option right now. He thinks we have the threat contained with the lockdown and can justify that with the buzz about Event Horizon. But evacuating three oil rigs at once, seven hundred miles away from the first threat, will cause a huge panic, in his opinion." Chuck pauses a second and then leans into the phone a little closer. "But The Legend then told me he would back up any play you call, Jacob. What do you want to do?"

Jacob does not hesitate. "You call naval command and tell them we need resources close enough to those other two rigs to respond to a threat. Tell them exactly what you told me about the president's desire to keep this quiet, but to be ready. Then contact that cruise ship out of Tampico and tell them not to come into our waters and to be prepared for someone trying to take over the ship. We're heading toward Deep Star. I'm positive this is not a typical terrorist attack. Someone is trying to cripple US oil production in the Gulf, and I don't want to let them get away with it, but that comes second to saving lives. We can be at Deep Star in two hours at top speed. Have Gunny Jones and Gustave's helicopter refueled and send them out to that rig. That's a Star Oil copter and they can help with the evac. Plus, I'll need Gunny Jones out there, too—I can feel it in my bones."

"Got it. Anything else?"

"Let me know if anything else comes up as soon as you know. Use the regular line for communication. I've briefed my crew about what's going on and everyone is as up to speed as they need to be."

"OK, Commander, will do."

Jacob ends the call and heads for the bridge. When he rounds the corner to make his way up, he spots Schuette and Bliss talking outside of Bliss's radio room. "What are you two talking about?"

Schuette responds. "Commander, Bliss and I were just discussing how well the communication setup we had during the drone incident worked. Being in contact with you and Seaman Bliss at the same time and tied into his radar reads really made a difference when I fired the OTO

Melara. We think we should leave that communication protocol and equipment in place should we need it again."

Jacob thinks about the suggestion for a moment and then responds. "Schuette, the OTO has its own tactical display and digital remote-control aiming. I tied in the extra protocols so we could stay real-time with the bomb squad on Event Horizon and track the stealth drone."

"Commander, the stealth drone is why Schuette and I thought we should leave the protocols. If a terrorist can get that kind of tech in the water, so can criminals, and so can foreign enemies."

Jacob puts both hands on his hips and smiles at the two seamen. "Gentlemen, permanently changing shipboard protocols is above my pay grade. But we still technically are under a terrorist attack, so I can keep them in place for now. After this is over, I want you two to work up a recommendation on this and I'll review it and pass it on to command."

Before the two men head off to their respective stations, Bliss thinks of something. "Commander, I sent two headsets up to the bridge for you and Lt. Commander Phillips, and I also sent one to Lt. Maelstrom in security. Just in case you decide to approve their use."

"Thank you, seaman," Jacob says, thinking what a couple of bright young men they are.

When Jacob steps onto the bridge he looks over at Lt. Commander Phillips and sees he is already wearing a headset. You really cannot call it a headset, because it is more like an earpiece and a thin, black wire that has a small microphone in it that leads down to the carrier's radio. The line allows for hands-free communication after the initial transmission is made. Once someone starts a conversation, the line stays open until Bliss closes it at his communication console. Jacob walks over to his station, grabs his headset and puts it on.

Phillips turns to him. "Commander, we're about an hour out from the Deep Star oil rig. Lt. Commander Yeager just sent a message. The cruise ship that left Tampico Bay this morning is unresponsive. He says the ship is still on course, but we can't reach anyone on the communication line."

Jacob walks over and looks at the radar display. "How long before we have an accurate read of them on the radar?"

"At least another thirty minutes, Commander," Phillips says.

"OK, how many Coast Guard and naval ships do we have at the closest rig to Deep Star?"

Phillips walks over to his tactical station and reads off the computer screen. "Seven altogether, Commander. Two Cyclones from the Navy, and six CBD Protectors of our own."

Jacob does some quick calculations in his head. "Cyclones have a complement of four officers and twenty-four crew, and a complement of four to eight Special Forces. The Protectors have ten in their crew altogether. Do either of those Cyclones have a Special Forces unit on it right now?"

"No sir, they both were in dock at Galveston refueling. They have only their regular crews on them. Wait a minute—Gunny Jones is on one. The order is right here.

Lt. Commander Yeager sent him out on your authority. He is supposed to join up with us any way he can."

"That means Gustave is flying solo," Jacob says. "Have that Cyclone with Gunny Jones on it and two CBDs meet us at Deep Star. Then have Bliss get us in contact with Gustave. How fast can that ship be here at top speed, Lt. Commander?"

Phillips looks at his console. "It'll be tight, commander. Fifty minutes, tops."

"OK, Phillips. You have the bridge. Have Maelstrom prep me a skiff and be ready to launch with two security specialists in twenty minutes. Call the captain of that Cyclone and tell him Maelstrom and I will meet up with him in forty-five minutes. Tell the captain that I want his men to prep his assault skiff and have it ready for Gunny Jones and me to use to board the cruise ship. I want you to take *First Responder* and place it between the rig and the cruise ship. We can't let the cruise ship run into that rig."

Phillips walks up to Jacob. "Jacob, what if you two can't get control of that ship in time? Are we supposed to blow it out of the water?"

Jacob puts a hand on Phillips' shoulder and shakes his head. "No, Larry. I want you to let it ram *First Responder*. You can maneuver her to minimize damage up to a point. When you collide, use grappling hooks and pull the cruise ship out of the way of the rig if you can. But if that ship hits that rig, pretty much everyone on it and the cruise ship will die. The Cyclone and the two CBDs will be there to respond and help you if you need rescuing."

"Sir, I don't understand. Why do you have to be the one to board that ship? You should be the one in command here, not me."

Jacob motions Phillips to the door and they step out onto the deck in the open. He sternly looks at Phillips and says, "Larry, those Cyclones usually carry a Special Forces complement of men, but you said they did not have one with them right now. If they did, I'd give the job of boarding the cruise ship to them. There are only two men out here that I know of who have Special Forces training and experience. One is Gunny Jones; the other is me."

Phillips stands there for a second, processing what Jacob has just told him. Then the corners of his mouth crease into a slight smile and he shakes his head. "You know, Admiral Billings told me that being under your command would be a little different. I only have one request, Commander."

"What's that, Larry?"

"Take your headgear with you. If the crew knows you're in contact with us, things will go a lot easier."

Jacob laughs. "Already planned on it. We'll also have Lt. Commander Yeager on the line with us. Just remember, you're the one on the ship and you're in command here. Follow my orders the best you can, but use your head and take the initiative when you have to, and that is an order, Lieutenant Commander."

Phillips stares back at his CO, then smiles, salutes, and says, "Aye aye, Commander."

Jacob reaches down and activates his communicator. "Bliss, contact Maelstrom and tell him I'm heading to the skiff launch port now. Have him and his team meet me there."

"Maelstrom here, Commander. We're already here, and ready to launch when you are."

Fifteen minutes later, Jacob, Maelstrom, and two security specialists are on the Hamilton's skiff, speeding toward the Cyclone that is headed toward the Deep Star oil rig. As they approach, Phillips's voice comes over the communicator. "Commander, we've just pulled up the cruise ship on our radar. They're about thirty minutes out from the rig and heading at top speed on a collision course."

"OK, Phillips, keep trying to reach that ship. We're about five minutes away from the Cyclone. Are any of those CBDs in the area yet?"

"Yes, Commander. Lt. Nelson and Master Chief Roberto Garcia from Station Brazos said they have rendezvoused with the Cyclone and are awaiting your orders."

"Pops is out here? How did he manage that?" Jacob asks.

"The captain of the CBD, Lt. Nelson, said Chief Garcia insisted on coming, saying that swim rescue is part of the protocol for situations like this."

Jacob rolls his eyes. "Yeah, I know that when a civilian ship is in distress, you need to have swim rescue available. *First Responder* has its own swim rescue unit aboard and he knows that. Tell Nelson to stand by. We'll be there in a few minutes. Have Gunny Jones prepare to launch the Cyclone skiff when I get there."

"Yes sir, Commander. The captain of the Cyclone wants to know if either you or Jones are qualified to do an ejection launch from the stern, or will they have to hoist it for you and let you board from the side?"

Jacob knows that the Cyclones have a lightweight, inflatable skiff with a high-powered outboard motor at the stern that can be launched from the back of the ship while it is still in motion. That's how most Special Forces units deploy from the ship. "I don't know about Jones, but I've been on five previous missions where we deployed from a Cyclone in one of those things. Just tell him that The Legend trained me in the maneuver. That should quell any fears he might have. What's the captain's name?"

"Captain Brian Anderson, Commander," Phillips responds.

Chapter Seventeen
The Commander

Five minutes later, Jacob and his crew are docking their skiff with the Cyclone. As Jacob climbs the ladder, he is greeted by Jones and a naval captain who turns out to be Anderson. "Permission to come aboard, Captain?" Jacob says as he steps on the deck and salutes the officer.

The salute is returned, and the man says, "Permission granted, Commander. Welcome aboard, Commander Edwards. Captain Brian Anderson at your service. I've been instructed by Naval Command to give you all the aid you require, and to follow your orders to the letter, sir."

"Thanks, Captain. Is the skiff prepped and ready for mobile launch?"

"Almost. Who will go with you?"

Jacob looks behind Anderson and nods toward Gunny Jones. "It will just be Gunnery Sergeant Jones and me. Lt. Maelstrom and his men will return to *First Responder* immediately." Jacob looks up and sees that Maelstrom is about to say something, but he holds his hand up to stay him off. "Alex, I'd love to take you along, and I think you could handle it, but to deploy in one of these things, you have to have a Special Forces rating, and to operate it you have to be certified."

Maelstrom's shoulders slouch a little and he throws a salute. "Aye aye, Commander," he says, and then he motions his men back to the ladder to get into the skiff and head back.

After Maelstrom pulls away from the Cyclone, Jacob, Jones, and Anderson head to the back of the ship where several of Anderson's crew are prepping the Cyclone's skiff for rear launch. Jacob looks over at Gunny Jones. "This is a stealth operation. The Legend wants no civilians to recognize us—ever. That means no interaction if we can help it; we dispose of any combatants with extreme prejudice; and we wear our black camo and masks until this is over."

Jones nods and they both put on their camo and equipment. Once ready, Jacob and Jones climb over the railing that encloses the inflatable skiff. Anderson leans over the side. "We'll be at five knots in fifteen minutes, then we'll deploy you."

"No time, Captain. Deploy now."

"Commander, we're at eighteen knots. I've only heard of one man ever jumping off a Cyclone in one of these things going that fast."

Jacob puts a thumb up and laughs. "Yes, I know. I was with The Legend when he did it. Scared the hell out of me, too."

Anderson looks over at his crewman manning the lever and yells, "You heard the commander. Deploy the craft!"

The hydraulics lift the little skiff's front end up and the gate opens in the back of the Cyclone and the craft slides out backward. Jones has been at sea enough to understand how hitting the water in a blowup skiff of this size will be like landing on concrete going thirty miles an hour. He grabs onto two handles, braces his teeth and watches Jacob gear the engine into full-forward throttle. When the back of the skiff hits the ocean, he can feel the tug of the drag pull the skiff in. The propeller going in full eases the drag slightly, but it still feels like riding a rollercoaster backwards as the craft hits the water and the front end stands almost straight up in the air. Jacob immediately throws the propeller in reverse and throttles it to maximum, looks over at Jones, and yells, "Lean over in my direction as far as you can!" Jones complies and the skiff tips sideways, and Jacob throttles back the motor to a minimum, then yells, "Lean forward!" The skiff slaps down into the water right-side up. Jacob waits a few seconds then throttles up the skiff and heads away from the Cyclone. He reaches down and activates his radio. "Bliss, give me a heading on that cruise ship. We can't see it yet."

"It's four miles in front of you and thirteen degrees to your port, Commander." Jacob makes the adjustment and Gunny Jones gets out a pair of binoculars and scans for the cruise ship and the Deep Star oil rig.

Captain Anderson and his men stare at the skiff that just deployed from his Cyclone while doing eighteen knots. Two younger sailors are standing with their mouths agape, wondering how anyone could pull off that maneuver like Jacob and Gunny Jones just did. Captain Anderson looks over at his XO and says, "Now I remember! I've heard some Special Forces talking about that guy. They say he's in line to replace The Legend someday. They didn't even know what branch of the service he was in." He takes a deep breath and turns around. "No one's ever going to hear who he is from me."

"Me, either," his XO says as they make their way back to the Cyclone's bridge.

Thirty Minutes Earlier, Aboard the Cruise Ship

Peter fully expected the bridge personnel of the ship to barricade themselves in. After 9/11, airplanes weren't the only form of public transportation that adopted that policy. The one thing that no one wants a terrorist to do is to gain control of a ship, whether air or sea. What the ship's crew did not take into account is that someone can cut off all navigating operations from the bridge of a vessel as big as a cruise ship, except for the emergency deployment of the anchor. But Peter had already taken that into account, as the bridge crew and its captain will soon learn when they try to deploy the anchor after seeing they are on a collision course with an oil rig.

Peter takes his laptop out and hooks up something resembling a game controller, then activates his Bluetooth signal and connects with the transmitter he installed in the engine room. An ocean map comes up on his display, along with a representation of the helm controls of the bridge. He punches in the coordinates for the Deep Star oil rig and puts the ship's helm on auto pilot, then locks in the controls and locks out the bridge. He then reaches for his radio and activates it.

"Natasha, we are in control of the ship. The bridge is completely locked out of helm control. In about forty-five minutes, they will try to drop their anchor. The explosion you hear will be your signal to move in for extraction."

"Superb, Peter. What is Dominik doing?"

"Exactly what we planned. He's at the back of the ship, scaring the hell out of everyone and keeping the crew away, so we'll have a clear path to escape."

Natasha laughs. "How that Neanderthal ever thought he was in charge of anything is beyond me. Don't you ever tire of picking up after his mayhem?"

"That Neanderthal caught and killed six security officers with his bare hands. Right now, he has the entire ship believing they're under siege by a large group of pirates. He's truly a one-man army."

Natasha laughs again. "You and Dominik be in position in thirty minutes. As soon as you're off the cruise ship and in your raft, activate your tracking devices. The mayhem the collision will cause should make it easy for us to move in and pick you both up."

Present Time, Cyclone's Skiff

Gunny Jones spotted the cruise ship a few minutes earlier, and now Jacob is maneuvering the skiff to its rear stern to use the ladders there to board. "It looks like they're dropping the anchor now."

The big anchor chain attached to the cruise ship starts to drop, but after a few seconds, they see an explosion right where the chain is attached to the anchor, and the anchor immediately falls into the water. The rest of the chain follows, but without the anchor attached, it will do little to slow down the vessel.

Jacob looks at his watch. "The ship will crash in thirty minutes." He takes a calming breath and thinks for a second, then says into his communicator, "Bliss, contact the Captain and chief Garcia's on that CBD and have them pull around to the back of the cruise ship. Tell them to have their lifeboats ready to deploy and figure out how to permanently patch me in with them. Then contact Captain Anderson on that Cyclone and tell him to get behind here with us. I want both ships here in fifteen minutes. Phillips, brace for collision and stand by with the maneuver we discussed. I have one more idea that might make it easier for you to grapple that thing, but be ready. Edwards out."

A few minutes later, the Brazos CBD becomes visible to Jacob and Gunny Jones, and a voice comes over the line. "Commander Edwards, Lt. Nelson here. I have Chief Garcia with me. What are your orders, sir?"

"Pull up alongside me and hand Jones your tow cable," Jacob answers. When the CBD pulls up, Jacob sees his father-in-law, Chief Garcia, and a young lieutenant at the stern of the boat, holding the thick tow cable they use when they have to pull another craft back to dock. As they approach, he sees the confusion written on both men's faces.

Lt. Nelson speaks first. "Commander, I don't understand what's going on. You don't expect my CBD to tow a cruise ship of that size, and why are we ready to deploy our lifeboats?"

Jacob yells over the ocean and watercraft noise. "Lieutenant, I have *First Responder* in front of this cruise ship ready to collide and grapple it. Best outcome with that scenario is we get clear of the oil rig with only two very valuable ships damaged, one with civilians and children on board. We'll use your CBD to stop it, or at least slow it down enough so that my ship can get it out of the way in time."

Before the lieutenant can respond, Chief Garcia does. "Sounds like a good plan, Jacob. What next?"

Nelson almost rebukes Chief Garcia, but Roberto solemnly looks at him first. "Lt. Nelson, I get that this is your first command and you want to do right by it. But you saw the memo from Admiral Bishop. Commander Edwards has complete operational control of the entire section until this is over. If you feel you need to, you can file a complaint later. But for now, your duty is to obey him."

Nelson reaches out with the end of the tow cable, hands it to Gunny Jones, and says to Jacob, "Aye aye, Commander. What are you going to do?"

"We'll attach this to the anchor cable, and then you'll try to slow the cruise ship down by pulling on it. If I tell you to abandon ship, I want you, your crew, and the chief off her, ASAP. Understood, Lieutenant?"

"Aye aye, Commander."

Chief Garcia yells over the noise, "You be careful, Jacob! Mary and Danielle expect you home for dinner, and I'm not leaving here until I know you'll make it!"

Jacob waves back at his father-in-law. "Pray for us, Pops!"

Jacob turns the little skiff around and heads to the back of the cruise ship. By his best guess, the ship is traveling a little under fifteen knots, which means the bridge crew slowed it down considerably before being taken over by the hijackers, because the normal speed of a civilian ship that size is between twenty-four and thirty knots. He knows he has to get it under ten knots before Phillips can be anywhere near effective in grappling it and towing it out of harm's way.

Jones secures the tow cable to the craft and Jacob maneuvers the skiff so that they are right next to the anchor chain being dragged behind the ship. Nelson provided them with an ultra-strong attaching belt to fasten the cable to. As Jacob gets right under the chain, which is about twenty yards behind the cruise ship, it suddenly shifts position and whips to the right, almost knocking Jones out of the skiff. Jacob veers to the right and repositions the craft. Jones jumps up and throws the end of the attaching belt through a chain loop and immediately shoves the tow cable out of the skiff.

Jacob activates his radio again. "Nelson, are you on this line yet?"

"Yes, Commander. I read you loud and clear."

"Good. Now let the cable get taut as you match speed with the ship, then slowly power down until they are towing you, and then put it in reverse. Our goal is to slow that thing down by five knots."

"Aye aye, Commander."

Jacob pushes the throttle to full and aims the skiff toward an area at the back of the cruise ship that has an access ladder that goes down to the waterline. When they get there, the water is rough from the propellers of the ship whipping them up. That, plus the fact that they are going fifteen knots makes the whole experience seem like an out-of-control whitewater raft ride down the Colorado River. Gunny Jones is at the front of the skiff with a grappling hook in his hand that is attached to the skiff's tow line. He whips it over his head a couple times and throws it at the heavy steel bars that hold the ladder in place. He makes it on the first throw, and Jacob yells, "Go!"

Both men jump out toward the tow line and use it to pull themselves to the ship. Fortunately, the inflatable skiff maintains its stability on the end of the tow line until they make their way to the ladder. When they are about a quarter of the way up, the skiff flips and flops over into the water. Jacob looks down, then at Jones. "When we're done, hopefully it'll still be attached."

A distant popping sound erupts from above. He looks up to see someone shooting at them. He draws his standard-issue .45 caliber pistol and returns fire, and so does Gunny Jones. Jacob activates his comm. "Nelson, someone at the stern of the ship is firing down on us. Cover us with the fifty cal so we can get to the top. Be careful. We don't know if any civilians are up there."

Almost immediately, a much louder *pop, pop, pop* erupts from behind them as one of Lt. Nelson's crew returns fire toward the area at the top of the ladder. Jacob and Gunny Jones wait a few minutes and then ascend. Just before they reach the top, Nelson comes back over the line. "Commander, we're ready to reverse engines and apply negative pressure. Should we wait until you get to the top in case you experience a good jerk from us?"

Jacob thinks for a second. "We can use that to board the ship. Wait until I say so, then give us the biggest jerk you can." He and Jones get to the top of the ladder, and both men hook an arm around part of the railing while holding onto their sidearms with the other. Jacob peeks over the edge and bullets fly as he ducks back down. "Nelson, now!"

He and Jones brace for the impact. Suddenly, the aft end of the cruise ship reels back and down, almost making both men lose their grips; but they hold tight and simultaneously propel themselves over the railing of the ship and onto the deck, both firing their weapons. Fortunately, there are lifeboats stationed right near them and they duck behind one and wait for a response. The wait is not long. Several shots ring over their heads and Gunny Jones returns fire. With gun in hand, Jacob says into his communicator, "Bliss, how much did we slow the ship down with that?"

"Not enough, Commander. It's down to twelve knots, but it's climbing, not falling."

"Dammit, we'll have to do it," Jacob mutters to himself.

"OK, Lt. Nelson, abandon ship, stat. Captain Anderson, once Nelson's men are off, target the bow of that CBD and put a hole in it big enough to sink it."

There is dead silence on the comm for about three seconds, and then Anderson responds. "Commander, you want me to sink one of our own ships?"

"Yes, Anderson, I do. That ship weighs a hell of a lot more than an anchor. If that tow cable holds out long enough, we should be able to slow the ship down below ten knots or better, and my ship can do the rest. If your gunner can make a clean enough hole in the stern while blowing nothing else up, we should be able to salvage the CBD and refurbish it."

"Commander, Nelson here. We're off and making our way clear now."

"Fire, Anderson!" Jacob yells as more shots are fired at them from the other side of the lifeboat. At the same time, a series of precisely placed shots explode into the stern of the CBD right at the waterline. The boat immediately takes on water and sinks.

Jacob puts his hand on Gunny Jones's shoulder. "Brace yourself, this'll be rough."

Just as he finishes speaking, the whole aft end of the cruise ship drops, and everyone and everything not fastened down jerks backward, which includes the two men on the other side of the lifeboat firing at Jacob and Jones.

Jacob and Jones leap over the lifeboat. The cruise ship jerks again and both men stumble and lose their sidearms as they fall. Luckily, Jacob notices that the two men on the other side do not have their weapons, either, so he attacks the man nearest him.

It is almost 8:00 p.m. and he can tell little about either man, aside from the one he is attacking is dark-skinned and the other is white. Jacob comes in low to his man and rockets a devastating right cross to the man's crotch, then stands straight up with a left upper cut to his chin. To his amazement, the man is still standing, so he hits him four more times square in the face with two lefts and two rights. He then wraps his right hand around the man's neck and places his right foot in his midsection, and as they are falling backward, Jacob extends his right leg with a powerful thrust. At the same time, the ship reels back again and the stern dips into the ocean so low at the rear that the man flies right over the railing into the water.

Jacob looks over at Gunny Jones to see if he needs any help. Jones and his man are up against the railing at the back of the ship. Jones throws a right ridge hand, two vertical straight punches, and follows with a left elbow strike. All of his hand strikes and the elbow strike are easily countered by his opponent. For a moment, it looks like Jones is in trouble. The man he is fighting appears to be using some wickedly proficient Wing Chun Kung Fu that is countering everything he's throwing. But before Jacob can move in to help, Gunny Jones, with the agility of a mountain lion, jumps straight up in the air and spins right, thrusting the outside of his right foot into his assailant's face, knocking him over the railing and into the ocean with a perfectly executed jumping spinning crescent kick.

Jacob immediately gestures to Jones. "Let's get control of the ship." He then talks into his comm. "Anderson, keep an eye on the stern of this ship. If anyone tries to climb that ladder, stop them."

"You got it, Commander."

Jacob and Jones run to the first entrance they can find but discover that someone has blocked the door shut. As they make their way around the outside of the deck, they find that every door is locked or barricaded with something. They surmise that the crew did their best to seal off the interior of the ship where the passengers were to protect them from the hijackers. As they make their way to the front, Jacob sees how close they are to colliding with *First Responder* and then the oil rig. He talks into his comm. "Phillips, what's the cruise ship's speed now?"

"Eight point five knots, Commander."

"OK, Phillips, it's your turn. Be ready to collide and grapple."

Jacob hears a helicopter and looks up to see Gustave flying toward the cruise ship in his Star Oil transport copter, dragging *First Responder's* huge tow cable underneath.

"Commander, Maelstrom and I came up with a better plan. When Gustave drops that tow cable, make sure it gets hooked to the main beam at the fore of the cruise ship, then get out of there. We'll pull her far enough out of the way so that she misses us and the oil rig. I'd have run this by you earlier, Commander, but you and Jones were in a firefight with the hijackers when we thought of it after Gustave contacted us and said he was still on the oil rig."

"You have the bridge, Lieutenant Commander. Good thinking!"

Jacob and Jones watch Gustave maneuver his helicopter to hover over the cruise ship, which is quite an accomplishment since the ship is still moving at 8.5 knots. He lowers the thick, metal tow cable down into both men's hands. The hook itself weighs over two hundred pounds, and the cable is thicker than a man's leg. It takes every ounce of strength of both men to loop the hook and cable under the heavy crossbeam fastened to the support structure of the cruise ship, and to loop it over the top of the beam and fasten the hook onto the tow cable. Once they get it, Jacob looks up at Gustave and gives a thumbs-up. "OK, Phillips, it's all yours."

Gustave releases the cable from the helicopter payload hook and flies away. When the cable falls, it crashes onto the deck with an ear-splitting boom. As it becomes taut, it grinds off the railing and any other upright thing that gets in its way. Jacob and Gunny Jones run away from the front of the ship and up to the next level, find a secure place and brace themselves. Within a few moments, *First Responder* moves away from the oil rig and the big towing cable pulls tight on the cruise ship beam.

At first, it seems like it's going to work; but then the cruise ship tries to adjust and maintain its course toward the oil rig. This causes a tug-of-war between the cruise ship and *First Responder*.

Jacob gets on his comm. "Phillips, the automatic pilot on this thing is fighting you. Anderson, see if you can get a clear shot at the stern of this ship and take out one of its propellers without causing too much damage."

Before the captain of the Cyclone answers, Bliss interrupts. "Commander, I detect a very strong Bluetooth signal coming from the engine room of that cruise ship that's not supposed to be there."

"Can you jam that signal, Bliss?" Jacob asks.

"Yes sir, doing it now."

Immediately Jacob feels the cruise ship engines shut down, and his admiration and respect for his XO grows as he notices that *First Responder* has already cut its power down to the minimum to soften the shock caused by the cruise ship no longer fighting them. He looks up and sees that his ship can now easily tow the cruise ship and its passengers out of harm's way. "Bliss, see if you can contact the bridge of this ship and tell its captain that we are sending a skiff over, and I'm coming up to meet him shortly. Tell Lt. Maelstrom to bring a full security detail with him, and to bring one of my shipboard uniforms, too."

Jacob heads to the rear of the ship as Gunny Jones says, "That was one hell of a Tomoe-nage throw you did on that hijacker back there. Never seen it done so well."

Jacob rolls his eyes and chuckles. "My old man taught me that one when I was nine years old. Said it saved his life once. Oh, and as long as we're handing out compliments, Gunny, you make Taekwondo look damn good."

Jones laughs and pats Jacob on the back. "Yes I do, don't I?"

As Jacob and Gunny Jones make their way to the rear of the ship, they see Gustave in his helicopter flying toward Deep Star. Jacob throws up a hand and waves, but a loud shriek catches his attention and he looks over to see a small missile headed right for Gustave's copter. Before Jacob can say a word, the missile obliterates the helicopter.

"NOOOO!" Jacob screams as the fragments of the helicopter crash into the sea. Jacob's face turns red as his eyes and veins swell with blood. Rage pumps through his heart. "Anderson, find whoever did that and blow them out of the f…" He then catches himself, takes a calming breath, and continues. "Pursue and capture whoever made that shot! I authorize lethal force. Edwards out."

Dominik Thrace stands on the deck of Boris's yacht, congratulating himself that he could at least kill the maggot, Gustave, who betrayed them. He lowers the handheld rocket launcher he used and turns to meet Natasha, holding a gun to his face. "You stupid Neanderthal, I should kill you right here."

Dominik ignores the gun, moves in on Natasha and grabs her shoulders. The rage he feels in his gut manifests in his hot, stinky breath as he yells in her face, "Look, you overprivileged little debutant, my patience only goes so far—"

But Natasha throws his hands off her, steps beside him, pushes his shoulder around so he is facing the other way, and says, "Are you going to blow *that* up, you stupid, testosterone-filled baboon! That is an American naval warship coming right for us, you moron."

Dominik dumbly stares at the Cyclone racing in their direction. Natasha turns to see that Peter is already at the helm and starting their escape. She yells, "Go!"

Peter pushes the throttle position to half power, turns the yacht in a southeasterly direction, and then pulls the throttle all the way back and yells, "Hang on!" The back of the modified Millennium stealth yacht dips low in the water as the engine's propulsion thrusts the vessel forward at maximum velocity. Within a matter of seconds, it skips across the waves like a pebble being thrown across a pond. To the observers on the Cyclone pursuing it, the yacht disappears into the horizon at unbelievable speed.

Captain Anderson gets on his comm. "Sorry, Commander, we were right on them and they powered up and rocketed out of here. I've never seen a yacht like that go so fast. They had to be doing sixty knots at least."

"Eighty-one point five, before I lost them on radar," Bliss interrupts.

Damn, Jacob says under his breath, then speaks into the comm. "OK, Anderson. They are your navy's problem now. Report their course and speed and ask Naval Command to keep us informed. Also, ask them to send a barge out with a hoist big enough to salvage Nelson's CBD. It's still attached to the cruise ship anchor chain, and I'm keeping it here until we can get it out of the water."

"You got it, Commander."

"Oh, and Captain Anderson..."

"Yes, Commander?"

"You'll probably get a call from Captain Williams at Naval Intelligence. The Legend will want no one outside of us ever knowing what went on out here."

"Understood, Commander. Pleasure working with you, sir."

"You, too, Anderson. Edwards out."

Jacob stands at the stern of the ship, waiting for Maelstrom to come over in the skiff. Still reeling from Gustave's murder, he gazes at Jones. "How much intel did you get out of Gustave about the people who set this up?"

Jones pounds his fist on the railing. "That's just it, Commander. I was focused on figuring out how to get to his contact in Houston. So that's all we talked about until we met up with Vivian Narcellas and got her to Lt. Commander Yeager. Maybe he found out who these guys are, because I sure didn't."

"You did what I needed you to do. If anyone can get us a step closer to figuring this mess out, Yeager can. It was good working with you, Gunny. What's next for you?"

Gunny Jones smiles and rolls his eyes. "The Legend called me before we met up today. I report to DC Naval Intelligence after you relieve me. Apparently, he wants me close for a while."

First Responder's skiff pulls up and Jacob waves down to Lt. Maelstrom, who is having his men secure the Cyclone's skiff that somehow stayed attached through everything. Before his men ascend the ladder, Jacob turns back to Jones, wraps a hand around the scruff of Jones's neck, and shakes it. "Been there, done that. Nothing like spending quality time with Captain Tommy Williams.

This will seem like a Tahiti vacation compared to going on ops with him."

Jones shakes his head and lightly laughs. "I know. I've been on ops with The Legend."

As Maelstrom comes onto the deck and hands Jacob his uniform, Jones mumbles, "You're a hell of a lot more like The Legend than you think, Commander."

Two Days Later, Office of Captain William Harrington, Sector Corpus Christi

Commander Jacob Edwards enters his commanding officer's office with Captain William Harrington and Lt. Commander Chuck Yeager next to him. The three of them stand at attention in front of Commandant Harry Rogers, Vice Commandant James Harrington, and a section commander of the Coast Guard admirals, Ryan Bishop. Seated to the right of these men against the wall is Captain Tommy Williams of Naval Intelligence.

"At ease, gentlemen. Have a seat," Commandant Rogers says. The men sit and the commandant continues. "First off, I want to officially offer our condolences to the Harringtons here for losing Mrs. Harrington this past week. I realize you both are still grieving, but I felt it was vital that you two should be in on this meeting."

"We appreciate that, Commandant Rogers, and we're here to do our duty." Admiral Harrington looks up to catch Jacob's eye and continues. "Although Commander Edwards grossly overstepped his authority in countless acts over the last three days, I do not think a public reprimand would be wise at this point. Since we are trying to keep this whole incident as quiet as possible from the press, perhaps a notation on his record and a block in his promotion status for a year or two would be sufficient."

The whole room is dead silent for a few seconds. Jacob is undaunted by the admiral's words, but when he catches Captain Williams out of the corner of his eye, he notices the man is doing everything in his power not to burst out laughing. Jacob looks at the three admirals before him, and with as much control as he can muster toward not letting the captain's thinly-veiled mirth affect him, says, "Sirs, I will accept anything you deem necessary for the good of the Coast Guard."

The commandant sits straight forward in his chair and looks to his right at Harrington. "Admiral, we are not here to reprimand…"

A hand reaches up from his left and touches the commandant's shoulder. "Commandant Rogers, if I may?" Admiral Bishop asks.

The commandant waves him on and leans back in his chair. Bishop looks at Jacob and smiles, then glares at James Harrington. "Vice Commandant Harrington, both you and your son were on grievance leave when this multilevel attack hit my section. Commander Edwards is the only command-grade officer I had with the experience necessary to competently counter a challenge like this. He acted under the umbrella of my authority over this section, and I was in constant communication with not only the commandant here but also"—he looks over and points to Captain Williams— "with Naval Intelligence.

Commander Edwards acted with intelligence, cunning, initiative, and courage. He, along with the crew of *First Responder*, spear-headed our counterassault that successfully protected two United States oil rigs targeted for sabotage by a very vicious and cunning adversary. Not only did they save both rigs, but also a shipload of innocent civilians, which included the South American Roman Catholic Children's Choir. During the time he had command of the operation, there was no loss of life save one, Gustave Landers, and no real damage to any military or civilian equipment or property, except for Star Oil's helicopter that Gustave was piloting when he was assassinated, and our own CBD boat, which is currently being refurbished. Frankly, sir, if I had my way, this man would stand in the oval office tomorrow being decorated by the president."

"Unfortunately, gentlemen, that will never happen."

All eyes go to Captain Tommy Williams as he stands up from his chair. He looks over at Jacob and then at the commandant. "Pardon me, Commandant Rogers, but I have been in conference with the president since this whole incident began. And yes, he is quite impressed and thankful for the job both Commander Edwards and Lt. Commander Chuck Yeager pulled off here, but he wants as little of what happened here going public as possible. We now know that the reason behind these attacks was not terrorism, but economics. Someone was trying to sabotage United States oil production in the Gulf of Mexico and make it look like a terrorist attack, or at least a compilation of bad decisions and use of faulty equipment by Star Oil. They wanted to force the president to put huge restraints on oil production in this region, thus crippling what energy independence we have. So, you see, making a big deal out of what Commander Edwards did, as impressive as it was, would be both counterproductive and detrimental to what he accomplished."

Tommy pauses for a second to take stock of the reactions of everyone in the room, and cannot help but notice the smug look of self-satisfaction on both of the Harrington's faces. He holds up his index finger and continues. "Although, I would like to say that if anyone in this room thought that Commander Edwards being awarded the Coast Guard Star, getting promoted, and then being given *First Responder* was a little premature, this incident should lay to rest any of those misgivings. Now, if you will excuse me, admirals, I will take my leave. I have a transport copter outside ready to take off for Miami. Because of some solid intel given to us by your own Lt. Commander Yeager here, we have arrested the man we believe is responsible for this incident. If you do not know, he is none other than Prince Abuella Hasheen of the Saudi royal family. Apparently, this operation was to help him stage a coup and usurp the Saudi king. Since it failed, he was going into hiding; but he stopped in Miami to sell some Arabian artwork he shamed the European aristocrats at the art show in Mexico City into giving back to his country. I am on my way to interrogate him now."

Tommy turns, salutes the admirals, then shakes each of their hands. He turns around and walks up to the side of Jacob's chair. "Nice work, Commander. Keep it up."

Jacob stands and turns and, with his back to the admirals, salutes and shakes Tommy's hand. He rolls his eyes, smiles, and mouths "Thanks a lot!" Then he says out loud, "Thank you, Captain Williams. Good luck in Miami, sir."

After Tommy leaves the room, Jacob turns around and waits for the admirals to continue. James Harrington is the first to speak. "So, that was the one they all call The Living Legend. Since he has the president's ear, I guess we'll have to follow his suggestions on this one." He then sternly looks at Jacob. "Commander Edwards, you are a maverick and a cowboy. People like you have no business commanding a ship like *First Responder*. I suggest that you don't let all the power you enjoyed over the last week go to your head; and if I have anything to say about it, you will never again be in that kind of position."

At this point, Commandant Rogers is staring at Admiral Harrington with a vehemence the whole room feels. James looks over to his son and sees him motioning with his eyes to notice his superior officer's glare. When he finally turns, the commandant leans in close and says, "James, say another word and I will put a public and permanent reprimand on your record. Now shut up and sit there while I finish."

Admiral Harrington sits back in his chair, red-faced and humiliated. "Yes sir," he mutters.

The commandant turns back to the three men in front of him. "Captain Harrington, command of Sector Corpus Christi is yours again. I trust you realize what an asset you have in Commander Edwards and will endeavor to take full advantage of his many profitable abilities."

"I promise you, Commandant, that the commander and I will have a very good and industrious relationship," Will answers with a nervous grin.

The commandant then looks over to Lt. Commander Yeager. "Chuck, we'll miss you. I've often said having you around was like having our own Sherlock Holmes in the Guard. The FBI better appreciate what we are sending their way."

Chuck smiles. "Thank you, sir. I have a little more time now that I missed the last class at Quantico. After Nancy and I are married in two weeks, we plan on taking a long honeymoon in Canada near Niagara Falls, then it's off to DC and Quantico."

"Sounds good, Chuck. Please stay in touch."

"Thank you, sir, I will."

The commandant looks around the room. "Well, gentlemen, that's all for now. Oh, Jacob, I am authorizing a three-week leave for you to get your family settled into the South Padre Island area near Chief Roberto and his wife, Isabella. *First Responder* is scheduled to do only one run down to Honduras and back in that time, and I think Lt. Commander Phillips can handle that without you. Don't you agree, Admiral Bishop?"

"Absolutely, Commandant. Phillips has come a long way in his short time with Commander Edwards. We could see a superb Hamilton captain out of him someday."

Jacob sits there and thinks that out of everything that was said in the meeting so far, that was the best. Larry Phillips has huge potential and he counts himself very lucky to have the man as his XO. The commandant then stands and dismisses everyone except Admiral Harrington.

When the rest of the group exits the Corpus Christi CO's office and steps out into the outer office, they find the entire room filled with as many of the Corpus Christi personnel that could fit. When they see Commander Edwards, someone yells, "IT'S THE COMMANDER!"

Every man and woman in uniform comes to attention and gives Jacob a salute. Jacob, though feeling a little self-conscious, returns the salute and smiles. The room erupts with thunderous applause and Jacob, Chuck, and Admiral Bishop make their way through the crowd with people slapping Jacob's back and shaking his hand.

Captain Will Harrington manages to slip away. The slimy tentacles of jealousy wrapping themselves around his being make it hard for him to breathe as he ducks into the nearest restroom and pulls out his personal cell phone to send a text to Natasha. "I really need you. When can we see each other again?"

He does not hear from her for weeks. During that time, he takes solace in the unlimited supply of pain medication his Corpus Christi doctor prescribes for him.

A few minutes later, Commandant Rogers and Admiral Harrington step out of the office. James is trying to explain that he is still emotionally upset over the passing of Will's mother and his ex-wife. They hear the commotion when the first group stepped out of the office, and the area is still filled with Coast Guard personnel, all talking about the same thing—Commander Jacob Edwards. They hear comments from around the room.

"Where did the commander transfer from?"

"Is the commander really the youngest, lowest-ranking person to ever command a Hamilton?"

"I was here when it all started. The commander controlled the whole response to the entire emergency. The president himself gave him complete control. Captains and admirals were following his orders. It was a complete win. The commander did all that and more."

James looks over at the commandant, disgusted. "Really, Harry? All this fuss over one little commander! These people better keep their mouths shut about this when they are off duty."

Harry just laughs jovially and shakes his head at James Harrington. "I have briefed them, Harry. That's why I let them do this, so they can get it all out now. You know, Admiral, there are a lot of fine young commanders in this Coast Guard, and every one of them is a credit to their uniform. But I believe from here on out that Jacob Edwards will always be THE COMMANDER!"

Next Day Headlines:
New York Times
Saudi Oil Mogul Prince Abuela Hasheen Assassinated
A member of the Saudi royal family, Prince Abuela Hasheen, was apprehended two days ago by United States intelligence operatives upon suspicion of orchestrating terrorist acts in the US. Some evidence has come forward to substantiate the claims. King Alos of Saudi Arabia

demanded the prince's immediate return after it was discovered that the prince tried to fence priceless Arabic art he had confiscated at the festival he attended earlier this month in Mexico City. The prince was stepping off his private jet when he was hit by sniper fire and killed instantly. The Saudi government refuses to comment on the motive or those responsible.

The Advocate New Orleans
Councilman Ferdinand Landers Found Dead in His House

Councilman Ferdinand Landers was found unresponsive in his bed by his housekeeper early this morning. After EMTs arrived and endeavored to resuscitate him for several minutes, the coroner pronounced him dead, saying the cause appeared to be a heart attack. Although the councilman did not have a history of heart problems, his family does. Councilman Landers achieved nationwide fame a few weeks ago when he offered to turn state's evidence concerning his brothers, who are suspected of being organized crime mob bosses in the greater New Orleans area. This is the second set of tragic news concerning the Landers family. It was reported just yesterday that Lander's nephew, Gustave, died in a fatal helicopter crash when his Star Oil helicopter had engine failure and crashed into the ocean off the port of Galveston, Texas, while delivering supplies to the Deep Star oil rig.

Houston Chronicle
Woman Suspected of Running a Local Escort Service Found Stabbed to Death in Her Cell

Vivian Narcellas, who was arrested three days ago under suspicion of running a local escort and prostitution ring that used minors, was found dead this morning in her holding cell at the county jail. Authorities believe the act was one of professional rivalry, instituted and carried out by competing criminal entities in the Houston area. Vivian and her brothers have owned and operated a local taxidermy and wild game meat-processing center in southern Houston for five decades. Her brothers declined to comment.

Associated Press News Release:
Admiral Ryan Bishop of the US Coast Guard Had a Busy Day

Such was the case this week on Wednesday when Admiral Ryan Bishop's section, which makes up most of the Gulf of Mexico, had numerous opportunities that required his attention. While having his New Orleans bomb squad respond to an unsubstantiated threat at Star Oil's Event Horizon oil rig, protocols forced him to make Star Oil evacuate the entire facility. They proved all threats false and returned the crews the same day. Because of the possible terrorist threat, he was also forced to put every port in his section on lockdown until all possibilities could be analyzed and discounted.

In the middle of the day, Bishop learned of an attempted hijacking of a northern-bound cruise ship that left Tampico, Mexico, earlier that morning. Bishop had two of his own ships respond—*First Responder,* captained by Commander Jacob Edwards; and a CBD cutter from Brazos, captained by Lt. Ron Nelson. The Navy also deployed one of their Cyclone-class cutters, captained by Captain Brian Anderson, to aid. The hijackers turned out to be two mentally disturbed ship security personnel who killed the rest of the ship's security officers and took control of the ship, endeavoring to run it into the offshore oil rig, Deep Star.

Investigation is ongoing, but preliminary reports show that both men were antireligious extremists trying to use the ship's passengers, the South American Roman Catholic Children's Choir, as martyrs for their cause. Bishop asked the navy Cyclone to spearhead the rescue. This class of Navy Cyclones carries a complement of four to eight Special Forces individuals. They deployed two to the vessel and they overcame and subdued the hijackers. Since they did no harm to US property or citizens, Bishop allowed the ship to turn back to Mexico to let their authorities handle the situation. When asked to comment on the day's happenings, Bishop said, "That is what the American people pay us to do—keep our coasts safe. I have a good team, and along with the Navy's help, that is exactly what we did." Admiral Bishop is retiring at the end of the year and has accepted a post in the State Department. Many of his comrades in the Coast Guard, which includes Commandant Harry Rogers, say the State Department is getting one hell of a fine man.

Office of Pedro Guerra, Shipping Mogul, Mexico City

Boris Rasmov sits in the office of his mentor, Pedro Guerra, drinking a vodka martini and smoking an exquisite Italian cigar from Pedro's private collection. Pedro summoned Boris for a meeting after the failure of his operation in the Gulf of Mexico. Boris surmised that his mentor had him come to evaluate the fiasco and work through the damage assessment to Boris's operations in the Americas. To his amusement, Boris once again finds his own timing to be perfect, because his mentor is already engaged in a delightful conversation with the Saudi Arabia king. "Your Eminence, it would honor us to supply your need in this category. Our product is the finest and most well-trained in the world. Most of the subjects start their training as early as seven years old. You will find that their skill set goes way beyond the pleasures of the bedchamber. We have trained some as bodyguards, assassins, as well as secretarial and administrative assistants. You can order other skills in advance, and we will forward an estimate of time and additional cost to you." Pedro pauses for a moment to listen to the king's response, then looks at Boris, who has already taken a seat, and smiles. "Excellent, Your Eminence. I will have my people make all the proper arrangements and then you and your family will have full access to our services."

Pedro hangs up the phone and looks over at Boris, beaming, and shakes his finger at the Russian. "You have been very busy these last couple of days. I have to admit, Boris, when I first saw what a complete disaster your operation for Prince Hasheen turned out to be, I was very disappointed. Other members of the council called and said I should withdraw my request that you be instated as a junior member of the High Council. I held off, and now I am glad I did. This little fiasco of yours has opened the Middle East to my services. With the Saudi royal family alone, I should see at least a twenty percent increase in profit. I understand that the king is using your services. Very impressive, Boris. I now assure your seat on the council."

Boris sets his cigar down in the porcelain dish next to his chair, takes a sip of his martini, and says, "As always, Pedro, I am grateful for your patience and support. Prince Hasheen's plan did not have a high percentage chance of success, but I had to try."

"Oh, come now, Boris, I'm not a child. You set this up from the start. You would win, no matter the outcome. Once you were sure that the attacks on the oil rigs would fail, you reached out to the Saudi king and offered your services to eliminate Hasheen. Then, in your usual clinical thoroughness, you took care of any loose ends by killing anyone that could connect you or your affiliates with the attacks. There is only one detail that bothers me."

"And what is that, Pedro?"

"How was Dominik Thrace so easily subdued and literally thrown off that ship? Fortunate for you that your daughter, Natasha, homed in on their beacons and picked him and your nephew up."

Boris takes his cigar from the dish, places it to his lips and draws in a deep drag of the smoke. He lets it linger in his throat for a few moments, then blows it out and says, "That is also a mystery. There is only one man that I know of that could challenge Dominik like that, and all my sources reported him to be advising the US president throughout the whole ordeal."

"You are referring to the one they call The Living Legend, Captain Tommy Williams, of course," Pedro states.

"Yes, so whoever was on that US Special Forces team must have trained under Captain Williams."

"Do you have any candidates yet?"

"One, but it's a long shot. He's the captain of the Coast Guard ship called *First Responder,* a Commander Jacob Edwards. Serendipitously, his father owns one of the biggest trucking and automobile wholesaling operations in Manheim, Pennsylvania. James Harrington sent me his name recently, a Jim Edwards. He recommended his operation as a target for me to pursue to further my money-laundering operation there. I think I will do just that and use the opportunity to learn more about the commander."

Chapter Eighteen

What Really Makes it all Worth It

South Padre Island, Texas

Jacob caught transport from Corpus Christi to Station Brazos on South Padre Island. Mary gave the keys for his Ford Taurus to two seamen who were sent by Chief Garcia to pick it up and have it ready when he arrived. When he grabs the keys from the receptionist desk, Lt. Nelson is there at the station and tells him that the chief is already with Danielle at the garage next to his property waiting for him. Jacob gets excited and heads out the door. Lt. Nelson steps up to him and holds out his hand. "I wanted to say sorry for giving you static about my boat the other day. You made the right decision, and you saved lives."

Jacob smiles, shakes his hand, and pats the young lieutenant on the back. "Nelson, if you had reacted any other way, I would have been very concerned. No captain of a ship should ever be easily talked into sacrificing his command. How is the restoration coming to that CBD, anyway?"

"Well, Commander, there was not enough line of chain left for it to sink all the way to the bottom, so damage was minimal. They should have it up and running within the month. Captain Harrington just put me on admin duty here until it's done."

"Well, I'm glad to hear that, and I know Chief Garcia will be glad to have an officer around here to keep his men on their toes for a while. I'm sure we'll work together again, Nelson. Got to go. I have a promised date with my daughter that is long overdue. See you later."

Jacob runs out the door, and as Nelson waves him on, he says, "Anytime, Commander, anytime."

Jacob gets in his car and as soon as he pulls out, his cell phone vibrates. He picks it up, flips it open and sees it is Captain Williams calling. "Hello, sir. The commandant himself told me I have three weeks off. So, if you need me for something, you'll have to go through him."

"Ha, ha, ha. He already told me I can't touch you for the next three weeks. I called to say you did a damn fine job on this one. I could not have done any better myself. You really pulled off a win for the home team, Jacob."

"Thank you, sir. It still would have been nice to have you around. Most of the time I felt like I was flying by the seat of my pants. It's not the same when you're not around for the big operations. But I know the president wanted you close, so we did the best we could without you."

"The president released me and sent me to the Gulf of Mexico when all this went down. I wanted to prove to him, and you, that you can handle it, Commander. So I laid low and watched from a distance. You didn't need me. If you did, I would have been there."

Jacob shakes his head and laughs. "Well, knowing you were close would have been nice."

"That's the point, Commander. You were in command. It was all on you and you did fine. Now, maybe someday I'll be able to retire and have a life of my own."

"Ha-ha, like that will ever happen. This is your life, c...." Click. The line goes dead and Jacob just shakes his head.

Once Jacob gets close to his father-in-law's property, his heart pumps at twice its normal speed. He quickly parks, gets out of his car and rushes over to the garage where the chief and Danielle are waiting for him. He walks up to the door, grabs the knob, opens the door, and walks inside.

His nine-year-old, Danielle, runs up to him and gives him a hug. She is covered from head to toe in green dust from sanding car paint, but that doesn't stop her daddy from bending down and giving her a big kiss on the forehead. He looks up and sees Chief Garcia walk around an engine that is hanging from a chain attached to a crossbeam in the garage. Jacob immediately recognizes it as a GM 350cc eight-cylinder engine that just came out of the car sitting next to it. Jacob walks over and devours the dark green 1972 Buick Skylark CP before him. He is undaunted by the rust on the rockers, faded paint all around, and the need for a new vinyl roof and leather upholstery. Danielle looks up at her daddy's smiling eyes and says, "What do you think, Commander? Can we bring her back to life?"

Jacob rubs her hair, then clasps both hands together. "You bet, spunky monkey. Now *this* is my idea of fun!"

The End